LOVERS & LIARS

Book 3 of
THE WARDEN

FELICIA JEDLICKA

For the ones who understand the importance of compliments.

SISTER WITCHES
THE DEVIL'S SHADOW
THE DEVIL'S SOUL

DESTINY REJECTED
DESTINY RECLAIMED
DESTINY RAZED
DESTINY RESTORED

DÉJÀ VU

SAVE THE HUMANS

THE NECROMANCER'S CHILD

THE NEBRASKA APOCALYPSE NOVELS
CORN COWS AND THE APOCALYPSE
COW TIPPING AFTER THE APOCALYPSE
CORN HUSKING AFTER THE APOCALYPSE

THE WARDEN SERIES
SUCCESSORS
RIVALS
LOVERS AND LIARS
BAD BLOOD
TENANTS AND TYRANTS
THE RING BEARER
GODS AND MONSTERS
BEASTS AND BURDENS
MAGIC AND MAYHEM
FORK IN THE ROAD
DETAILS AND DEADLINES
*CURSES AND SACRIFICES**
*WITCHES AND WOLVES**
*SAINTS AND SERPENTS**
*ENEMIES AND ALLIES**

MARRIED TO DEATH*

LOVERS & LIARS

FELICIA JEDLICKA

1

D aniel McGrath stomped up the stairs to the offices of Bailey, Kumpf, and Walline—a decoy law office that masked the operations of his employer. Aside from the intentionally curt secretary—who never answered the phone, always told people the lawyers were out, and constantly smelled like mothballs—there was nothing to recommend the place as a viable law office. He had learned through a quick succession of visits that the seventy-year-old woman would not remember his face. Rather than acknowledge her when he entered, he simply stormed past her and made a beeline for the stairs.

If any unwelcome visitors managed to make it past the crotchety receptionist, the elevator—that was perpetually out of order—discouraged them from roaming beyond the second floor.

By the third flight, Daniel was sucking air, but his irritation lengthened his strides and he finished the fourth flight by skipping every other step.

He arrived on the fifth floor and passed by several offices that were piled high with empty boxes, a useless tactic to make the rooms look appropriated for storage, if nothing else. At the end of the hall was a wooden door, with a fogged-glass window that read, *Criminal Division*—a vague description that hardly offered explanation for the room, let alone the work assignments that were delegated from it.

He charged toward it, unfastening his thigh-length jacket. He wiped away the sweat that had developed on his forehead from his quick ascent, and combed through his flyaway hair to make sure his gel was still working.

He had let the auburn mess grow out a little to help keep it under control. Along with that, he was trying out a mustache and goatee that made him look chancy. He hadn't noticed it contributing to his bounty hunting success, but it had reduced his failures in the bars, and that was reason enough to spare his razor.

He pushed his shaded oval glasses higher on his nose. The lenses didn't improve his vision, but his abyssal black eyes always made people uneasy, so it was best to cover them. Exposing them might have added to his bold entrance, but there was no reason to terrify the poor woman.

With a firm twist of the handle, he flung open the office door. It clattered against the adjacent wall, scaring the wits out of Sophie Plum. The peroxide blonde was bent over a file cabinet—or had been just before he came in. She hugged her confidential paperwork to her slim frame and gaped at him. Her fear quickly changed to fury as she registered the identity of the trespasser. "Daniel! What the hell?"

"What the hell is right, Sophie?" He closed the door behind him, giving it another hardy slam. He sat down in the leather armchair in front of her mahogany desk. The office set was well above her paygrade, but Daniel had assumed it was a private purchase. Like many of the "interns" that had held this position over the years, she came from money. Unlike her predecessors, though, she actually seemed to like her job—apart from his visits.

Sophie was just one in a very long line of caseworkers he'd had the privilege of pissing off. Much to her regret—and shame, as it turned out—she was also one in a very long line of his one-night conquests. It didn't take her long to realize he had no intention of offering her a second date, so their relationship had remained strained. He probably should have known better than to sleep with someone he had to see on a regular basis, but he wasn't discriminate in that way, or any way, really. If they were willing or drunk enough not to object too strongly, he was going to take a shot.

"What were you thinking, assigning us a woman?" Daniel picked up her nameplate and flipped it in the air.

"Uh," Sophie rumbled in exasperated realization. She slapped her files down on her desk and pulled her high-backed leather chair out to sit. "What is your issue?"

"Heaton and I lost a partner to unfortunate circumstances," Daniel explained.

"He got married. How is that unfortunate?"

"It's the most unfortunate circumstance I can think of for a friend of mine."

"Does that include death?" Sophie droned.

"Aye, but now you give us a replacement. It's a hard enough task to have a fella come to fill the shoes of a great man like Ethan Pierce, but for you to send us a *scanger*."

"She graduated top of her class. She was a top pick by the American FBI."

"What the feck does that have to do with bounty hunting?"

"She was highly recommended," Sophie said.

"You did this, didn't you?" Daniel chucked her nameplate at her, which she barely caught. "You just had to get back at me for slickin' you up and leaving you to dry out."

Sophie clenched her eyes shut like an image had popped into her head that would take a good deal of effort to remove. "First off." She opened her eyes and positioned her nameplate where it belonged. "You know I don't have that power. Second, please don't make me ill. I wouldn't go near you with a... I don't even want to be *this* close to you." She motioned to the distance between them.

"You do a bird a favor." Daniel crossed his arms in feigned astonishment. "Get her off on her first few days in town, and suddenly she thinks you owe her."

Sophie stared at him, temporarily paralyzed by his audacity. "Daniel." She clenched her palms together before continuing. "You are an exceptional asshole. I am familiar with the way one-night stands work. I take full responsibility for my part in it, but never before have I been demeaned for doing so by the other person involved. I was fooled so briefly into thinking you were a human being, but clearly, that is beneath you." Sophie paused to pick the precise word she needed. "The *odium* I feel for you is only limited by my faith, because it demands that I have respect for all living creatures... including the cold-blooded ones."

Daniel uncrossed his arms and leaned back in his chair to take in the insult. He rarely had the opportunity to engage with the women he had thrown away over the years, but he imagined they would share this same conviction.

"All right, I'll apologize. Not because I feel that there is anything wrong with a man and woman being honest about their desires, but because I won't have you think me inhuman." He paused in thought. "You were an excellent lay."

"Geez, Daniel," she scoffed, but he continued unfettered.

"I shouldn't have been such an arse when I threw you out of my apartment. I'm an eejit and I'll never be otherwise, but I'm sorry that my behavior has put you at odds with your faith."

Sophie arched her brow. "You think one apology is just going to change what I feel toward you?"

"I don't need you to like me." Daniel leaned forward. "Just forget about me and let yourself enjoy the company of other men. Men who would be honored to wake in the morning next to your lovely face." Daniel leaned back and let her come to terms with his sincerity.

Sophie frowned at him and continued where they had left off. "The woman we've assigned to you has a rare talent. We aren't sure it will come in handy, but we aren't going to dismiss it. She was assigned to you so you can field-test her. The hope for you is she will detect transmorphs without any extraneous efforts, and possibly track known offenders."

"What is this rare talent she possesses?"

Sophie pursed her lips sourly, apparently lamenting the words before she even spoke them. "She can smell transmorphs."

Daniel smirked. He stood and walked around the desk and leaned against it beside her chair. She shook her head, refusing to look at him. "Sophie, did you just assign me a bloodhound in the form of a petite, pixy-cut brunette?"

Sophie looked up at him. He barely contained his laughter, and she was pinching her lips to hide her smile. "She is very smart..."

"Every good dog should know some tricks," he added.

"She is physically fit." Sophie pointed a finger to reassert the serious nature of the conversation.

"I'll walk her every day to keep her that way."

Sophie pushed back her chair to put some distance between them. "Daniel, please," she said earnestly. "I know she is going to be a strain on your razor-thin patience, but think how many people you could save. Think how many minds could be recovered before they're irreparably tangled."

"Yeah, I guess." Daniel didn't want to get too excited. There had been several plots over the years to stop the parasites, but none of them had panned out.

"If she doesn't work out, then we reassign her, but not before we know what she can do. She's already very good with human detection, but she hasn't had hands-on experience with many supernatural beings. Her nose should improve over time, but we can't know for sure until she gets a chance to... smell live transmorphs." Sophie shook her head. She seemed to know how ridiculous she sounded to him.

"Fine, I'll give her a go, but I can't condone someone so miniscule in this line of work. She's likely to get eaten before we even notice she's missing." Daniel pushed off the desk and circled back to the door.

"Daniel," Sophie interjected before he could leave. He turned back. "Don't sleep with her."

Daniel furrowed his brow and scoffed. "Yeah, like that's possible." He left, slamming the door behind him.

2

T HAT EVENING, DANIEL STALKED into the pub where Heaton had agreed to meet him. Much to his disappointment, their new partner, Nevia Jordan, was sitting at the table with him. He yanked back the chair she had been resting her feet on under the table. She slipped down in her chair, barely catching herself before she fell off the edge.

Daniel sat down, lounging his long legs to one side. Nevia resituated herself and gave him a dubious glance. She probably suspected that his slight was intentional, but he didn't care.

"What the hell?" Daniel asked, throwing his hands up at Heaton.

The slim, handsome black man widened his eyes in a silent scold. Short, tight spikes that splayed every which way off his head had recently replaced his long dreadlocks. It was an improvement, but he wasn't pulling this hairdo off either.

Heaton leaned forward and pulled his wallet from his back pocket. "Jordan." Heaton pulled a twenty-pound note from the brown leather. "The bartenders here are a little nicer to the ladies. Would you mind speeding up our path to drunkenness? Two pints and whatever you want."

Nevia gave him a subdued smile and took the note. "One *m-scra* coming up," she mumbled as she headed to the bar.

"What the feck is wrong with you?" Daniel said before she was safely out of earshot. "Why did you invite her here?"

"Because she is new to this job and new to this country, not to mention she is our partner. Since when do we not take our partners out to the pub?"

"Since our new partner is a fecking woman."

"What did Sophie say?" Heaton asked, downing the last of his pint and shoving it to the center of the table.

"Apparently she's a bloodhound for transmorphs, or so they hope."

"You're kidding." Heaton tipped his brow. "You mean she senses them?"

"She smells them, literally."

Heaton stared at Daniel, blank-faced for a moment. "You're joking with me, aren't you?"

"No, ask her yourself. Sophie said she smells the difference between humans and transmorphs. They are hoping that she can tell when a transmorph has enveloped a human."

"Is that even possible?" Heaton asked.

"You tell me," Daniel said. "The bitter gene, color blindness, cankles—the human body has an array of mutations. Maybe her mother shagged a werewolf, I don't know."

"What are we supposed to do with her?"

"We are supposed to put up with her until she proves to be accurate or inaccurate, and then they'll reassign her."

"If she's accurate, won't they want to keep her on?" Heaton pointed out.

"No, because after we determine her use, I'm going to sleep with her. She'll be asking for a transfer by high tea the day after."

"You do know that you're becoming a sociopath." Heaton perked an eyebrow at him.

"Becoming?" Daniel gave him a wry smile.

Heaton shook his head and lost all amusement from his face. "Seriously, Daniel, you're getting worse."

"Aren't you going to call your pet back? She's waiting at the bar for the signal." Daniel wanted to get out of this conversation as quickly as possible, and he also wanted his beer.

"Are you going to be nice?" Heaton narrowed his eyes.

"Not likely," Daniel admitted. "But I won't scare her off, if that's what you mean."

"It is. Like it or not, we need a third," Heaton said as he got up and left the table.

Daniel watched Heaton rush over to help Nevia carry the three pints she had purchased. Listening to Heaton's concern for his social behavior made him wonder if Sophie had it right. Was he really inhuman?

Nevia rejoined them and took a long swig of her beer before turning to Daniel. "Everything settled then? Can the new girl hang out in the boys' clubhouse?"

Daniel smiled at her intuition. The way her hair wrapped around her ears made them seem pointed. In fact, all her features were sharp, not round like some women. All she needed were the wings and she could fly away to be with the other fairies.

"I'm told I need to be nice to you. Sophie says you have something to offer me... us," Daniel corrected himself. Heaton glared at him. He gave him a quick grimace to let him know he had honestly misspoken—for a change.

"They think I have a nose for your criminals."

"How exactly did you come to be here?" Daniel reached for his pint. "Sophie said you were going to be an FBI agent." He took a long drink, not losing eye contact with her as she answered.

"Yeah, I was about to sign the W-2s when I was approached to apply for a top-secret international job. It was all very intriguing, so I couldn't resist. I'm not entirely sure how they found out about my talent, but my interview was just one long scratch-n-sniff test. In the end, they offered me a job. The pay, as you know, was irresistible."

"That's how they hook you," Heaton said. "They got me right out of the British army. They said I showed potential. Hadn't even finished my term. I'm told I should be flattered."

"What about you, Daniel?" Nevia asked.

"*I* found *them*." Daniel glanced at Heaton for a rescue.

"So, Jordan," Heaton chimed in. "How do you like England so far?"

"It's fine. This is the base of operations, I take it?"

Heaton glanced at Daniel. The statement wasn't entirely accurate, but there was no reason to get into the details just yet. "For us it is," Heaton answered.

"How often do we get to leave here?"

"Despite the brochure highlights of world travels, most of our assignments don't take us outside of Europe. There are several teams scattered around the world, so generally it's more about proximity than talent."

"What will we be hunting?" Nevia whispered.

"I would say vampiric creatures are about fifty percent of our workload. Wouldn't you, Daniel?"

"Aye, the fecking things breed like rabbits, and they're a nuisance to livestock."

"After that, transmorphs," Heaton said. "We get all the transmorph reports."

"All?" Nevia asked. "Is that your specialty?"

"It's my specialty," Daniel said.

"Well, I'm not on a coffee break for them," Heaton protested.

Daniel shrugged, realizing his offense. "Yes, it's our specialty. Now that you're aboard, we might as well go into business for ourselves."

"I've never smelled a real one." Nevia patted her chest to let out a not-so-ladylike burp. "I just want both of you to know I'm not here because I think I have any skill at this. I'm here because some bureaucratic paper-pusher, who couldn't keep his hands off his nose, suggested that I would be an invaluable asset to your work. My plan is to just stay out of your way until I can be of use."

"Well then," Daniel said, "we should get along just fine."

"Yeah, I think—" Heaton's cell phone interrupted, chirping like a bird. Daniel stared at the device as he took it out. "Sophie," Heaton announced, reading the screen. "Excuse me. Hello."

"Change that ring, you poof!" Daniel scolded him loudly enough for Sophie to hear on the other end.

"Hang on, Sophie." Heaton punched Daniel's shoulder as he left the table for more privacy. He grunted and rubbed his shoulder before taking another swig of beer. He should have known that Heaton would never pull his punches.

"Just so you know, Sophie warned me about *you*," Nevia said.

Daniel choked on his drink, sending a bubbly blast of beer up his nose. He set down his pint and wiped off his face as he coughed up the offending liquid. "Did she now?" He cleared his throat to get a better grip on his voice. "What exactly did she say?"

"Just that you're a hard man to know and an even harder one to like. She said that I shouldn't let you fan my skirt up with flattery. She said you hate women."

The last statement dragged down Daniel's smirk. He narrowed his eyes. "I don't hate women," he defended bitterly. "I love women. I can't get enough of them."

"You love sex," she corrected. He must have sneered at her because she averted her eyes. "That much is true of any man, I guess."

"And what about you?" Daniel snatched up his pint so fast the beer splashed out onto the table. "Do you like sex?"

She looked back as he took a drink. She waited until he had finished and put the glass down before answering. "Very much."

Her calm demeanor surprised him; she didn't blush or avert her eyes. She wasn't flirting, though, just being honest. "Are you worried about me... fanning your skirt up?"

She looked him over as if she was evaluating his potential as a mate. Her eyes held on the deep neckline he always wore to show off his chest. The black shirts made him look pale, but the smooth skin peeking from beneath it drew attention to his natural physique. Years of hard work, not workouts, had earned him his lean, broad body, and he had no intention of hiding it.

"I'd like to think that I'm smarter than that, but I wouldn't be the first woman to fall for the bad-boy image."

"It's not an image," he said somberly.

She stared at him. "If I do have a moment of stupidity, I hope you won't hold it against me."

He took his turn to evaluate her. She was small, but she had a nice shape. Her chest was not as bountiful as he preferred, but that preference usually came with a bigger body to match. He had forgotten to look at her butt when she last got up—an oversight he would not repeat.

There was nothing especially appealing to him about her—at least no more than any other woman. However, he had learned many things in his years of casual sex. One, condoms are not optional. Two women lie just as much as men. And three, great physical attraction does not guarantee great sex. Some of the best lays he had ever had were with women that most men would have turned their noses up at.

"Nevia—" he started, trying her name on his tongue for the first time.

"Jordan, please," she corrected.

He frowned. "Most people correct someone to call them by their first name."

"Not me." She shrugged.

"Jordan," Daniel amended, but the name didn't sound right to him. He leaned forward on the table, careful not to put his sleeve in his beer puddle. "You're not being very coy. I'm not used to that."

"Would you prefer I announce my indifference to you, and purport that I will never sleep with you, when clearly

I've only just begun to know you? I'm sure that would only provide the type of challenge that a man like you would aspire to."

"Well, feck!" Daniel slumped back in his chair. "Now you've just taken the fun out of all of it. We won't be flirting, because you're not coy. We won't be arguing, because it won't build any sexual tension. We won't be avoiding the potential for a sexual encounter because you're too honest. What could we possibly have left to do with one another?"

"We could try working together, as platonically as the relationship allows. If you think you can tolerate doing that with a woman."

Daniel threw up his hands. "I don't hate women. I can work around you just fine."

"Good, then between me staying out of your way and you endeavoring to not get me into bed, we might actually tolerate this arrangement."

Daniel picked up his beer and begrudgingly submitted to clanking her proffered glass before they took their respective drinks.

Heaton returned and leaned over the table. Daniel could already tell from the irritation on his face that Sophie hadn't given him good news. "Sophie got a message through the taps from Belus. Ethan's wife is in trouble."

"Mermaids?" Daniel smirked at the thought. He didn't envy her that debt. Those slithery bastards could hold a grudge over generations.

"No, Daniel, it's a transmorph." Daniel stood up and Nevia followed suit. "He wants us there yesterday."

Daniel didn't bother asking about the specifics. Belus wouldn't have called him in unless it was serious. He guzzled the last of his beer. Nevia did the same, even though hers was a great deal fuller. Heaton eyed her as she finished and let out another not-so-ladylike burp. Daniel scoffed and shook his head. "Come on, bloodhound. Time to get you field-tested."

3

T HE ALARMS SHRIEKED INCESSANTLY throughout the prison. Ethan climbed the stairs to the transmorph level to meet Belus. Despite the excitement, he was still shrugging away the last vestiges of what would have been a good night's sleep.

The buzzing phone in the study had awakened Cori and him at four in the morning. He wasn't aware the device was capable of such an obnoxious noise, but apparently it got louder with each ring.

Belus reported to him that a transmorph had gone missing, and he needed their immediate presence.

As Ethan jogged up the stairwell, several armed guards ran down on the other side of him, giving him respectful nods as they passed. Belus had shut down the elevators to limit mobility between floors. He was probably already barking out orders for the guards to inventory the entire prison.

Although Ethan had been officially named the warden's successor, he never felt the need to usurp Belus's authority. He respected his experience and his fervor. He saw no reason to throw his weight around unless he actually disagreed with his tactics.

Normally, Danato would be the one trudging up the stairs to meet Belus—or rather, Danato would have restarted the elevators, since he wasn't likely to hike up three flights of stairs no matter what the risk. Danato, unfortunately, was on a two-month leave of absence. It was his wedding present to Cori and Ethan. It was the closest thing to a proper honeymoon he could allow them. Not to mention it had been a decade since Danato had left the prison for more than a few days.

Danato had left Ethan, and consequently Belus, in charge while he was gone. Aside from a rocky first week of married life, the last six weeks had been pleasant and without excitement. Ethan had hoped that the next two weeks would be just as boring, but life was never quite that generous when you were responsible for containing supernatural beings.

He made his way through the transmorph level. The alarms blared even louder inside the area. He covered his ears as he approached Belus. "Can we shut off the damn alarm? We know it's an emergency."

Belus looked up from his clipboard. The confusion slowly drained from his face as he observed the racket that was forcing Ethan to yell. Years of working through emergencies in the prison must have deafened him to the unbearable sound. Two guards towered on either side of him, eagerly awaiting their instructions. "Where's Cori?" Belus asked, looking behind him.

"She's coming. She's a little slower in the early morning hours."

"That's no excuse. I need her here."

Ethan nodded and resisted the urge to roll his eyes. In an effort to reward Cori's tied score for warden, the judges and Danato had made her Belus's successor. Although Belus's responsibilities were highly subjective and open to interpretation, he took them very seriously. As such, he had started to train Cori. He took her under his proverbial wing—or, in Belus's case, his proverbial foot—to guide and mold her into the perfect soldier.

Ethan had expected Cori to rebel against Belus's authoritarian teaching style, but she seemed eager to please him. She had become quite the little appendage to him and had been spending more time with Belus than she had with him.

He would have been offended by the late days, but somehow he forgot about such trite conversations when she walked in the door, stripping away more than her coat. Cori's hesitations in the bedroom had all but disappeared since they'd married. She was finally comfortable with herself and, at long last, with him. He couldn't blame her for her apprehension, given her history, but he was relieved that he didn't have to be so cautious with his advances anymore.

"She'll be here. Seriously, Belus, the alarm?"

Belus snorted before giving the guards the order to shut it down. The look of amusement on his face told Ethan that Belus thought a real man should be able to tolerate a loud noise. Ethan wanted to interject a comment about ears not being muscles, but he bit back the caustic statement.

When the alarms went silent, he sighed in relief and unclamped his ears. "Thank God. Okay, fill me in."

"The men are doing a cursory inventory on all the floors," Belus rattled off from his clipboard, as if he had already logged the details to speed up his paperwork later, which, of course, he had. "No one has reported any duplicates yet. Next, we'll have to check the guards. I told Danato we needed to chip the guards."

"How did this happen?"

Belus stared at him a moment before speaking. "As I said on the phone—"

"It's four fucking a.m. Belus, cut me some slack." Ethan cleared his throat, trying to take back his intemperate tone.

Belus didn't seem to take offense, but he gave him a once-over before tucking his clipboard under his arm. "Once a month, a guard goes through the levels to check cell conditions. They check for damage, contraband, and whatnot. The point is, on this month's rounds, they saw one of the transmorph cells empty."

"So he went missing between daily rounds yesterday and the monthly round this morning?"

Belus scratched the back of his neck. "That appears to be the case, but I'm not sure yet. I would like to consult with Cori. She's taken over the daily rounds for this level the last few weeks. She's checked off on the roster for the last five weeks."

"I'm sure Cori wouldn't miss something like that," Ethan said defensively.

"Something like what?" Cori asked as she approached. "Sorry I'm late."

Ethan couldn't help but smile when Cori jogged up beside him and looped her arm in his. As unprofessional as it was, he loved having her by his side. He hated to be a territorial brute, but he loved having contact with her body in the presence of others. It always reassured him that they were really together, really married, and really forever.

Until he came to this prison, forever was an unimaginable word. Family wasn't forever, friends weren't forever, and belongings—forget it. Since Cori had slipped off her cracker-jack ring in return for his final tenth gold ring embedded with a diamond that only a bounty hunter could afford, he had been fighting the urge to wrap her in his arms and never let go.

"What did I miss?" She smiled back at him, wrapping her grip tighter on his bicep, which he unconsciously flexed for her. Her hair had grown out since the dragon. It was still shorter than before, but long enough to put back in a ponytail.

Today, however, she was wearing it down. Her usual jeans and t-shirt were a fading memory. These days she was wearing the black cargo pants like the other guards, and black t-shirts. It made no difference to him, but he was once again surprised at how quickly she had given up her trademark tees and adapted to being Belus's little soldier.

"You've been logging in for this level the last five weeks," Belus said. "Why is that?"

"You told me to take on more responsibility," she said, pulling away from Ethan's arm. "So I did."

"Did you do full floor checks daily?" Belus persisted.

"Of course, why?"

"Was the floor accounted for at your check-in at four o'clock yesterday?" Belus asked.

She looked at Ethan, no doubt withholding the usual eye roll that Belus's conversations inspired. "Yes. The count was the same as it was every day since I started checking."

"Hmmm." Belus's brow pinched as he looked over his clipboard again. "I'm going to need you to go over the cells with me. I want you to tell me which transmorph is missing."

"Don't you know which one is missing?" Ethan asked.

Belus nodded. "Yes, but if *she* doesn't, that means the transmorph went AWOL between the last check before she started and the day she started."

"You think she misread the chart?" Ethan glanced at Cori. She crossed her arms and frowned into a borderline pout at the accusation.

Belus patted his clipboard against his leg. "Are you planning to take over this investigation? Because if you have better ideas, I'd love to hear them."

Ethan debated whether he *should* take over, but he didn't want to create an uncomfortable relationship with Belus. He certainly didn't have the option of quitting this job if he didn't get along with his coworkers. "I have no arguments. I'm just asking questions."

"Let's answer my questions first. You two need to stop playing tag-team defense so we can get down to the facts. I don't have time to worry about whose toes I'm stepping on. Danato never has a problem with my techniques, and when he does, you'd better believe he tells me about it."

Ethan nodded and gave a half-ass salute. "Have at it." He put his hand out to usher Cori away, but she was already leading the way to count down the cages with Belus.

Ethan hadn't had many opportunities to work with the transmorphs, but since Cori had discovered a way to identify them and keep their forms, he didn't think they were the menace everyone had made them out to be. However, with one of them out of containment, there was no way to differentiate it. Not unless they started throwing acid on everyone—which Belus may not have ruled out yet.

Or they could use the photos.

"Hey, Belus, we should use the photos to clear the guards," Ethan hollered after them, but they were already through the airlock.

When he turned back, he saw the last person he expected to see on the transmorph level, or any level other than the basement.

Ethan watched two of his guards escort Cleos toward him. The photophobe psychic arrived wearing shackles and a long brown hooded cloak to protect him from the harsh fluorescent lighting. Ethan wasn't sure if the attire reminded him more of a monk or of Obi Wan Kenobi. Either way, Cleos was neither.

"What the hell is he doing here?" Ethan snarled.

Cleos smiled at his irritation. He seemed to find pleasure in anything that Ethan did not. It was just another personality trait that added to his hatred of the photophobe.

"He insisted on speaking with you," one guard answered back.

"And I insist on having HBO. It doesn't mean I'm going to get it," Ethan retorted dryly.

"He said it was a matter of life and death," the guard answered a little more quietly, as if he suddenly realized how stupid it sounded. Ethan could hardly reprimand the man for his mistake. Cleos only needed to touch him to influence his thoughts.

"This freak," Ethan said, not bothering to fly above childish name-calling, "has been requesting to talk with me the last few weeks, but I haven't bothered with him since the issue he wishes to discuss is out of my hands." Ethan took a few steps toward Cleos. "She doesn't want to see you anymore. She read your file. She knows you're a monster. Get over it. Put him back in his cage," Ethan ordered the guards and turned on his heel to leave.

"The life I'm concerned with," Cleos said hastily, "is Corinthia's."

Ethan slowed his departure to a stop. His muscles tensed with vexation. He hated the way he called her Corinthia, as if he was above her nickname. He knew he should walk away and ignore him, but he couldn't.

"Are you threatening her?" Ethan asked as he turned back to me.

"Never." Cleos's face crumpled at the accusation. "I am not the one who has put her in danger."

"Oh, really?" Ethan crossed his arms. "Who has put her in danger, then?"

Cleos looked down at the guards, holding his arms, and then back at Ethan. "Is this really necessary?"

Ethan nodded for the guards to release him. "Keep your hands to yourself," he warned.

"For now," was the only contention Cleos offered after the guards removed his cuffs and stepped away from him. He strolled over to Ethan, keeping the guards at his back as he spoke in a hushed tone. "I assume the alarms mean you have a missing transmorph?"

Ethan nodded and shifted to create a more comfortable distance between them without actually backing away. "Let's jump to the climax of your story so I can get back to my job."

"Yes, I didn't get a chance to congratulate you on that. It was nice of Cori to step down so you could rise in the ranks."

Ethan clenched his jaw but said nothing. Cleos was always going to be an itch he couldn't quite scratch. It had frustrated Danato immensely that Cori had formed an attachment to Cleos, but it had only taken Ethan five minutes with the photophobe to realize he disapproved of their friendship as well.

Jealousy aside, Cleos was dangerous. Cori had refused to see it. As much caution as she took with their contact, she persisted in visiting him on a weekly and sometimes daily basis. Before Danato left for his vacation, he put strict orders down that she stay away from Cleos. He even threatened to have her restricted from the level by an armed guard.

The conversation had gone about as well as asking a teenage girl to stop seeing her motorcycle-driving boyfriend. Besides a torrent of cuss words she'd spat at Danato, there were also a few choice phrases directed at Ethan for his involvement. They held their ground, despite her insistence that they were overreacting.

It took a week for her to cool down enough to accept Cleos's file. It had lain on her nightstand, unopened, for several more weeks. She'd blamed her exhaustion as an excuse not to read it. It wasn't until a week into their honeymoon that Ethan revealed his intent to uphold Danato's orders and demand they dissolve their acquaintance. After an intense argument, he'd forced her to read the document. Once she was finished, she went straight to Cleos to confirm the vile acts revealed in it.

"Ethan." Cleos spoke with a sternness that didn't seem to fit him. "If Danato were here, I would take this up with him. Since he is not here, I have no choice but to confide in you about my concerns."

Ethan scoffed. "I'm surprised you didn't try, Belus."

"No," Cleos snapped. "I want nothing to do with that small-minded man."

Ethan tipped his head, making a mental note to ask Belus about the incident that had led to such revulsion. "Cleos, what exactly is your concern?"

"What the hell is he doing here?" Cori called over as she and Belus returned to the section.

Cori was holding a picture of the missing transmorph. Ethan always found that transmorphs looked very similar in their original shape. He wondered if the pictures served any purpose other than to make them look the same, therefore *less* identifiable.

Belus observed Cleos with some confusion, but Ethan couldn't see anything in his body language to hint at the animosity Cleos had expressed toward him. Perhaps it wasn't mutual.

"Cori," Cleos drawled with a sparkle in his eye. "Good to see you again. How about a hug?" She frowned and stopped her approach, leaving a significant distance between them.

Cleos took a step forward, but Ethan raised his hand and shook his head. The photophobe clenched his jaw, but stayed back.

"You thought of the picture. I was just going to suggest that." Ethan nodded at the photo in Cori's hand.

"What else would we use? Acid?" Belus said with a finely sharpened stab of condescension.

"We're going to make copies and show it to the other inmates," Cori chimed in before he could respond to Belus.

"If we find anything, we'll let you know," Belus said. "You need anything here?" He nodded at Cleos.

Ethan glanced back at Cleos, who was watching Cori. "No, I can handle this from here. I have my walkie." Ethan grimaced and pulled the slim device from his belt. He clicked it on.

Since he only used the radio for designated operations and emergencies, it was easy to forget about it. The outmoded technology wasn't without its risks, but short, direct conversations didn't seem to spark any possessions, unlike radios and televisions that transmitted constant, autonomous sound waves.

Belus frowned at his belated adherence to the protocol, but withheld his criticism. "Come on, Cori."

Cori gave him a solemn smile before following Belus.

Ethan turned back to Cleos and jumped when he found him right behind him. "We need to talk," he insisted.

Rather than back away from the overly personal encounter, Ethan grabbed his shoulders and pushed him back. Cleos had an inch or maybe two on him, but his frame didn't support enough muscle to be a physical threat. If anything, Cleos had the same build as most vampires: wiry but starved muscles. It made Ethan wonder if vitamin D was a little more important in muscle building than anyone gave it credit for.

Before Ethan could remove his grasp and once again ask for the conclusion of his badgering, Cleos grabbed his bare forearm with his cuffed hands. The bare-skin touch made Ethan want to rip himself away, but the panic that Cleos's grip exuded, as well as his eyes, gave him pause. "If you love her nearly as much as you claim to, then one discussion with me can hardly be a waste of your time. Especially if there is even the slightest hint of danger to her." The guards jumped on Cleos and pried his hands off Ethan.

Ethan shook away the feeling that Cleos had injected with his touch. He didn't like being influenced by a criminal, but he was right. Cleos seemed to care for Cori in whatever deviant way he was capable of. If he was as troubled as he was portraying, Ethan needed to at least hear him out.

"Wait." Ethan took in a deep breath and huffed out his dissatisfaction. "Take him down to the office," he instructed as he headed that way himself. "And get these damn elevators going! Transmorphs know how to use stairs!"

4

WITH THE GUARDS STATIONED just outside the office door, Ethan settled into position, leaning against Danato's desk. Despite his new title, Ethan still couldn't bring himself to sit in the chair. Not only did it feel like an insult to sit on the throne of a king, but it was uncomfortable as hell. No matter how Ethan situated himself on it, the wretched springs poked him.

He had broached the idea of using one of the many empty rooms down the hall for his office, but somehow the topic kept getting underplayed or outright ignored. At first, Ethan assumed it had something to do with a tight budget, but how much could a set of thirty-year-old office furniture cost?

Cleos sat in one chair in front of the desk, inspecting the room. The rusty old furniture and pervasive diesel smell must have disappointed him—much like everyone when they first encountered the room.

"This is where great decisions are made?" Cleos went so far as to wipe his fingers along the vinyl-covered chair arm to check for dust or grease. It was clean, of course, but that didn't stop him from wiping his fingers on his cloak.

"Yes, this is the warden's office. I suppose it is too much to ask for you to get right to the point." Ethan stood to circle around to the swivel chair, but he remembered it was outside of his comfort zone, so he took up a different spot, leaning against the desk. "Can we at least introduce the product before the sales pitch, so I know what I'm supposed to be buying into?"

"Cori is missing," Cleos said flatly.

Ethan tried not to smile, but the grin that spread across his face most likely didn't depict his restraint. "You just saw her upstairs. She was the cute blonde, rosy cheeks, yay high." He raised his hand to show her height; he wanted to add 'great rack,' but thought better of it.

"That is not Cori. That is your missing transmorph."

Ethan took that in, losing his smile as he gave the suggestion honest consideration. "I'm afraid that isn't possible. The transmorph would have gone missing last night. Cori was with me all night. Not to mention, where is Cori then? I doubt the men would have missed her tied up in a corner somewhere."

Cleos's eyes shifted into a glare; he obviously didn't appreciate Ethan's mockery. "I hope Danato didn't choose the wrong person for this job. Think about the two different types of transmorphs."

Ethan knew it was already skirting five a.m. but his brain was still back at four a.m. He was still not accepting anything about Cleos's suspicions, but he was realizing what he was alluding to.

There were two types of transmorphs: the ones that could manipulate their appearance to mimic someone and the ones that outright enveloped their prey. Both types could emulate voices and mannerisms to frightening accuracy, but it was the enveloping types that could read minds, accessing their victim's memories to disguise themselves more accurately.

"You think that the transmorph enveloped her sometime yesterday and is still riding on her now?"

"No," Cleos said. "I think she was enveloped five weeks ago."

"Five weeks! Don't you think I... we would have noticed a missing..." Ethan trailed off as he remembered Cori was the one observing the transmorph levels' daily checks. The monthly check, conducted by a separate person, had revealed the discrepancy. "I would know if she were different," he rationalized.

"I had hoped that, but no such luck." Ethan opened his mouth to object, but Cleos continued. "I'm sure the subtle differences weren't all that objectionable."

Ethan creased his brow. "What does that mean?"

"You must have been relieved, albeit surprised, when she came to you, determined to give me up."

Ethan wanted to inform him it had been *her* decision to end their friendship, but that wasn't what this was about anymore. "That's why you think she's a transmorph. She broke your friendship, therefore she must be under the control of a foreign being. That is some ego, Cleos."

"Indeed, it is." Cleos elevated the intended insult to a compliment. "She would never have given me up; at least, not that easily, not cold turkey. She certainly wouldn't have treated me that way when she did."

"She saw what you were, and she hated you for it," Ethan said, justifying the cold manner in which Cori had dismissed Cleos at their last encounter five weeks ago.

"Yes, we can discuss how she reacted to my file at a later time. For now, let's discuss her last few weeks with you." Cleos leaned forward and looked Ethan over. He wasn't sure if the gaze looked carnivorous or carnal, but either way, his eyes were unwelcome. "You're a young, virile man. I bet the subtle changes in her sexuality were lost on you, so long as your dick was slapping into something."

Ethan wasn't sure what steps took place between him leaning on the desk, and his fists constricting Cleos's cloak around his throat. The only thing preventing Ethan from choking him to death was the vinyl chair tipping back on two legs, reducing the pressure he could impose.

"Think, Ethan," Cleos said through his obstructed windpipe. "Think about every night since she disavowed my friendship. How receptive was she to your advances? How often did she instigate? Did she ever ask you to stop to rid her mind of bad memories before you could continue?"

Ethan pulled back on Cleos's cloak, pulling him up with the chair. He backed away, feeling a sickness in his stomach. He had made love to Cori every night since she broke her friendship with Cleos. She had almost always instigated it.

Prior to their marriage, Ethan had discovered the burden of making love to a woman familiar with rape. Although some intimacies were without interruption, he often had to stop to talk her out of her memories, so she could concentrate on being with him. She was also far more comfortable being on top, where she could control the act.

Ethan counted the many missionary evenings he had spent with Cori over the last five weeks. He couldn't think of a single interruption to their sex life. To add to it, he couldn't think of any quarrels outside of the bedroom either—a rarer event still.

"It's not just your sex life, Ethan," Cleos continued, ignoring his discomfort at the conversation. "There may be subtle changes to how she behaves, or the way she presents herself. Transmorphs aren't as thorough in their reads as I am. They wouldn't understand the noticeable difference of her hair being worn down, when she normally wears it up in a ponytail."

Ethan glared at him. He hadn't meant to. The expression was only in response to his knowledge. Cori did normally wear her hair up, but in the weeks past, it had been down more often. It disgusted him that Cleos knew her from the inside out. He'd never understood why Cori hadn't viewed that intimacy as the ultimate violation, especially given her past.

Ethan looked away and cleared his throat. "She usually wears jeans and a clever t-shirt. Now she wears the cargo pants, and her t-shirts are always black." Even as Ethan said it, he knew he was admitting to what a fool he had been, but he had to add something to defend his knowledge of his wife.

"You believe me." Cleos didn't seem to ask so much as confirm what they had established.

"I don't know. This is all very circumstantial. These changes could all be because of her getting more comfortable with me and her new duties here."

"Yes, because stubborn women with trust issues live happily ever after when they marry Prince Charming."

Ethan moved over to him. "I need more proof. I can't accuse my wife of being a transmorph just because she's more sexually available and doesn't put her hair up."

Cleos thought for a moment. "I can show you proof, but it's a memory. My memory of the night Cori came to denounce me."

"I was there, remember?"

"Not for all of it. You left us alone. The last bit was the important part. I can tell you, but I doubt you'll take my word for it. I can't manipulate my memory. You have to trust what I saw as fact. Are you willing to take my memory?"

Ethan extended his hand, denying his fear any hold over him. Cleos smiled and touched his hand with the tip of his finger. Ethan looked at his hand, trying to find a physical manifestation of the transfer. As soon as he did, he felt his mind fade away. Not to blackness, but to a previous memory. This time, however, he was watching it from another set of eyes.

5

ETHAN COULD SEE AND hear what Cleos saw and heard, but his physical connection to the photophobe's body was numb. He had no sense of what he thought or felt emotionally. He wondered if Cleos had blocked that aspect of the transfer, or if it was an inherently different fragment of the memory that he simply couldn't or didn't add.

He saw himself and Cori approach the cell, and the familiar memory unfolded with a slightly different slant. The creatures in the adjacent enclosures were atwitter about the prospect of fresh blood passing just out of their reach. The vicious, licentious monsters were far from the glamorized heartthrobs of teenage romances.

Cori approached Cleos with a cold, calculating sneer already on her face. He was surprised to see his own face didn't hold any retribution. He recalled that at that moment, fleeting as it was, he felt guilty about what Cori was about to do.

"Cori. Ethan," Cleos said after activating the intercom. "What brings you by so late?" He placed his hands in the pass-through, prepared to receive Cori's usual donation of *mental cake,* as she had put it once.

"I've come to say goodbye," Cori said, without the slightest hint of pain in her voice.

"That's rather unlike you to give up on your pet project. Don't tell me you're letting this tyrant bully you?" Cleos said, looking to Ethan for some reaction. As angry as he had been at Cleos for suggesting he was an oppressive husband, he could see now that he hadn't shown it. His face remained indifferent to the conversation.

"I made this decision on my own. You know very well I make my own decisions," Cori said, with a hint of cynicism in her tone.

Cleos reached for her. "I don't believe you. Let me see the truth."

"No." Cori hadn't said it with any more resignation than the latter statement, but a shiver went through Cleos. Ethan wished he could sense Cleos's thoughts at that moment. Was this anger for him? Shock? Or was it something more mournful?

"What about our conversation before?" Cleos lowered his voice, as if Ethan wouldn't be able to hear him standing only inches away from her.

Ethan recalled feeling uncomfortable at that moment. He had recognized Cleos's distrust, but he had attributed it to his influence on Cori's decision. He hadn't wanted to be accused of playing the puppeteer to Cori.

Ethan cleared his throat. "I'll give you two a moment." He watched himself lean over to kiss Cori. It should have been a discreet peck on the cheek or lips, but his territorialism had the better of him that day, and he gave her a deep, sensuous kiss. He remembered that he even probed with his tongue. Looking at it now through Cleos's eyes, he regretted his display. He may as well have pissed on her leg before he left.

Cleos's eyes didn't avert as he'd expected they might. Either he wanted to watch or he couldn't look away, or his assumptions were wrong all together. Perhaps he had been indifferent to Ethan's affections.

When he broke from Cori, he walked back through the airlocks to the west elevator. That was where his own memory of the encounter had ended, but now he could see what had happened after he left. He knew Cori didn't stay much longer, so he couldn't imagine what epiphany Cleos had come to in that time that would lead him to believe she was not herself.

"Talk to me! What's changed?" Cleos slammed his fists into his plexi-glass cage.

"Everything has changed. I've read your file. You're a monster. I want nothing to do with you," Cori recited.

"What about our last conversation? Do you still want my reason?"

"You said you'd never give it to me." Cori shrugged, seemingly disinterested.

"I'll give it to you." Cleos thrust his hands back through the pass. "I'll show you what you wanted to know. Just touch me."

Cori's eyes looked over his outstretched hand. His knobby fingers pointed out to her, begging to wrap around her hand. Her face darkened in disgust, and she took a step forward, just inches out of his reach. "I couldn't wash enough from touching that," she snarled. "I don't care what anyone says, you'll always be an impotent vampire to me." Cori flipped her hair over her shoulder and walked away.

"Corinthia!" Cleos banged on the glass. He watched her stalk down the hall. Vampiric creatures fled from view as she did. Ethan could hear Cleos's ragged breath. He felt his heart throbbing in his chest, but instantly knew it was his own. The blur in his vision turned out to be a side effect of being pulled out of the memory.

Ethan shook his head at the disembodied feeling of waking in a strange place after an unintentional nap. He snapped his head up to check on Cleos, but he hadn't moved. He was sitting patiently in his chair, observing. He looked at the clock. He hadn't checked it before he received the memory, but the hours hadn't ticked away.

Ethan stepped around the desk and sat in Danato's chair, ignoring the pokey springs. He rubbed his face before settling his stare on Cleos. There was something sympathetic about the calm scrutiny Cleos conveyed. He obviously knew what Ethan was going through, and he didn't intend to rush him past it.

"That was interesting," Ethan said, trying to define the experience that spanned the spectrums of creepy and freaking awesome.

"Yes, I have my uses."

Ethan tilted his head, trying to discern what emotion he was putting behind that statement, but Cleos wasn't giving anything up at the moment. "I can see why you were suspicious. That last statement was more than cold. She was just trying to hurt you, and I can't believe she would have treated you like that."

"You still didn't see it, did you?" Ethan had no trouble recognizing Cleos's frustration. "I was suspicious the minute she wouldn't offer me her hand. I was concerned when she wasn't interested in finding out what she had so desperately wanted to know the night before."

"What was that about, anyway?"

"Another time, Ethan. I was convinced she wasn't who she claimed when she insulted me." Cleos leaned forward, putting a dramatic pause before his next statement. "I knew she was a transmorph when she left."

Ethan had hoped the dramatic pause would be leading to more information than he had started with, but he could see by the look on Cleos's face that he wanted him to figure it out himself. He either gave Ethan's 5a.m. mind more credit than Ethan did, or he just wanted Ethan to see it himself, so he would believe it more.

He thought back to her exit. Something about it *was* different. Something Cleos saw that he wouldn't have seen. She came in with him, but left without him.

Ethan stood before his mind had fully wrapped around the entire summation of the theory. "The vampires were quiet when she left. They should have been screeching and reaching. They didn't even stay at the bars. They shied away."

"And what prisoner in this facility can impersonate our Cori, while still remaining unappetizing to a bloodsucker?" Cleos asked, leaning back in his chair.

"Fuck."

6

E THAN COULD FEEL HIS legs shaking as he made his
way through the second level to find Belus and Cori.
He could have contacted Belus over the two-way radio, but
he couldn't risk the transmorph suspecting anything. If
she continued to pose as Cori, he at least knew who his
enemy was. There were still too many questions to answer
before he made a move. One of which was, where was the
real Cori? Followed quickly by, how did they save her?

A flurry of emotions ran through him alongside those
unanswered questions. He was concerned for Cori, but
she was likely still alive within the transmorph. She was
also just as likely severely dehydrated and malnourished.
He feared losing her when he had only just begun his life
with her. He was also furious at himself for not noticing
the changes, which was partnered with an equal share of
guilt for being so stupid.

He focused on his bravado and let his military strut
portray his urgency over his panic. "Belus," he called over
to the dwarf. He was holding a picture up to one of the
mermaid tanks. Cori was on the other side of him, holding
the picture to another tank. He made a mental note that

at no point had she looked at the picture herself, although that may not matter now.

"What did you find?" Belus asked.

"Diddly-squat, but I need to pick your brain about a few things. It's quicker to ask you than look them up. Cori, can you finish up this floor and report back to us when you're done?"

"Sure." She nodded and moved to the next tank.

Ethan nodded for Belus to follow him and he started toward the airlock.

"What happened with Cleos?" Cori asked before he was through the door.

Ethan looked back and gave her a scrunched face with a headshake. "You knew he wasn't going to give you up that easily. Just forget about him and focus on getting that transmorph rounded up." He gave her a wink for good measure. She gave him a simple smile before proceeding to show her photo to the inquisitive mermaid in front of her. Ethan couldn't help but notice how calm the mermaid was being. No fangs bared. No incessant screeching. If he had any doubt about Cori's identity before, it was gone now.

After the first airlock, Ethan kept a few steps between him and Belus in case Cori—or rather, the transmorph—was still watching them. "Belus, keep walking, and don't turn around," he said as sternly as he could without sounding as if he was going to mug the man.

"What's happened?" Belus asked, already on board with the intrigue.

"I got some information from Cleos, which I'm inclined to take seriously. Unfortunately, I got it five weeks later than I should have, because he's a conniving bastard who can't be trusted. Except, I think I trust him on this."

"And?" Belus said, to speed his rant into report mode.

"Cleos believes Cori was enveloped by a transmorph five weeks ago, and the transmorph we are looking for is the Cori we just left behind."

"Any evidence to support that?" Belus asked without any hint of concern or shock.

"Sort of. He gave me a memory." Ethan paused to see if Belus would dispute it. "He saw Cori leave the lower level, and the vampires didn't try to attack her. They were even a little afraid of her. And just now, the mermaids were calm, too." Ethan glanced back and saw him mulling over that thought. "There are other things, but they're just atypical behaviors."

"I've noticed some things myself," Belus finally said. Ethan wanted to turn around, but they hadn't quite made it to the elevator. "She just isn't as stubborn as she usually is. She's been surprisingly compliant." Ethan thought about that and agreed. He wondered how many things he had missed that even Belus had noticed.

"We need to contain her... the transmorph. We need to find out if Cori is inside, and then we need to get her out."

Ethan pushed the button for the elevator and waited. "Any ideas how we can do that?"

Ethan looked down at Belus as he stood beside him to wait for the lift. He was starting to run through the gamut of emotions that Ethan was already entrenched in. "I need to make a call. You may need to freshen up your chapters on transmorph possession."

"Right." Ethan nodded. He didn't want to freshen up his knowledge. All he remembered was that long-term possession by a transmorph was usually fatal.

7

Ethan approached Duke without his usual smile. Duke, however, had a broad one for him. "Hey, boss-man." He took Ethan's outstretched hand and added a slap on his shoulder. "What brings you to the roof without a coat?" Duke looked him over, slowly losing his smile as he did.

Ethan was in his usual black t-shirt and black cargo pants, just like the other guards. He had never seen a reason to distinguish himself, even after receiving his title. Bundled to the nines, Duke wore a hooded jacket, ski mask, gloves, and something that looked like chaps. The spring season wasn't as cold as the winter, but it was still too damn cold to be stepping outside without the proper attire.

"Could I have you step away from your post for a bit?" Ethan said, trying to smile but failing.

"Sure thing, boss," Duke said, propping his weapon on his shoulder. Ethan didn't like when he called him that. It made him feel separate from him, but since Duke wasn't the type to give up a nickname, Ethan never requested he stop. Somehow asking him to stop calling him "boss" seemed... well, bossy.

They stepped back into the stairwell, and Ethan stopped at the first landing. Duke must have realized the seriousness of the situation, because he gripped his weapon tightly with both hands. Ethan could see the furrow in his brow, even through the ski mask.

"Why the long face, boss?"

"I have a job for you to do."

Duke chucked his shoulder and guffawed. "Is that all? You know I ain't too proud to do my job." His Texan accent laced his words with a friendliness that couldn't be beat by any other burr. "What can I do for ya?"

"I need you to arrest my wife," Ethan said.

Duke pulled off his hood and mask, revealing sandy-blond, static-frenzied waves. His cheeks, still rosy from the cold, looked chapped from the long days of roof duty. His golden eyes were normally bright and eager for mischief, but Ethan's request had stunned them into a state of alarm.

Duke swallowed hard and looked around in case someone was waiting to jump out with a video camera. "That's a strange order. She make a bad meat loaf?" he joked, but didn't smile.

"She's been taken over by a transmorph. I'm not sure if she's inside or not, but I can only assume she is. I can't bring myself to do it. I can't trust myself to do it. I don't trust the others... not with my wife. You know what I mean, don't you?"

"You need me to take her into custody, forcefully if need be, but not hurt her when I do it."

Ethan nodded, feeling relieved that Duke understood. "I knew you would be the man to ask. The friend to ask."

To Ethan's surprise, Duke pulled him into a full hug. It wasn't long, but it was heartfelt and in many ways he needed it. "Don't you worry; I'll get your girl locked up. You just work on getting that parasite off her."

"Thanks Duke."

Duke gave him a half-mocking salute before descending the stairs to find Cori and arrest her.

8

"WHAT IS THAT SUPPOSED to mean?" Ethan glared at Cleos from across the office. He was still idling in his vinyl chair, waiting for his tea service, among other delusions. Belus sat in Danato's chair, apparently unaffected by the obtrusive spring.

"Exactly what I said," Cleos responded. "Neither of you has the skills or patience to deal with a transmorph. Danato is the only one who's dealt with them. Tiny Tim here has never been alone in a room with one." Cleos brandished a finger at Belus.

"How do you know?" Belus asked flatly.

Ethan once again searched for evidence of a feud between the two men, but so far, it seemed to be one-sided. If Belus had anything against the man, he was hiding it extremely well.

"He's too by the book," Cleos continued. "You're barely off the book." He gestured to the book in Ethan's hand. "You know who would really excel at dealing with a creature so off the cuff as a transmorph? Cori. Too bad she's going to die because of inadequate staffing."

"Are you done?" Ethan asked, exasperated. He took a few threatening steps toward Cleos. "Let's forget that I could body-slam you with one arm. Let's forget that the structural integrity of my fist could outlast your face. Let's just focus on one thing: Cori is in danger and I will do whatever is necessary to save her."

"Then send for Danato," Cleos drawled.

"Ahem," Belus interjected. They both looked over at him. "I've already sent for help. I sent the message out on the taps right away. I already know that this is too much for us. It doesn't mean we're going to sit around and wait, though," he added.

Cleos sat back in his chair, seeming somewhat floored by the admission. "Well, you're smarter than I would have given you credit for."

"I'm a lot of things people don't give me credit for," Belus mumbled. "We need to question the transmorph. Find out if she is the one enveloping Cori, or if she put her in one of the others."

"And I suppose she's going to give up her location, just like that?" Cleos challenged.

"Will you shut up?" Ethan was losing what was left of his patience. He couldn't stand the whiny rebellion of a grown man. Especially one he could drop-kick.

"He's right," Belus said, breaking the tension. "She won't give herself away. That's why you're going to help us." He pinned Cleos with stern eyes. "You know her better than anyone, right? Even her lover."

Ethan barely contained his chuckle. He hadn't expected Belus to turn Cleos's greatest boast against him.

"I can't guarantee that I'll be able to tell between the two minds," Cleos demurred. "Transmorphs are very good at mimicking thoughts as well as faces."

"But you will feel two minds?" Belus asked.

"Yes, that shouldn't be a problem, as long as you ask the right questions to throw her off her game. Otherwise, the minds will just blend into one."

"Alright, we have a room on level four we can use as an interrogation room. I'll have Duke move her there," Belus said. "Cleos, you do whatever you need to do to prepare. Ethan, you just remind yourself that she is not your wife, no matter what she says."

Ethan nodded, but everything about that creature was his wife. Not only did she have her mind and body, but for the last five weeks, she'd had him as well. He shivered at that thought and wondered how many times she could have killed him. Since she didn't, it made him wonder what her ultimate plan was.

9

"SOMEONE WANT TO TELL me what this is all about?" Cori rocked back in her yellow plastic school chair with one leg crossed over the other. They had set up the interrogation room in a soundproof cell on the transmorph level. Along with several old school chairs was a long metal table that still bore the etched engravings of Peter and Erica's forever-love. There were also a few less than loving remarks about Derek Penn.

Belus came in and sat down at the long end of the table. Ethan took the center chair, and Cleos stood next to him. Cori and Cleos eyed each other carefully. There seemed to be an unspoken challenge being raised between them. Ethan knew it wasn't his wife, but he still didn't like the connection between them.

"What is he doing here?" Cori griped. Her resemblance to the real Cori still impressed Ethan. He could already see her haughty attitude pushing through her attempt to remain civil. "Hell, what am *I* doing here? What's with the cuffs?" She raised her shackled wrists from her lap as if Ethan might not have been aware of the treatment she had received.

"Cori—" Ethan started to explain.

"Ethan," Belus interrupted. Ethan glanced at him, but he already knew what his hard stare was telling him. This wasn't Cori, and there was no point in perpetuating the ruse any longer than necessary.

"Actually, I'm not sure what to call you." He turned back to her, offering her a scowl. "Transmorphs don't really have names, do they?" Her eyes didn't waver or hint at any surprise. "Not really much point when you're always pretending to be someone else. We should call you something, though. Do you have a preference?"

"What are you three smokin' out there?" She glanced over all of them with a disapproving motherly concern. It was a look she often used on Danato when he didn't abide by her diet regimen.

Ethan resisted the urge to explain things to her again. "How about..." He leaned closer to the table to see the names embedded in the heart. "Erica." He tapped the name. "That seems simple enough; a little less confusing. I suppose I could just as easily use Peter, since you don't really have a recognizable gender, but given the last few weeks, I thought I'd save on my gag reflex."

Her eyes sparkled, and she smiled at this comment. "I've enjoyed our honeymoon, too."

Ethan looked away, even though he didn't want to. He hated the guilt that was prickling up his spine. "Cleos." He looked at Cleos to hide his discomfort. "Why don't you sit next to... Erica?"

"My pleasure," Cleos said without a glance.

"Touch me and I'll claw your eyes out," Erica threatened when he brought a plastic chair around to sit beside her.

"Erica." Ethan leaned over the table to speak.

"Stop calling me that! I'm Cori!"

Ethan shook his head. "No, you aren't, and I think we both know that aside from your ability to change your appearance, you really have no exceptional talents for strength or agility. Hell, you can barely move except to walk and sit. Let's put aside any objections you have about Cleos's proximity, because if you really prefer, I'll *force* the issue." He arched a brow and waited for a snide remark, but none came.

She instead leaned forward and touched his hands with hers. His instinct said to pull away, but he let her touch him. He wanted to see if he could feel the difference now.

Her hands were soft, too soft. Gardeners never had soft hands. Her fingernails pinched his skin as she gripped his hand. Her eyes watered and she frowned. "Don't you know me?"

"Yes," he said. He could sense Belus shift. He was prepared to break him away from her at the slightest hint of weakness. "I do know Cori. I know that her fingernails are constantly dried out from digging in the dirt. They break all the time." He lifted her hand and reflected on the perfect length on each nail. "She can never grow them out." Erica ripped her hand away. Her tears instantly dried up and her sneer returned. "It's all in the details. You could never be her."

She laughed—a deep cackle that didn't belong to Cori's vocal cords. Her face didn't change, but the spurious shadows that darkened her features made the otherwise innocent face look malicious. "For five weeks I was. It would have been for a few more if it weren't for him." She shot Cleos a scowl that, surprisingly, made him back away.

"Cleos." Ethan didn't want to let her rant go on any longer than possible. "Touch her." Erica actually hissed at Cleos when he reached for her, but he clamped on to her arm hard with his shackled hands. Ethan was sure the pressure he was using would likely cause bruises, but he shoved away the unnecessary concern. "Where is Cori?" Ethan asked, using his best cop voice.

The police had interrogated him many times, and it was always the same. First, they tried to intimidate you, then they reasoned with you, then they threatened you, and finally they wore you down with repetitive questions, bad coffee, and unpredictable spikes in anger. Ethan wasn't sure any of those tactics would work here, but he would start with what he knew and work his way up to impromptu genius.

"She's right here. She never left," Erica said, leaning her elbows out in place of her hands.

Cleos offered nothing in the way of confirmation. His eyes were shut and his lids flickering.

"Is she safe?" Ethan asked, trying to hide his anxiety about her condition.

"Snug as a bug in a rug," Erica quipped.

"You've been feeding her?"

"A little here and there. She's pretty tough. I had to make sure her mind stayed quiet." Erica pressed a finger to her lips. "She's sleeping now. I don't want to wake her."

Ethan knew he was going to have to come up with better questions than this, but he was running out of ideas. All he really wanted to know was where she was, and if she was okay. He needed to ask her something that separated her from Cori. "Why didn't you kill me?"

Erica arched a brow. "No need. I was having fun."

"I don't get it." He looked her over, trying to pinpoint what disturbed him about this. "You could have transformed into a guard or a dock loader. You could have escaped the minute you had access to Cori and her keys. Why did you stay?"

Her head tipped as if she were trying to see through his plan. Little did she know; he had no plan.

"I hardly think revealing my ultimate goal is helpful to me now. Especially if I get a chance to do it again."

"You spent a lot of time with Belus instead of me." Ethan glanced at him. He was staying quiet, but his eyes were trained on Erica. "I figured that was because he didn't know you as well as I do, or at least wouldn't question those subtle differences like I might."

"Seems I didn't have to worry, did I?" Erica beamed.

"You had to be around to monitor the level. That way no one discovered the empty cell." Ethan leaned back, thinking about that further. "Still, five weeks. What was keeping you here? Did you want to take over Belus? You would have had to kill Cori before you could take over another body, or maybe not. You could have left her in a dehydration coma. It would have taken at least a few days for her to be capable enough to explain what had happened, if her memory was even intact."

Erica drummed her fingers on the table. Ethan wasn't sure he was doing the interrogation any good, but he wanted to get his thoughts out, anyway. "Five weeks in this body. Hiding yourself from Belus and me, without the intention of escaping or switching bodies. What would you accomplish in another few weeks that you hadn't accomplished in the first five?" His eyes froze on Erica. He could see her glower deepen even as his mouth turned to a grin. "Danato." Cleos's head jolted back, as if new information was pouring into him via electric shock. "You were waiting for Danato to get back."

Erica's face actually changed form and replicated Danato's for a brief moment before returning to Cori's again. "Two more weeks, and I would have placed him in my cage instead of me. I would take his form and I could dispose of Cori. I would have had lots of fun running his prison while he sat in jail screaming to be let out."

"You thought we would fall for that?" Belus asked.

"You already did." Erica raised her arm and looked at Cleos, who seemed to be in a good deal of pain. "Had enough?"

Cleos ripped his hand away. His face poured sweat, and he panted from the encounter. He leaned over the table, scarcely staying in his chair. He looked up at Ethan, worry etched on his face. "We have a problem."

10

AFTER CLEOS HAD CAUGHT his breath, they made their way through the airlocks away from the interrogation room and toward the imprisoned transmorphs. Cleos had been vague about what he needed them to see.

As Ethan approached the first section of dual transmorphs—the type that could transform separately or envelope another living entity—he saw why Cleos had brought them there. There were only half a dozen type-two transmorphs in custody at the prison. One of them was down three sections in a cell, sitting on a plastic chair, taking the form of Ethan's wife. The other five were here, standing in their cells, also in the form of his wife.

Ethan walked in front of the cells. Five beautiful Cori replicas lined up to greet him, each with a slightly different interpretation of her. Five different facets of her personality were on display—the playful Cori, the motherly one, the scared one, the angry one, and the manipulating one.

Ethan shook his head and turned back to Cleos. "What does this mean?"

"When I was reading her, I got a very distinct read from Erica, as you called her. I searched for Cori, but at first I couldn't find her. I thought that meant she wasn't there, but then I got a read on her." Cleos paused and stepped forward. "She's alive."

Ethan set his jaw and closed his eyes. It took everything in him not to react to that statement with an outburst of joyous tears. "And?" He opened his eyes.

"She's weak and scared, but she could sense my presence right away. Erica was right. She has a strong mind. That's good. She'll need it."

Ethan had always hated that Cleos could read Cori's mind, when he himself struggled to interpret her vague signals to get a bearing on her thoughts. He hated even more that Cori could recognize Cleos in her mind, but he was grateful for any contact they could have with her at this point.

"Even as I started to make contact with her," Cleos continued, placing his hands as if in prayer, making him look so much more like a monk. "Other minds started to infringe on us. They blocked out Cori's voice. I couldn't tell where I was hearing her from. The other minds were transmorphs." Cleos paused and looked back at Belus. He must have already understood, because his face had fallen along with his shoulders. "The transmorphs have linked minds."

Ethan stared at Cleos. It must have been a grave statement, but not only had he not been aware that it could happen, he didn't even understand what that meant. Of course, it meant something bad, but how bad? He waited, refusing to ask for more information.

"Although I strongly suspect that Cori isn't in Erica, I can't be certain. It's possible that she is in one of these transmorphs. At any rate, with their minds linked, I'm hardly going to be useful to you in determining which one is harboring her."

Ethan looked over the cells of Cori. The motherly one reached out for him. Her eyes begged to ease his burden of worry. "Even if we could get her pinpointed, do we have any way of getting her out of the transmorph?"

"Let me worry about that," Belus said. After a brief pause, he continued. "We can't do any more without assistance. Erica is detained. Let's take a break from this. Cleos needs to be getting back to his cell, and Ethan, you need to get some rest."

"Yes," Cleos mocked. "I've so missed my confinement."

"I'll take him back down," Ethan volunteered. He needed a reason to leave his Coris behind. He didn't bother grabbing Cleos by the arm. He just motioned for him to follow.

11

ETHAN WAS SURPRISED THAT Belus had permitted a break in their efforts. He was normally eager to solve problems. It was possible that he was just taking pity on him—letting him have time to adjust to the new burden on his shoulders. However, it was more likely that Belus knew their efforts were fruitless, because the time they considered to be so precious had already run out.

After an awkward ride in the lift, they arrived at the lower level. Barking, hissing vampires grabbed for them through the bars. Ethan walked slowly and Cleos matched his pace, staying only a half a step behind him so their shoulders didn't bump as they stayed on the midline path.

"That was a good catch," Ethan admitted, thinking about the memory he had been given. "I only wish I had come to see you sooner. I just assumed you were trying to convince me to let you see Cori."

"In a nutshell, but for different reasons than you thought," Cleos said.

"I don't get you and her. I probably never will, but thank you for your help." Ethan felt like he was lying to say the words, but even if he wasn't thankful for Cleos, he should have been. If it weren't for him, he would still be with Cori's doppelgänger, and Danato would be in danger when he returned.

"That must take a lot out of you to say."

"It does," Ethan acknowledged.

"I've noticed that about you—your pride. It's different from Cori's. She likes to prove people wrong. You, you like to prove people right. You like living up to the expectations of others."

"I know who I am. I don't need to be psychoanalyzed."

"Fair enough. Still, it must bother you—Cori and me."

"Just figuring that out now?" Ethan stepped through the airlock and pulled it shut behind them. A new round of vampires symphonized their appreciation of fresh blood.

"What we have, or rather, what I have of her, is something you couldn't comprehend. I don't imagine that with another decade together, you'll know her as well as I do. That is such a shame."

Ethan resisted the urge to shove him into the reach of one of the hungry vampires. "I understand your obsession with her. I just don't understand why *she* tolerates *you*."

"I'm an addictive personality." Cleos smiled.

"I must be immune," Ethan mumbled.

"For now. You forget, I've been there for Cori when you haven't been. I helped her study for the warden's written test. I helped her free the prison from elemental control."

Ethan stepped through another airlock and shut the door after Cleos was through. Yet another band of slobbering bloodsuckers begged for their appendages. "It doesn't matter. She gave you up," Ethan said.

"No, she didn't. The transmorph did, because she knew I would read right through her."

"She would have given you up either way."

"No, Ethan, she wouldn't have. Not the way you think, anyway. Cori is devoted to me. Maybe that makes no sense to you, but rest assured, she is as loyal to me as she is to you and Danato."

"I think you're reading outside your scope again." He stopped at Cleos's cell and wrenched open the door.

"Perhaps it's time we discussed the last night Cori was herself. The night she became Erica." Ethan removed Cleos's handcuffs. "You argued that night, didn't you?" Ethan glared at him. He clearly knew the answer. There was no point in asking. "It was a knock-down, drag-out fight. You forced her to read my file. You told her she would either read it or you would read it to her."

Ethan remembered that argument vividly. They had been only days into the honeymoon. She had planned a dinner for two with pot roast and scalped potatoes. He was ravenous. He ate two helpings of each. When they went upstairs to make love, he saw the file missing from her bedside table. He asked her about it. That simple question drew angry accusations of mistrust from her.

The argument persisted over the next hour. He raged about the necessity of her reading the document, and she tried to justify her right to be ignorant. In the end, she attempted to leave, but he blocked her way. He remembered how livid she was when she realized he would not let her leave her own home.

In the end, she sat on the couch and read the document aloud, to prove she was reading it. Her eyes watered more with each atrocity on Cleos's record. He had hoped when she was finished, she would understand the danger to her and forgive him for being so overbearing. She didn't. She ran out of the house with the record in hand.

"She came to *you*, didn't she… after she read it?" Ethan asked.

"Yes. She was still her then, but what happened when she came back to you later that night?"

Cleos knew that answer as well, but he likely wanted Ethan to remember it for himself—confirm the details in his own mind. "I was in bed already, not quite asleep. It was late, after midnight, but I don't remember exactly." He paused. He didn't want to be explicit about how Cori, or perhaps then Erica, had come in and made love to him. "She called you a memory-sucker. She said she wanted nothing to do with you anymore. She begged me to forgive her."

"Yes," Cleos said as he walked into his plexi-glass cell. "It was everything you wanted, handed to you on a platter. I can imagine why you didn't question it. Who would?"

Ethan couldn't tell if Cleos was being sarcastic or making an excuse for him. He latched the cell door and pressed the intercom button so they could continue the conversation. "Somewhere between you and me, she turned into Erica," Ethan pondered aloud. "Why would she even go up to that level?"

"We'll ask her when she gets out," Cleos said, sounding remarkably reassuring. "Do you want the memory of our last conversation?" Ethan crumpled his brow. "You won't like it, of course, but who knows? Maybe a second pair of eyes will see something I didn't."

Taking the memory served no purpose other than flaunting Cori's attention to him, but he couldn't resist seeing her again. He hated not seeing her and hearing her.

He placed his hand in the pass-through and Cleos tapped it. He pulled his hand back out and waited, but nothing happened. He looked at Cleos for an answer.

"Get home and settle in. Once you are relaxed, the memory will come to you. Don't try to force it."

Ethan checked the door to make sure it was secure, then headed home.

12

T HE HOUSE WAS QUIET and cold, almost as if the entity that embodied it was sad at the loss of Danato, or maybe even Cori, if she could recognize the change. Ethan turned on a few more lights than needed and started a fire just to make the place look lived in.

He rummaged through the cupboards for something resembling lunch, or perhaps it would be his supper now. He settled on canned spaghetti, which he didn't bother to warm, and toast with extra butter. He scarfed down the non-nutritious meal and sprawled out on the couch.

As Ethan listened to the silence in the house, he wished Danato was home. He didn't understand how he had tolerated living in the house alone for so long. Without a television or radio to make noise, he desperately wanted voices to fill in the void.

He heard a gentle knock on the door and eagerly answered it. "Belus?" Despite the shrunken list of people likely to knock on his door, he didn't expect to see him. Visiting was uncommon for him. Cori had invited him to dinner a few times to encourage it, but Belus always seemed uncomfortable being around the three of them together—as if he was interfering with family time. What he didn't realize was that they thought of him as their grumpy old uncle. "Come in." Ethan waved him inside.

"Thank you." Belus came in and shook a few stray snowflakes off his coat as he hung it up.

"Have you eaten?" Ethan asked, moving into the kitchen to search for something more civilized to serve his guest than canned spaghetti.

"No, but don't trouble yourself. I have a lady friend in the cafeteria that keeps me fat and happy. I had something else in mind." Belus moved to the living room and slid open the hidden panel beside the fireplace.

Ethan smiled, knowing how alluring Danato's private stash was to the dwarf. "Knock yourself out." He hadn't been privy to the private cocktail parties Cori had, but he supposed Belus wasn't willing to wait for her to return to partake.

"You'll have one too," Belus dictated rather than asked.

"You have bad news." Ethan's stomach roiled.

Belus pulled out a bottle of gin and poured it into two glasses. He didn't bother to water it down before handing it to Ethan, who took the glass and sat on the couch to wait for the bad news. Belus took a sip of the liquor and settled into Danato's usual chair. He never had qualms about taking the big man's chair. Had he been six inches taller, it might have been *his* chair.

"Danato won't be coming back early," Belus finally said.

"What?" Ethan gaped. "Didn't you explain the situation?"

"Yes, he understands the dangers. He doesn't feel that this situation is any different from predicaments he had to face in his early years. He wants you to handle it."

"This isn't just an escaped prisoner. It's Cori!" Ethan yelled at him as if he was the embodiment of Danato. To his credit, Belus didn't take any offense.

"I know it is. So does he. He knows you will find a way."

"Cleos is right. We aren't prepared to deal with these creatures."

Belus chuckled. "Cleos doesn't know everything. I've taken the liberty of calling in someone who can help. He won't be here until tomorrow, so you should rest tonight. In the morning, we will interrogate Erica again, if for no other reason than to have Cleos read her again."

"I feel so useless."

"Being warden isn't always about saving the day. Sometimes it's just about directing those who do save the day. Danato and I have saved lives by letting our guards do the jobs they are trained to do. All we usually do is give them a leader that is worth doing it for. Those men in that prison respect you as a colleague and a commander. Don't assume that you have to be on the front lines to have a successful battle."

"Spoken like a general." Ethan clinked his glass and downed his gin. He held back the cough that his throat demanded. "When we find her, how do we separate her body from the transmorph?"

"I think that's best discussed when our friend arrives tomorrow." Belus took the last sip of his liquor and set the glass on the coffee table before heading to the door. "Sleep, kid. You're going to need it." Belus slipped on his coat and left.

Ethan's stomach gurgled, objecting to the alcohol. He didn't usually drink hard liquor, though he was painfully acquainted with the result of too many empty beer bottles. Either way, drinking was not his strong suit.

As he relaxed, he felt the world spin and his eyes forcibly close. When he reopened them, he was no longer at home and he was no longer himself. Back behind the eyes of Cleos, he saw Cori approach his cell, tears in her eyes and a manila folder clenched in her hands.

She slammed her hand against the intercom while Cleos moved to meet her at the glass. He placed his hand in the pass-through, but she just looked down at it with revulsion. When her eyes returned, she shook her head. "You're eating my memories!"

Cleos pulled his hand away and turned his back to her. "I see you've finally read my file."

"I thought you were reading my mind, not eating it."

He looked back at her. "Microscopic trash memories. Things you would never miss, and don't even remember, anyway."

"You had no right. Those are *my* memories."

"The names of people you met only once at a party. The smell of the worst-tasting food you ever ate. The recipe for a dessert you've never once made. They are useless memories that you would need me to recall for you, anyway. They are too deep for you to find. They are scrap memories. I am hardly damaging your brain."

"What about Sasha Gellen, Elenor Reiding..."

"I know their names!"

"You lobotomized five women!"

"No, I erased their minds. It's different. They will create new memories."

"They couldn't walk or talk when you were through with them!" Cori slammed the folder against the glass. "If that's not lobotomized, I don't know what is!"

Cleos looked away. He paced the short depth of the cell before returning to Cori. Her face crumpled and tears freely flowed down her cheeks. "I'm a criminal. What did you expect? I wasn't put in this cell for kicking puppies and pulling kitten tails. My powers come with their own set of burdens. Nothing in my world is cut and dried."

Cori shook her head vigorously. "You said you were nothing like them." She pointed to the slobbering beasts down the basement alley.

"I'm not." Ethan could feel Cleos clench his fists. His nails dug into the palms of his hands painfully.

"Tell me what the difference is between sucking blood and sucking memories."

"You don't need all your memories."

"That's not for you to decide!" Cori screeched, losing control of her voice through the emotions.

"How many times did I tell you to read my file? It was there all along. You chose to be blind to my faults. You wanted to keep me under the category of the good guy. Don't blame me for your self-inflicted ignorance. I *am* a bad guy. I deserve to be in this prison, and I never lied to you about that."

Cleos turned away again. He jumped at the sound of his door opening. He looked back just as Cori entered his cell. Ethan could see her sorrow was gone, replaced by conviction.

"Show me." She held out her hand. "Show me what you took from these women. Show me why you took all their memories, when you clearly have the ability and control to take only a little."

Cleos looked at her hand. His eyes narrowed and his fists tightened again. "No."

She took his hand in hers, forcing the clamped fingers to open. She placed her hand in his. "Take my seventh birthday party. It was a fiasco anyway."

"You can keep your parents' arguments. You'll need a foundation for that sharp tongue."

"Show me!"

Cleos looked down at her hand in his. He moved forward, embracing her body. Ethan wanted to close his eyes. He didn't want to see what was about to happen, but the eyes weren't his.

Cleos grabbed Cori's ponytail and pulled her head back. The position put her neck open to him. Still holding her hand and her head, Ethan could feel what Cleos was observing. Her body was trembling in his hands. Cleos could even feel her heart thumping in against his chest.

"Even now, you're terrified of me." Cori didn't deny it, but she didn't move away. "Is your arrogance that strong? You just can't admit that maybe they were right. Maybe I *am* a monster."

"No, I don't believe it. You had a reason to do what you did, and I want to know what it was."

"What if I told you that I wanted to? What if I told you I enjoyed it?"

"No, that's not the reason!" Cori yelled, gripping his hand tighter. "Tell me the truth!"

Cleos moved away from her, ripping his hand from hers. "No. It has nothing to do with you. I won't justify my crimes just so you can feel better about our friendship, even if that means you hating me."

"Then tell me to ease your conscience," Cori persisted, taking yet another step forward toward an already cornered man.

"I don't need to ease my conscience. I did exactly what I did because I wanted to, and I would choose it again."

Cori moved at him again. Cleos stepped back, but the wall stopped his retreat. She put her hands on his shoulders, leaning her forehead into his chest. "Tell me why you chose to do it?"

Without warning, Cleos pushed her off him. She fell to the floor. She looked up at him, appalled. "Get out!" Cleos yelled at her at a volume that made his throat croak.

She shrank from his fury and scrambled to leave the cell. She secured the door and slammed her fists on the glass. "Why won't you just tell me?" she whimpered.

Cleos approached the glass. "Because it has nothing to do with you. They are my actions and you have no right to pass judgment, nor lift it."

Before she left, she slipped her hand through the pass-way. She waited for him to take his token memory snack. She was offering more than that, though. Cleos didn't move.

"Go home, Cori," he whispered. She ripped her hand from the pass-through and stomped down the hall away from him.

Ethan felt himself slip from the memory, but his eyes never reopened. He went from remembering to dreaming in an instant.

13

E THAN THOUGHT ABOUT THE memory as he came into the prison the next morning. Cori must have stayed late that night to work on something in the transmorph area. That explained her abduction. She didn't care what it was she was doing. She always found something to keep her busy when she didn't want to come home. What he was concerned about was what had made her lose concentration enough to step into the grasp of the transmorphs.

Ethan wanted to redo everything. He wanted to refuse Danato's request to help end her relationship with Cleos. He wanted to stuff that blasted folder in the trash and never think of it again. If he hadn't made her read that file, she never would have left the house. She wouldn't be dying inside a transmorph. No matter how he looked at the events that transpired that night, he was the one who'd started it all.

"How did you sleep?" Cleos asked as Ethan approached the interrogation room. He was shackled next to Belus in his full monk garb that protected him from the light.

"We're going to interrogate the other type-two transmorphs," Belus interjected before Ethan could think of a sarcastic response. "I'm hoping that we can figure out which one is holding Cori."

"What about Erica?" Ethan asked.

"She's reading as multiple minds now. I don't even hear Cori in her now," Cleos said.

"I think we should assume that Erica isn't holding her," Belus said. "It takes a good deal of energy to maintain an independent being. I think she's been getting psychic readings off the other transmorphs so she could concentrate on imitating her."

"The others are getting the same readings so we can't tell where she is located," Ethan clarified.

"Right," Belus agreed. "So nothing has changed. We need to figure out where Cori actually is."

"Can't you just use your photos?" Cleos asked.

"No," Belus said. "The photos only change their outer image. Cori could still be inside and we wouldn't know it." Belus nodded to the room. "Suspect number one is already inside. Are you ready?"

Ethan nodded. He knew he was about to see another version of Cori today, one that was so far from real, it made his heart ache.

He stepped into the room and seated himself right away. Belus took his position at the long end of the table, and Cleos sat down beside Cori, putting a hard grip on her arm. She glanced at the manhandling, but turned her attention back to Ethan.

"What do you expect to accomplish here?"

Ethan smiled. "I need Cori's recipe for stroganoff."

"Cute." She sneered.

"No, actually I was hoping you could tell me which one of you sick bastards has her."

Cori leaned forward, giving him a sideways smile. "Why would you want to know that? You'll never get her out."

Ethan found it strange to be negotiating for the release of Cori with a creature that looked and sounded exactly like her. "I'm willing to discuss the terms of her release after you tell me where she is. I like one-on-one conversation. This six on one isn't really working for me."

"I'm pleased that you're willing to negotiate with us, but I think you missed something very key in our attack."

"And what's that?" Ethan crossed his arms.

"Revenge," Cori smirked.

"Yes, I know you and Danato have a rocky history."

Cori shook her head. "Yes, that revenge was planned out as well, but I'm talking about Cori herself." Ethan tipped his head, waiting to hear more. "She threw that vial of acid on us. She made us identifiable. Do you really think we would let that go unpunished?"

"This is about revenge on Cori. Danato was just an afterthought."

"Chicken and the egg, my friend, but rest assured, we have no intention of letting her go. You can save your negotiations for someone who cares what their living conditions are."

Ethan glanced at Cleos. He was out of his trance, but he wouldn't meet Ethan's gaze. "Humor me, *Number One*. What exactly transpired to cause Cori to be captured?"

Cori thought about this for a moment before answering, as if she needed to consult the five minds before proceeding. "A mere distraction when she was logging us. Nothing we could have predicted, but we grabbed her, knocked her out, and took her keys. It's been a grand ole time ever since."

"What are your plans now that we've discovered you? Don't you desire your freedom?"

"Freedom has never been our goal, only revenge. Cori's mind and body is ours now. We can keep her on the cusp of death for years to come. Don't fool yourself into thinking you can separate her. Even if you could, you'd still have to disconnect our minds, and that, my love, will be impossible."

14

"**W**HAT DID SHE MEAN?" Ethan followed Belus out of the interrogation. Cleos stayed inside to collect himself. Despite his psychic abilities, he seemed to struggle to deal with multiple minds simultaneously.

Belus didn't face him. He leaned against the wall and took in a deep breath. When Ethan couldn't stand the silence anymore, he circled around to look at him. "Has Danato ever told you about his wife?" Belus asked.

"Cori mentioned her, but no, he has never spoken of her to me."

"Don't be offended, but he probably never will." Ethan wanted to shake Belus and ask him what the point of this was. "He couldn't save her. He very much wanted to, but he couldn't."

A hot wave of fear slithered up Ethan's spine. "Can I save Cori?"

"I'm not sure yet." Belus shrugged. "The mind is far more fragile than the body. Once it's been shattered by psychic interference, it can't be mended. It would take a good deal of strength to release her mind without harming it."

"So, Cleos will need to break the connection."

"No." Belus chuckled under his breath. "Cleos can't. And we are well past a purely surgical removal. Her mind and body have to be severed from the creature simultaneously." Belus shifted, and his jaw locked. "The only way to remove her now is to utilize a tactic that has its own risks. I don't want to pretend that we aren't on the cusp of losing her even now."

"At what point is she irretrievable?" Ethan asked.

"By normal standards..." Belus pinned him with a stern gaze. "Three weeks ago."

Ethan felt the knife in his heart. He had never considered that she was already lost. Belus had never hinted that there wasn't a chance.

"You son of a bitch," Cleos snarled. He was out of the interrogation room. His voice was quiet, but his face was screaming his fury. At first, Ethan thought he was directing it at Belus. "This is all your fault." He pointed a knobby finger straight at Ethan.

Belus gave the exchange a momentary evaluation before stepping clear of Cleos's wrath.

"You were with her for five weeks," Cleos continued, closing the distance between them. "You could have stopped this. We could have saved her."

"I didn't know," Ethan defended himself. "How could I?"

"You should have known the difference!"

"Don't you think I haven't been torturing myself with that thought for the last 24 hours?"

"Was it worth it?" Cleos lowered his voice to a hissing whisper, and he leaned into Ethan's face to taunt him. "Five weeks of pleasant conformity from an obedient wife. Or was that not the best part? Perhaps you liked the unrestrained sexuality of a wife without baggage. You know what they say." Cleos tipped his head. "Once you go transmorph, you don't go back."

Ethan's fist flew before he could think it through. Cleos's nose cracked on impact. Driven to the floor by the young man's strength, he floundered and sat up. He touched the blood that was pouring from his nostrils, then glared at Ethan from under his brow.

Ethan lunged at him, intending to wipe that sneer off his face, but his body caught on something; two arms looped under his and dragged him back from the brink of murder. He tried to wrench free, but a familiar Irish voice stilled his efforts.

"Easy lad, he can't take much more of that."

Ethan looked back to see a familiar face. "Daniel!" He turned to look at the man clasping his other arm. "Heaton!"

"Hey Ethan." Heaton smiled with an abundance of amusement for his surprise. "Heard you were in a spot of trouble."

"Aye, they sent for the cavalry," Daniel said as they released him.

Ethan gave them both short, severely tight hugs. "Belus called you?" He looked around for Belus. He was back in the interrogation room with two guards. They were collecting Cori number one to take back to her cell. He noticed the short young woman standing behind his friends. She gave him a curt nod, which he instinctively returned.

"That's right." Daniel pushed up the rim of his tiny shaded spectacles. "Were you expecting someone else?"

Ethan's heart sank. As happy as he was to see his friends again, he would have preferred that Belus call someone who could help them. "Yes, actually," he admitted. "A shaman maybe, or an exorcist. I'd take a voodoo priestess at this point."

Daniel and Heaton exchanged glances.

"Well, I don't know about Daniel," Heaton said with a shrug, "but I've been voodoo-free for about six years now. I kept the dolls, though. Kind of cute."

Ethan nodded at Heaton. He wished he could laugh at the joke, but things were just too serious. "Listen guys, I appreciate this, but I just can't focus on anything but Cori right now."

Daniel patted his back. "It's alright. Belus has filled us in on the basics. Why don't you tell me what we're up to now?"

"We suspect that Cori is in one of five transmorphs. The original one that was filling in for her seems to be singular."

"Is that a for sure?" Heaton asked.

Ethan nodded back at Cleos. "He's our resident mind reader."

"What do you say, brain-sucker?" Daniel asked him. "Is the Cori impersonator clear?"

Cleos spat blood at him. The trail of red on the white floor didn't come close to reaching him, but it still brought a glimmer of mischief to Daniel's eyes. He smiled and flapped back his black jacket as he crossed over the corridor.

Daniel crouched down in front of the psychic. "Now, I don't know you, but my friend back there was just about to mop the floor with you. In case you hadn't noticed the size of his biceps, I think it's safe to say you had about two punches left before he permanently dented your face. So, let's just ask that question one more time, with you remembering that I'm the one who saved your face from being a fender bender." Daniel lowered his spectacles on his nose so he could look Cleos in the eye.

Ethan had gotten used to his friend's unnaturally dilated eyes, but he still avoided staring into them straight-on. It gave him the willies and then some.

Cleos shrank away from him, losing what was left of his pomposity. "Erica was alone when I first caught a glimpse of her," he explained. "Cori didn't come in until later, along with several other minds. I think she is clear."

Daniel pushed up his glasses and turned back to Ethan. "Erica?"

"We renamed her, so we didn't have to call her Cori." He shrugged, seeing it as stupid now.

"That was smart." Daniel stood up and moved back to him. "It's best we continue to call her that for our next meeting."

"'Devil creature' would also work," Heaton added.

"Aye, that too." Daniel pointed at Heaton.

"We're going to interrogate her again?" Ethan asked. He didn't understand why they would waste time with that.

"Well," Daniel said, exchanging a look with Heaton. It irritated Ethan when they did that. It made him feel like an outsider, but considering Heaton and Daniel had been partners for nearly five years, he really *was* an outsider. "I thought I'd take the lead on this one, if that's all right? It won't be so much an interrogation this time as an example."

"What does that mean?" Ethan said, feeling yet another shroud of ignorance fall over his eyes.

"Ethan." Heaton touched his arm. "Daniel's going to save your wife's life."

Ethan stared at Heaton, trying to read the words off his face that his ears just couldn't understand. He looked back at Daniel. His usual faint smile didn't convey anything new. "How?"

There was another shared glance between his former partners.

Daniel squeezed his shoulder. "I couldn't and wouldn't try to explain, but you'll know soon enough. Nev—Jordan!" Daniel beckoned over the short-haired brunette. "We'll need a bit of your expertise as well."

The woman joined them. Standing next to Daniel, she looked like an elf, sans jingling shoes.

"Ethan Pierce," Heaton extended his hand to him, "Nevia Jordan."

Ethan shook her hand, and she gave him a tight smile. "I'm sorry. Who are you?" He glanced at Heaton for more explanation.

"She's our new partner," Heaton said. "Your replacement."

"No." Nevia shook her head severely. "I've been hearing a lot about you on the way up. I am not even close to being your replacement. I am just..."

"She's our resident bloodhound," Daniel supplied.

"Please don't make that my title." Nevia grimaced at Daniel.

"She is going to double-check Erica to make sure she is empty. Think you can do that?"

"Sure." Nevia smiled, but it was a strained smile that told Ethan she wasn't sure.

"She's ready," Belus called over to them. Erica had been put into the interrogation room in place of Number One.

Daniel gave him a nod before turning back to Ethan. "Why don't you join Belus and me? You'll need to see this up close."

Ethan didn't understand, but knowing Daniel, he knew he soon would, so he didn't ask questions. He just followed him into the interrogation room.

15

A T THE DOOR, ETHAN offered Nevia the lead in. She stepped inside and shuffled to one side as close to the wall as she could get without actually becoming a fixture on it. Heaton hung back, not showing any interest in joining them. Ethan couldn't discern his mood, but he seemed anxious.

Three chairs lined the table opposite Erica. Belus sat on the right. Ethan took the left seat, leaving the center directly across from Erica for Daniel. Behind them, Heaton shut the door to the windowed cell and observed from outside with his arms crossed tightly.

Daniel removed his coat and, unbelievably, opened yet another button on his shirt before settling into the chair. He didn't so much sit as sprawl. Reclined in the chair with his legs crossed and his arm resting on the back of it; they may as well have been in the bar together.

Daniel hissed before clicking his tongue. "Mmm, mmm, this is going to be a damn fine shame. I forgot what a beauty your wife is." He reached across the table and took Erica's hand. She perked an eyebrow at him. When he drew her hand forward to kiss it, she ripped it away.

Daniel laughed and turned to Ethan. "She never did like me much. Too bad. It wouldn't be cheating with her." Daniel winked at her.

Ethan reminded himself this wasn't Cori, and Daniel deserved some leeway if he was actually going to do what he said he was. Nevertheless, he cleared his throat.

"What do you want?" Erica rolled her eyes.

"Oh, I want all of it." Daniel scanned her body, so far as the table would allow. "But I want the real thing. You don't happen to know where the real Cori is?"

"I am the real Cori." She looked at Ethan with begging eyes. Despite the jig being up, she still wanted him to believe her, and he wanted to believe, but it was all a lie.

"We'll see about that. Jordan, you're up." Daniel looked over at her when she didn't move.

Nevia pulled herself from the wall and circled the table. Erica kept a watchful eye on her as she approached. When she abruptly shifted in her chair, Nevia froze. Ethan looked at Daniel for permission to help, but Daniel kept his eyes pinned to his new partner.

"Nevia," Daniel said quietly. She looked at him. "You remember what I told you about Ethan here? Our tough-guy hero." She looked at Ethan. "He's not going to let anything happen to you." Ethan nodded in agreement, and she took the last step to reach the transmorph.

Nevia touched her hair, pulling it up to smell. She moved down her neck and sniffed behind her ear. She withdrew a moment and bit her lip. She glanced at Daniel before swiftly lifting Erica's arm and smelling her armpit.

"What the hell?" Cori yanked her arm away. "Freak!"

Ethan looked at Daniel with wide eyes. His jaw clenched and his lips tightened into a thin line. He looked angry, but Ethan could tell he was trying to hold back a grin.

Nevia withdrew and shook her head. "She's a transmorph. I don't smell human on her." She stood a moment, seeming unsure what else to say.

"Thank you." Daniel bobbed his head to the back of the room and she scurried away. Rather than pin herself to the wall again, she slipped out the door to observe with Heaton.

"So, Erica, now what do you have to say?" Daniel asked. "You haven't fooled our psychic or our bloodhound."

"I am as close as you'll ever get to her. She's gone, Ethan!" Erica yelled at him. "Let's just move on. We can start where we left off. It's not like you noticed any differences."

Ethan clenched his fists on the table. Daniel covered his tensed hand with his own. "Of course he didn't notice anything. You're an exact copy. You've flourished the last 800 years on that little talent. If you weren't good at it, you wouldn't have survived this long." Daniel gave Ethan a look of sympathy before removing his hand.

"I myself have a special talent," Daniel continued. "Inherited, just like yours. However, where your talent is a bit like hiding in the woods, mine is a lot like burning the woods down." Daniel removed his spectacles and placed them on the table gently. Erica's eyes flickered over his. "I don't suppose you'd like to discuss Cori's location again?"

"You'll never be able to free her," Erica said more urgently. "You'll kill her trying to remove us." She turned to plead her case. "He'll kill me, Ethan!" She brushed away the moisture that was beading on her forehead and stared at her hand with terror. Since transmorphs didn't naturally sweat or bleed, Ethan wondered what this phenomenon represented for her. "Please, don't let him do this!" she screamed at him.

Ethan leaned forward, trying to see what Daniel was doing. From his perspective, his companion wasn't doing anything except looking at her. Before he could get a view of his eyes, Daniel's arm pushed him back in his chair like a mother's seatbelt.

Erica frantically ripped at her cuffs. She backed out of her seat, toppling it as she moved away from the table. The distance didn't seem to make a difference, though. She was still in a frenzy.

Ethan looked at Heaton through the glass door. The man's somber eyes met his gaze. Ethan furrowed his brow, silently questioning him, but he looked away again.

"Tell me where she is." Daniel's voice was hard, but there was no grand inflection of anger or evil. Yet the transmorph before him covered her ears to block him out. "I will kill every last one of you until I find her."

"I'm here! Ethan, help me! I'm inside! He's going to kill me!" Ethan looked at Belus behind Daniel's back. Belus wasn't looking at him, but he shook his head, silently answering his concerns. Daniel's arm pressed harder against his chest.

Ethan knew it was a trick. It wasn't Cori. Daniel wasn't hurting Cori. This was a transmorph ruse. However, every logical analysis of the scene brought him right back to the same conclusion. *Save her!* He wanted to go to her.

Ethan braced his hands on the table and planted his feet, prepared to rescue the damsel in distress. "Daniel," he said—or warned, or questioned. He needed something from him. Some explanation for what the hell was going on.

Daniel's fingers gripped his t-shirt. "Beyond stopping," his voice trembled.

Erica screamed. Daniel's hand shook against Ethan's chest. The transmorph's body vibrated and her scream took on the tone of multiple voices.

Daniel's face contorted as the intensity of his power shook him as well. Ethan didn't know what was happening on his end of the staring contest, but he got the sense this wasn't an easy undertaking for Daniel.

Erica's vibrations increased, blurring Ethan's view of her. The color of her clothes fuzzed into obscurity.

Her voice ceased. The indistinct humanoid shape faded, replaced by a fine gray dust that rained onto the floor.

Daniel released Ethan. He took in a few ragged breaths and flopped his head down to the table.

Ethan slowly stood and examined the tiny pile across the room. He moved around the table, approaching it cautiously. He bent down and swiped his hand through the fine dust. The gray ash stuck to his fingers.

Ethan turned his attention to Daniel. His head was still down on the table. He looked back at Heaton through the glass, but he no longer questioned the somber expression his former partner was wearing.

Daniel peeked up from his restful position. He fumbled with his glasses, replacing them before exposing the rest of his face. "Is it too early for beer?" he chimed—slightly out of breath—from purplish blue lips.

16

E THAN STOOD IN THE kitchen, watching Daniel get situated at the dining room table. He sagged into a chair, cracked open his beer, and took a long swig before settling back into a steady shiver.

Nevia sat on the opposite end of the table, staring at her unopened bottle. She looked a little pale. She looked how Ethan felt: shocked and a little sick.

Heaton clinked his bottle, drawing Ethan's attention back to him. Ethan gaped at him, trying to find the right words. If there were even words for what he had just witnessed. "You knew about this?" he asked.

Heaton shrugged. "I've been with him for the last five years. It wasn't exactly a secret."

"Except from me," Ethan pointed out, taking a drink from his beer.

"It just hadn't come up yet," Heaton said. "Besides, it's not the type of thing you just mention."

"Are you two going to continue this conversation *about* me *without* me?" Daniel asked, without looking back at them.

"I was planning on it," Heaton said even as he rounded the island to join Daniel at the table.

Ethan took a seat across from Heaton, facing Daniel at the long end of the table, while Nevia stayed on her end. Ethan felt guilty for leaving her out of the conversation, but she wasn't paying any attention to them, anyway.

"What exactly did you do in there?" Ethan asked as delicately as he could without passing judgment.

Daniel inhaled and huffed out his breath. "I incinerated her... it. I..." He put his hands out and brought them tightly together. "I crushed it. I..."

"He energized her molecular structure—" Heaton assisted with a hint of annoyance, "—and magnetized it to collapse in on itself like a black hole. It's an implosive incineration on a cellular level."

Ethan crumpled his brow. He had seen many unbelievable and strange things since coming to this prison, but this floored him. "What are you?" Ethan knew that question made him sound like a bigot, but he couldn't think of any other way to ask it. He was relieved when Daniel laughed, but there weren't many serious discussions he wouldn't laugh at, as long as he had a beer in his hand.

"I know what you're thinking, but I'm not an animal—at least, not outside the bedroom."

"Dude, this isn't the pub. You have no audience," Heaton scolded.

"Oh." Daniel looked around as if seeing the house for the first time. "Holy hell, does this house ever change its motif?"

Ethan chuckled. Something about Daniel's casual attitude toward everything irritated and amused him at the same time. Even with the urgency of the situation, he was in no hurry to provide an explanation. Ethan could only laugh at him because he didn't want to strangle him.

"I think it's Danato's choice, not hers." He thought about asking when Daniel had been in the house, but he resisted, since it would only take them further off topic.

When Daniel didn't continue, Ethan shifted his gaze to Heaton. He just shrugged in response and rolled his eyes. Heaton was more patient with Daniel than most people, albeit discontentedly.

"You know how werewolves and vampires are sworn enemies, at least in the movies?" Daniel asked.

"Sure." Ethan leaned back into his chair and downed half his beer.

"Transmorphs and what I am are kind of like that."

Ethan cleared his throat. "So, do you have a name or something? What do the storybooks call you?"

"Some people have called us exorcists," Daniel said, then quickly added, "but I don't like that. What I do is kill. It has nothing to do with gods or demons."

"No superhero name?" Ethan smiled widely, hoping that would come across as a joke.

Daniel returned his grin. "Not outside of the bedroom."

Heaton and Ethan chuckled at Daniel's unabashed arrogance regarding his sexual antics. Ethan had always known him to be a one-night stand type of guy. They had joked that the reason Daniel had one-night stands was because the women would never make the same mistake twice. However, despite his arrogant approach to women, he always found new takers.

"My particular magic," Daniel continued, "has been passed down through the ranks of my family. It's like a birthmark or a receding hairline." Daniel pushed his fingers through his hair—a habitual tick he was probably barely aware of. "It skips a generation at times. It's only passed on to the men, but women can be carriers."

"Do the women of your family have any abilities other than... killing transmorphs?" Ethan asked.

"Yes, nagging." Daniel chuckled. "My mother's always had a commanding presence. She's a big ole gal, but strong. She and my father ran a farm in Ireland. Hard work—made harder by my father running off to *answer calls*, as he put it. My mother was a carrier, and my father was an active hunter. I would have been on the skipped generation if it weren't for my mother. Anyway..." Daniel paused as his eyes glazed into a memory.

Ethan looked at Heaton again. He seemed to be glaring at Daniel, but it might have just been five years of exasperation translating as animosity. Heaton met Ethan's eyes, losing the harsh expression. He flicked his empty bottle, making it *tink*.

Heaton got up from the table and headed to the fridge. He tangled three bottles of beer in one hand before kicking the door shut. He came alongside Nevia, who was still entranced by sublime thoughtful nothingness at the opposite end of the table. She was no doubt contemplating the sudden change in her partner's job description.

Heaton gave her a nudge. She looked up at him. With his free hand, he moved her unopened beer closer to her. She grabbed it and twisted off the top. A long swig later, she seemed to wake up.

Ethan downed the other half of his beer just as the second round arrived. Heaton settled into his chair again.

"My mother often had to do the work alone when he left," Daniel continued, as if the record player in his mind had just found purchase again. "Made her strong. Made me strong too. It wasn't until I was about ten that she figured out Dad wasn't always answering calls. We'd go into town for supplies and find him at the pub drinking himself into a stupor. I suspected there had been a few floozies, though Mum would never confirm it."

Ethan wasn't sure if it was the beer, the fatigue, or just the exposure of a hidden secret that had prompted such honesty in his usually impersonal friend. Daniel had always been a devoted mate. He had always been more than happy to listen to all of Ethan's problems, especially when he went on drunken rants about Cori, but never once had Daniel instigated a conversation about *his* personal life—let alone spouted his life story.

"She didn't leave him, of course. She couldn't run the farm without him. It was too much, even with my help. Six years she nagged that man. I honestly don't think she ever touched him after she found out he'd been drinking to get out of his duties at home. I even felt sorry for him the way she kept at him. When I turned sixteen, I started taking on a lot more of the workload. Between school and the farm, I barely slept. Meanwhile, my father got lazier and more absent.

"One day in particular, she was naggin' on him something fierce. He finally hit her. After six years, it was bound to happen. I mean, you can only press a man so far." Daniel looked at Ethan as if he needed to rationalize his father's behavior. "He kept at her, though. Wouldn't just let that one clatter be the lesson? I think one good bruise on my mother would have put the balance back in their marriage. You know?" Daniel looked up again, still looking for that approval. Ethan nodded, though he didn't agree. He had taken enough hits in his life to know that violence only made things worse. "He had to take out all his repressed rage on her. All six years came back in that one day."

Daniel froze. His beer drifted down to rest on his thigh. His eyes dropped to the floor as years-ago memories drowned out his voice.

Heaton shifted and took another swig of his beer. Ethan wasn't sure, but he got the sense that Heaton had already heard this story. He still looked aggravated, but also sympathetic. After so long as partners, there probably weren't a lot of gaps in their knowledge of each other. Ethan felt envious of that. He loved his wife, and his relationships with Danato and Belus felt like family, but he missed having friends. He was glad they were here even if the fun was being muddied by exploding secrets and a parasitically challenged spouse.

Ethan glanced over at Nevia. She was also patiently waiting for the end of the story. Since she was new to the group, it was unlikely she had known this much of Daniel's backstory. At least he wasn't the only one in the dark.

"So." Daniel spoke up abruptly, breaking the silence. "I came in with a shotgun and killed him." The words fell out of his mouth like directions to a train station. Ethan didn't move. He didn't dare if he wanted to maintain his indiscriminate appearance. "The first time I ever had to use my power wasn't on a transmorph, but to dispose of my father's body to keep my ass out of jail. What a bitch irony can be?"

While Daniel slammed down the last of his second beer, Ethan gaped at Heaton, hoping for some recourse. Heaton closed his eyes and shook his head in exasperation.

Ethan looked at Nevia again. She was wearing the facial expression he was trying to hide. Wide eyes, mouth agape, struggling to add yet another level of reality to the man sitting at the table with them.

"Where were we?" Daniel asked with a chipper pitch in his voice. "I'm a transmorph hunter." Apparently, the reminiscing was over. "Along with hunting down all the other creatures that come into this prison, Heaton and I locate transmorphs. Well..." He glanced at Heaton.

"We don't usually find them," Heaton took over. "We get calls. People recommend us under the radar to help with "demon possession." That's why the whole exorcist thing got going."

"But we don't exorcise demons. We aren't priests," Daniel reiterated, as if that point couldn't be clear enough.

"Right," Ethan said.

"When people start noticing strange things about their loved ones," Heaton continued, "they eventually get referred to us. Especially when the real priests don't have any luck getting the offending creature off of them."

"People think they are possessed when this happens?" Ethan asked, feeling his stomach growl. "Keep talking. I'm going to find us some food." Ethan moved into the kitchen to scavenge for edible, guest-worthy snacks, while Heaton continued the background information.

"You have to understand," Heaton said, raising his voice despite the short distance between the table and the kitchen. "Transmorphs can leech off a living body for years. By the time we get called in, their loved ones have been observing subtle changes in behavior, compounded by what is usually a sudden shift in morality."

"How's that?" Ethan asked as he debated if breakfast cereal could be considered a snack.

"At some point in the custody of the body," Heaton said, "the transmorph gets tired of acting like the person it has taken over. They don't want to be caught so they play the part as best they can, but anywhere from three to nine months, depending on the patience of the transmorph, they get antsy. I mean, let's face it, if you were driving a rental car, would you really care if you got a few dents in it?"

Ethan found a full bag of chips stuffed to the back of a low cupboard; no doubt hidden there by Cori before her abduction. He smiled, thinking of her, but it faded when he realized she was still so far away from him. He brought it over to the table with what he laughably called a relish tray: three fat pickles, a handful of radishes, and a jar of olives.

"So what do they do?" Ethan asked as he set down the food. Despite obviously being yesterday's leftovers, they eagerly accepted it. He fetched four more beers and sat down again. "What moralities do they challenge?"

"At first, there is usually an increase in spending," Heaton explained between bites of his pickle. "Most transmorphs prefer to prey on the wealthy; it's just a more enjoyable lifestyle."

"Next is sex," Daniel jumped in. Any conversation involving sex was likely going to be guided by him. "If the victim is single, there is a spike in dating and one-night stands."

"Should I be worried about you?" Ethan asked, fishing an olive out of the jar.

"Ha, ha," Daniel said. "If they are married, then the partner, if receptive, is usually pressured non-stop." Ethan couldn't help but think how sexually available Cori had been to him over the last weeks. Stupid him. He'd thought he was in the honeymoon phase. "If they aren't receptive, the victim will start an affair."

"Next is alcohol and drugs," Heaton added. "Followed by vandalism, theft, rape, murder, whatever pleases the transmorph."

"So, why do they do it? I mean, why be someone else to begin with, but also, why sabotage their cover?" Ethan wiped the orange cheese from his hands and passed the chip bag to Nevia. She had yet to attack the food, and he didn't want to leave her out. She took a handful of chips from the bag and handed it back to him.

"Imagine it, Ethan," Daniel said, blowing a pimento from his green olive at Heaton. "Imagine you could just jump into someone else's life. Live in their house, work their high-paying job, shag their wife, and spend their money. It would be the ultimate vacation." Daniel described it as if he envied them. "When they get bored with that life, they don't just leave. They..." Daniel paused, marring his face with a grimace, before he continued. "It's never good enough for them. They always want more. They want his life, or her life, never their own."

"The temptation is too great for them just to leave," Heaton said, interrupting Daniel's irritated reflection. "They can jump ship any time. They don't have to take responsibility for any of it. The frustration of our job is not catching or killing transmorphs, it's watching the person left over suffer for what the bastard did to their life. Try explaining to a judge that you were possessed. Try asking your spouse to forgive you for screwing your secretary because you weren't in control of your body."

"Don't they understand after you remove the transmorph? Don't they get that it wasn't them?"

Daniel scoffed and leaned forward to tap the table for emphasis. "Do you know what shit people believe in?" Daniel turned his dramatic finger to Heaton. "I've got this quarehawk reading me his horoscope every morning, just like it's a damn weather report. People believe in God Almighty without a shred of proof, and yet these people won't believe what they see with their own fecking eyes."

"It's the face," Heaton said, more to Daniel than to him. "They can't get over it because it's the same face that hurt them. It doesn't matter if the person inside is different."

"Okay," Ethan said, "that explains the type-two transmorphs, but what about the ones that just morph without encasing their subject?"

"Technically," Daniel interjected, "they are the same creature; they just lack the malleability to encase. If they never acquire the skill and activate it, or they never kill someone in order to take their identity, we don't touch them."

"If they play it straight and narrow," Ethan asked, "they get to be regular citizens?"

"Correct," Daniel said.

"The ones you have here," Heaton said, crunching on another bite of his pickle, "are type ones that have killed, and type twos that have encased."

"So, the type twos don't usually kill their host?" Ethan asked.

Heaton and Daniel exchanged a look. "Not usually," Heaton said, "but don't mistake that for mercy. They... the one holding Cori will threaten to do that. You must trust us when it comes time to remove her."

"You can remove her, though, right?" Ethan asked. "You can save her?" He volleyed his anticipation between them.

"We've taken transmorphs off of people who have been enveloped for years," Daniel explained. "During their captivity, the victims are essentially in a coma. The transmorphs dehydrate them and deprive them of nutrients. This keeps them weak, but the weight loss also allows for a more convincing overlap. Because the victims are in this state for such a long time, they sometimes require physical therapy to build up enough strength to walk again."

"You think Cori is that bad?" Ethan took another drink of his beer.

"No, not physically, not after five weeks." Daniel shook his head.

Ethan could see the sincerity in his face, but he could still sense that there was something being left out of the conversation. They probably didn't want to scare him with the details. "What's the catch?" He looked at Heaton, but he only stared blankly at Ethan. "You have to tell me the truth. Belus said the procedure is risky. What are the risks?"

Heaton shifted away from the table and took a swig of his beer.

"Killing the transmorph, like I did today, is relatively easy. Removing one from another being is kind of like using a sand blaster to knock off chipped paint."

"You could hurt her?" Ethan said, feeling the weight of the day that the beer had lifted press back down on him.

"It's a delicate procedure, but that is secondary to finding her." Daniel pointed across the table. "First, I've got to take Nevia—"

"Jordan," she corrected.

Daniel glared at her for the correction. "Jordan and I have to go see if she can pick out which one of these creatures is not like the others."

"That's what you do?" Ethan asked, remembering the odd spectacle from earlier. "You smell transmorphs?"

Nevia's eyes darted between them as her mouth gaped with a delayed stammer. "Sort of."

Daniel jumped out of his chair. "Yup, she's a regular bloodhound. We're just breaking her in." Daniel came around the table, grabbed his coat from the rack, and handed Nevia her puffy white bubble coat. "I would prefer to be breaking her in in other ways, but after a very honest discussion we both decided against that." Daniel smiled and clicked his tongue at her. "Didn't we?"

"Yes," she said in a daze as she slipped on her coat.

Daniel turned back to him. "Don't let her stimulating conversation fool you. She's actually quite smart. We'll be back." Daniel tugged on her coat, drawing her out the door behind him.

As the door slammed, Ethan looked back at Heaton. "What was that all about?"

"I don't know. This is her first case and frankly, I don't think she was prepared for all this."

Ethan frowned and nodded. He hadn't realized she was that new. He took a sip of his beer and looked at his friend. "So what's *your* superpower?" he asked. Heaton chuckled and sipped his beer. "Seriously, I can't take any more secrets. What's your power?"

Heaton's brow rose, and he shook his head. "Nothing, I'm just boring old me. The only reason I've survived this long is because I know when to hide behind that nut job."

"Good plan." Ethan smiled.

17

Daniel stalked ahead of Nevia, letting her struggle to keep up with his long legs. He knew her fashionable coat would fail to keep her warm. As it was, he was wishing he had brought along his dorky-looking earmuffs to keep his ears from burning bright red after every trip to and from the prison.

He pushed open the building's heavy metal door and slipped into the foyer. He let it close behind him for a few seconds and reopened it when he anticipated Nevia's arrival. She ran inside with her hands tucked in the pockets of her blue slacks—also not warm enough for the arctic climate.

He plucked open the buttons on his jacket and ripped it off, along with his leather gloves, which he stuffed into the pockets before hanging it up in an available locker. "What the hell was that?" he asked, turning back to her.

She hadn't taken her coat off, nor did it look like she was going to. "I'm sorry. I..."

"That's my friend back there." He moved forward and unzipped her coat for her. "His wife is in danger." She turned to let him slip the coat off her arms. She removed her pointless cotton gloves and handed them to him. He searched the coat for a pocket, but couldn't find one.

"I usually stuff them in a sleeve," she directed.

Daniel eyed her before stuffing the gloves in her coat sleeve. He stuffed the coat in with his, not bothering to give it a hook, since the puffball would stay wherever he crammed it. He slammed the metal door and turned back to her. "How sure were you that Erica was only a transmorph?"

"I thought it was almost certain, anyway. The mind reader said—"

Daniel narrowed his eyes and took two menacing steps toward her. She recoiled and looked away from him. He couldn't comprehend how she could have made it as an FBI agent. She hadn't an ounce of backbone in her. "How sure were you?"

"I haven't smelled one since they tested me."

"How sure were you?" Daniel yelled. He hated yelling. He hated the way his voice, topped on his burly frame, made him seem like... his father.

"Not sure enough for you to do what you did!" She turned away, covering her mouth. The shaking in her body made him think she was crying, but when she turned back, her eyes were dry. "I was confused about the scents. I just need to refresh my senses. I can do this. I can help your friend."

"*That* was what you needed to say back there." Daniel pointed to the door. "That was what he needed to hear."

"Yes, sir." Her eyes lowered, but her chin lifted. Daniel hadn't thought he had much attraction to her, but her petite body playing the part of a dutiful soldier, and him being her commander, was enough to make him want to have her right then and there.

He stepped forward and put his body as close to her as he could without threatening her. "Nevia."

"Jordan."

He scoffed at the correction. "Jordan, don't call me sir." *Outside of the bedroom.* "I'm not your boss. I'm your partner." She met his eyes. "You don't owe me any explanation about your abilities, but you do need to be honest about them. If you are sure, I'll trust you at your word. I sure as hell don't have a keen sense of smell. Just check my fridge." She smiled. "If you aren't sure, then we need to be cautious. You saw what I can do." She averted her eyes again.

"It was remarkable," she said, still not returning her gaze to him.

"What?"

"What you can do. It's remarkable," she said.

"You mean it's fecking weird and downright unnerving," he corrected.

She looked back up at him. "It's the scariest thing I've ever seen in my life," she said, holding his eyes with more bravery than she had shown so far.

Daniel wondered if she was normally a bit sturdier. Perhaps the day had just taken its toll on her. It wasn't every day you were partnered with a man who can obliterate a being just by looking at them. He pushed up his glasses to be sure they were masking his eyes.

"I'm sorry. I didn't mean to make you afraid of me. I don't like being the scary one."

She raised her hand and caressed his cheek. He jumped, shocked by the intimacy of her touch. With her other hand, she removed his glasses. He didn't stop her, but he bowed his head, averting his eyes. He refused to let her see his perpetually intimidating eyes without a veil.

He didn't have to wear the glasses. His power wasn't contingent on the removal of the glasses, and wearing them didn't hinder it, but his cavernous open pupils just freaked the hell out of people.

"Look at me," she whispered.

He reached for his eyeglasses, but she pulled them away. "Nevia, please," he scolded. "I don't want to frighten you."

"I'm already frightened. I want to see the worst of it, so I can begin to get over my fear. I don't like being afraid. It's an irrational emotion, and I don't wear it well. I like to confront my fears head-on."

"You took a lot of psychology classes in college, didn't you?" Daniel chuckled, but didn't look up. He didn't want to see the discomfort in her eyes. He had seen it from too many people to count.

She stood on her tippy toes and kissed his forehead—another gentle gesture that seemed so out of place. He reached out for his glasses again, but when he couldn't reach them, he settled his hand on her left hip. She didn't pull away like he expected her to, so he put his other hand on her, cupping the little girth she had on her slim body. He stood before her, bowing abjectly and holding her.

He pulled her forward. His mind was so wrought with conflicting emotions, he didn't know what he intended to do. He was angry that she had the audacity to hold his glasses away from him; he was uncomfortable with her sensitive gestures; and his hands pressing against her body turned him on.

Somewhere between wanting to see her lips before he dove in for a kiss, and wanting to show her just what she was getting herself into, he looked at her. Her steely gray eyes looked over his, first with surprise, but then she analyzed him.

He waited for her to draw herself back. He waited for the terror to unhinge her bravado. He waited for her to see the demon that everyone else saw when they looked into the black recesses of his eyes.

"Fascinating."

Or not.

"What?" He drew back, losing his façade of bravery.

She stepped forward again, trying to get another look at him. "How do you see in the day? Isn't that blinding?"

"No. I don't know. I don't exactly visit eye doctors."

The open pupils should have left him blinded by the sun, but for whatever reason, the sun never bothered him, no matter how bright. He did, however, have the added benefit of excellent night vision, which hadn't come in nearly as handy in bounty hunting as it had in the bedroom. His shy women liked to keep the lights off, but it made no difference to him, since he saw everything anyway.

"You see well at night though, don't you?" she guessed.

He furrowed his brow and reached down for his glasses, which she pulled away again. She must have seen the annoyance on his face, because she looked down at them as if she'd forgotten they were in her hand. She gave them back.

"Yes, I see well at night." He slipped the glasses on and pushed them up tightly on the bridge of his nose. "How the hell can you stand looking at me?"

He moved to the elevator and pushed the button, requesting its presence. If the elevator had any understanding of urgency, based on the pressure of one's push, it would have fallen to their floor. It did not, of course. It was nearly lunchtime, and the lifts were busy with the guards delivering meals to the inmates.

"They're just eyes, Daniel," Nevia said, joining him at the elevator.

"I have never had anyone say that about my eyes. I destroy people with these eyes."

"Hardly."

"Excuse me?" He turned back, prepared to challenge her blasé attitude toward his power.

"Your eyes may be the barrel of the gun, but clearly it is your mind that pulls the trigger, otherwise I would be vaporized for looking at you."

"I just mean that you are... insane." He settled on the only word that could describe her indifference to the mark of his birthright.

"I guess I'm more interested in their function. I'm kind of a brainiac. Math, science, engineering, theoretical physics. I can build a bomb," she presented slightly spiritedly. She was apparently very proud of this feat, but he didn't offer her any kudos. "Not just a shrapnel one, either. I mean, I could literally build a nuclear bomb if I wanted to—which I don't," she added, as if worried her words might sound threatening.

Daniel looked at her, giving her another once-over. He kept seeing different things every time he looked at her. "No one has ever looked into my eyes without shrinking away in fear," he admitted, so she would understand his frustration with her inquiries.

She gave him a flat smile. "I'm sorry. I guess I'm the one scaring you now."

"Not scared, just... uncomfortable."

She turned away and stared at the elevator doors. He joined her in silent gazing. When he once again felt comfortable, he caught her glancing over at him. She said nothing, but her lower lip was tucked between her teeth.

"What is it?" he asked when it was clear she might implode if she wasn't allowed to speak her mind.

"I thought I should say something in regard to your admission earlier, but given that I'm already making you uncomfortable, I don't think I should. However, I do want you to know that I was thinking about a condolence, so you won't think your admission was presented to apathetic ears."

Daniel narrowed his eyes. "You're sparing me the embarrassment of discussing my past, because you know I don't want to, but you want me to know that you did want to discuss it, so I don't think you're a cold-hearted bitch," he clarified with his own dizzying interpretation.

"Essentially," she said with a nod.

"Hmm, well, your avoidance of that conversation is appreciated, and your sympathetic interests will be noted as a positive in my assessment of your character." He shook his head and chuckled at the strangeness of the interaction. The elevator thankfully arrived with a *ponk*.

18

Daniel signed out a set of keys from one of the guards that wasn't rolling around a rack of food trays and led Nevia to the type-two transmorph section.

"Can't we just x-ray these things to find Cori?"

Daniel shook his head. "I wish we could, but the bastards absorb the radiation. Pictures just come back white."

Daniel stopped at the first barred cell and opened the sliding door. The Cori transmorph within huddled herself into a ball on her cot. She looked up as he slid the door open, but she buried her face when she saw him.

"Time for some scratch-and-sniff, Number Five."

"Leave me alone," Cori-5 mumbled into her knees.

Daniel leaned against the door and waved his bloodhound inside. "You're up, pup."

Nevia slipped past him apprehensively. Her nose lifted high, sniffing the air. She stepped a little closer to the prisoner and stopped.

"Do what you gotta do," he said, bracing his foot in the doorway.

Nevia glanced back at him before taking a breath and approaching Cori-5. She grabbed a lock of her hair to sniff.

"Don't touch me, you freak!" Cori-5 snarled and ripped free.

Nevia looked back at him for a solution.

"Do you want me to hold her down?" he asked. The transmorph's head whipped up and stared at him with terror in her eyes. He hadn't intended to bait her fear, but since it was working... "Because I'd be more than happy to straddle that fine body." Daniel smiled as Cori-5 moved back into a position for her sniff-test.

Nevia started by sniffing her hair and the back of her neck. She lifted her arm to get a whiff of her armpit. He expected that to be the bulk of it, but then she lowered her head and sniffed the woman's crotch.

Daniel knew humans had scent glands there. He knew she was just trying to smell the most pungent areas to get an accurate read. However, that didn't stop him from bursting into a childish giggle fit.

When she finished, Nevia backed away, stopping just short of barreling through his leg to get out of the cell.

"Well?" he asked, not moving his barricading leg.

"I'd like to smell them all first." His heart sank. He didn't like the sound of that. "It's not as easy as smelling a flask in a lab," she defended.

"I told you, you don't need to rationalize. It's your talent."

"Fine, then move your damn leg so I can finish my work."

He dropped his leg and stood upright so she could move by him. "Yes, ma'am." He smiled as he shut the cell behind them.

Daniel moved down to the next cell, futilely searching for the corresponding key. "Next up, contestant number four. And how are you feeling today, Four? Are you excited about potentially having the life ripped right out of you?"

"You know, Daniel," Cori-4 said, threading her arms through the bars of the door, "I think I misconstrued your personality when we first met.

"Did you, now?"

"Mmm. I think there was potential for a relationship between us."

"Oh, really?" Daniel dropped his hands and gave up the effort to find the key. "Please tell me you're getting this directly from *her* mind."

"I think you and I could have had a go." Cori-4 drew her finger down his chest.

"I'm not one for long-term relationships," Daniel warned.

"You'd like my version. Just think, once every two or three months, a shag in the broom closet. You can head back to wherever you belong, and I stay behind to anticipate your next visit."

"Oh, that is very tempting, Four. In fact, if my partner weren't here right now, and if it wouldn't totally freak out Ethan, we could start that relationship right now."

"Don't let me hold you back," Nevia mumbled from behind him. He looked back at her. He expected to see revulsion in her eyes, but she just looked bored. "I could come back in five if you like."

Daniel smiled, turning his attention back to Cori-4. He had to admit the proposition was appealing. He hadn't really approved of Ethan taking on such a high-maintenance woman, but he had approved of her physically. Five minutes alone with her...

Daniel dropped his smile abruptly and looked back at Nevia. "Five?" He looked her over. "Did you just insult me?"

She shrugged. "I thought I was being generous."

"Oh, you're a vixen, throwing that wick at me." He shook his head and located the key. He shoved Cori-4 away from the door and slid it open. "First things first. If you're a good girl, Four, and my partner clears you, maybe we can discuss a rendezvous for later," he whispered, even though Nevia was clearly within earshot.

Nevia slipped through the door, and he propped his foot up again. He watched her approach Cori-4, who, for the most part, wasn't shying away from her. She started her cursory sniffs—hair, neck, and armpits—but then she looked back at him.

He was grinning in anticipation of the upcoming fanny sniff. She rolled her eyes and settled into a hard glare. "Can you not watch me do this?"

"What?" He laughed. "I'm just observing your work."

"Please, this is humiliating enough as it is."

"I'm not leaving you alone with her," Daniel said, firmly losing most of his smile.

"Just turn around so I don't have to see you snickering when I'm supposed to be concentrating."

He mouthed "okay" and turned his back, bracing his arms in the door instead of his leg. He listened to her sniffing for a few seconds. "Are you getting Cori's scent on either of them? Any human scent?" When she didn't answer, he glanced back.

Nevia's hands grappled toward him as the transmorph embraced her body from behind. Her face was red, desperate for air, since part of the creature was smothering her mouth. In the brief span he had not been observing, the parasitic bitch had activated her impossible elasticity and curved her body around Nevia. Although it took several hours to complete the muscle and organ shifts, the initial encasement took only seconds.

Daniel whipped around and rushed over to them. He punched what was left of the transmorph's face. The punch was hardly enough to harm it, especially in its stretched state, but he kept at it, peeling the thing off Nevia, until it had no choice but to surrender its hold on her.

He pulled Nevia out of the cell. She bent over, coughing and gasping. He locked the cell before moving back to aid her.

"There's something in my throat," she gagged.

"Nope, nope, lift up." He drew her body erect and lifted her arms, clasping both her wrists with one hand. "Breathe deep, fill up those lungs." She took in the deep breath and coughed. Something milky wet her lips, and she spat it out. With his free hand, he maneuvered to pat her back and then settled into a gentle rub. "That's it. Don't think about it, just get it out."

She looked up at him with bloodshot eyes. She hadn't broken into tears. As her breathing steadied, he became aware of the tiny wrists clasped in his hands. He probably shouldn't have found the pseudo-bondage situation arousing, especially given the seriousness of the situation, but he was seeing potential in her small frame.

A glint of silver caught his attention, and he looked down at the gap between her blue trousers and white shirt. A silver ring hung from the taut flesh of her navel. He hadn't expected to see a body piercing on her.

He looked up to ask about it, but he found her eyes already on him. He closed his mouth and tried to read her emotions. "What is it?" he finally asked when nothing revealed itself in her expression.

"Thank you," she said hoarsely. A stray tear finally made it out of one of her stubborn eyes. She started to shake—possibly her adrenaline catching up with her.

He released her hands and pressed gently on her back. She followed his lead and moved forward to embrace him. He wrapped his arms around her and rubbed her back. "I'm sorry. I should have been more careful."

She drew away from him, wiping her eyes. "I'm the stupid one who asked you to turn away."

"I shouldn't have made you uncomfortable in the first place. What you're doing is important. I shouldn't have laughed at you." He huffed in frustration and looked around. "Why don't we get a coffee or something before you do the next one?"

"I don't want to delay us."

"We aren't going to solve this in one day. Besides, I don't have the energy to get her out yet." Daniel started walking away. When she didn't follow, he turned back. "Come on, Nevia."

"Jordan," she corrected before following him to the elevators.

19

D ANIEL STUFFED CREAM AND sugar packets in his shirt pocket and carried over two beige mugs of coffee to where Nevia was already sitting. When he arrived, she pulled her foot off the chair across from her and sat up straight.

He set down the coffees and tossed the packets on the table before sitting down. She dumped a creamer packet in her coffee and looked around.

"Spoon." He snapped his fingers and jumped back up. He moved back to the condiment bar and pulled a silver spoon from the cache of utensils. He jogged back over and handed her the spoon before sitting down again.

"Thank you," she smirked at him.

He nodded but didn't afford her the usual *no problem* he might normally have. He brought the mug of black coffee to his lips and took a sip. It would be a few minutes before he could take a full drink of the hot beverage. Nevia continued to doctor her coffee until it no longer resembled coffee.

She took a cautious sip before taking a full gulp. She furrowed her brow and looked at the cup as if it were something she had never drunk before. "This is good," she declared. "Really good." She went back for another gulp.

"Danato keeps this place well stocked with the finer things. Granted, everything else is shit," Daniel added, noting the hairline fracture running through his mug.

"Too bad I won't get a chance to meet him," she said. Daniel smiled widely. He tried to cover it with his cup, but she saw it. "What's so funny?"

He chuckled. "I was just picturing your petite five feet up against his plump six plus."

"Five foot two, thank you. I imagine it would look similar to the dwarf standing next to him."

Daniel shrugged. "Belus never looks quite as small as he should once you get to know him."

"And me? Has my height improved any in your eyes?"

Daniel held her gaze for a moment. "I don't know that you've gained any height, but I can safely say I'm not nearly as pissed to have you with me—us—as I thought."

"So, you aren't going to toss the bloodhound out on the side of the road?"

Daniel lowered his eyes to his coffee. "Let's just say I'm rooting for you."

"I really am sorry that I'm not better at this."

"It's not your fault. You have an undeveloped skill in an extraordinary situation."

"You still wish I could just point to her, though."

"I wish she wasn't in this situation to begin with, but wishes are as useless as prayers. At some point, you just have to pick yourself off your knees and do the work, even if it takes longer than anticipated, and even if someone tries to kill you on the way."

She smiled at him. "I appreciate your patience."

He nodded. "It's not my strongest characteristic, but it's like riding a bike."

"If we can locate her, do you really think you can save her?"

"I have no choice. Failing would mean destroying my friend. I won't do that to him."

"You're surprisingly loyal," she said.

"Only to my partners."

She paused mid-sip to take on the meaning of that statement. He caught her gaze. He almost made a comment to contradict his statement, or somehow exclude her from it, but that wouldn't have been true. Although he didn't know her well, he would still make his best effort to save her from danger.

"I will endeavor to earn that loyalty," she said.

20

ETHAN STARED AT HIS bowl of goulash, wondering for the hundredth time how much longer it would be. Daniel had called back to let them know it was going to take a while longer. Nevia had insisted on rechecking each transmorph before she would make any judgments.

He looked at the clock on the wall over the sink. It was after 5:00.

Heaton looked back at the clock as well. "I'm sure they are—"

The front door opened, and Ethan nearly jumped from his seat. Daniel entered with Nevia shortly behind. Daniel slipped off his coat and smelled the air. "Oh, grand, dinner. I am so hungry."

Daniel moved to the stove and loaded up a bowl of goulash, which he apparently didn't need an invitation to. He tossed a spoon in the overflowing bowl and shoveled in a few bites as he made his way to the head of the table, opposite Danato's usual spot.

Nevia shut the door and slipped off her coat. Ethan jumped to her side and hung it for her. "Well? Good news, I hope," he probed when he noticed her bloodshot eyes.

"Of course, I think I can at least narrow it down for you."

"Narrow it?" Ethan asked, not quite hiding the disappointment in his tone. "To how many?"

"Two. I am confident that three of them are not housing any human being, nor have they in the last few days."

Ethan nodded. "Two." He could see the shame on Nevia's face. She obviously would have preferred to give him an exact location. "That's wonderful. I'm so grateful." He took her hand and squeezed it. "Really. I'm sorry if I sound unappreciative."

She looked down at his hand and squeezed it back. "I'll check again tomorrow. Perhaps the subtle notes of scent are confusing me."

He nodded and smiled. He knew the sound of false hope when he heard it. "Hungry?" he asked, breaking away from her hand before she misinterpreted his appreciation as something else.

"Starved," she said.

"Please eat, before Daniel takes it all." Ethan directed her to the food before sitting down to enjoy his own.

"What's the plan?" Heaton asked.

"Sleep," Daniel interjected over a mouth full of food before Ethan could say anything. Daniel swallowed his food. "Nevia has worn herself out." She glanced up from the stove, looking confused, but said nothing to object.

"I am about three bites from passing out, and Ethan, you look like you could use a night's sleep."

Nevia joined the table at the opposite end away from them. Ethan wondered if she was intentionally separating herself from them, or if she just didn't want to strain her neck to observe the conversation. She bowed her head in a silent prayer over her food before she ate. It had been a long time since he had seen anyone pray before a meal. When she raised her head, he observed her bloodshot eyes again. He also noticed a bruise on her neck.

He frowned and looked back at Daniel. "What happened at the prison?"

"What?" Daniel said over another bite of food.

"Why is Jordan's neck bruised?" Ethan asked in a tone that he'd inherited from Danato.

Daniel swallowed his bite. "I got sloppy, but rest assured, we ruled out that one right away." He snickered.

"It wasn't his fault," Nevia added, but Ethan didn't take his gaze from Daniel.

"It's his fault when I give him permission to open cell doors in my prison."

Daniel shifted away from his bowl. "One minor mistake, *Danato*. Oh, I mean, Ethan. She isn't hurt."

"She could have been?" Ethan hated the blasé attitude he was taking with the transmorphs. He may not be in any danger from them, but others certainly were.

When Ethan didn't release his glower, Daniel leaned forward over the table. He lowered his voice to a whisper. "Are we still talking about Jordan?"

Ethan glanced back at Nevia. She was staring intently at her goulash.

"I always take care of my partners, Ethan. You know that," Daniel said, trying to calm him.

Ethan cleared his throat. "I'm sorry. I didn't mean to accuse you of neglect. I just don't want anyone else to get hurt."

"Nevia won't get hurt. I will make sure of that. Cori's going to be okay, too. I will make sure of that as well."

Ethan nodded and slid his chair away from the table. "I think you're right about sleep. I put your suitcases upstairs. I put Jordan's in Danato's room. Would someone mind cleaning up the dishes so we don't get any goblins?"

"We'll take care of it," Heaton assured him. "Get some rest."

Ethan headed upstairs. He hated being the one people had to tiptoe around. It was as if Cori was dead and everyone was doing their damned best not to bring it up, lest his emotions erupt onto them. He stumbled up to his room and forced himself to slip into his cold, lonely bed.

21

ETHAN GOT A FEW hours of sleep before the sheer emptiness of his bed woke him. He stared at the blank spot beside him. His hand gravitated to the space that Cori should have been in, but the unnatural cold made him draw it back again.

He ripped off the gray comforter and slipped on his robe and slippers. He opened the translucent Asian shade that separated their bedroom from the living room. Since they'd started sharing the room, it had changed shape several times. They both blamed it on their changing needs, but the fact was, if they had been completely simpatico, the house wouldn't have been indecisive.

The apartment had gone from variations of separated rooms to an open studio style. Along with that, the décor had swung the expanse of a decorator's portfolio. The house tried modern abstract furniture that Cori referred to as Alfred Hitchcock's sub-textual death threats. The shabby chic phase was short-lived, because Cori refused to sleep in the apartment while it looked like an Applebee's.

Now it was in the modern Asian theme. Although the transmorph he had known as Cori didn't object to this theme, he wondered if it wasn't a sign that something was wrong with her. The house had always given Cori simple, comfortable furnishings and it gave Ethan bold, modern furnishings. He knew it was a tough match to balance, but somewhere around the French country theme, he probably should have suspected something was wrong.

He stepped through the living room, kicking floor pillows as he did. He headed out of the apartment and downstairs to the kitchen. At the base of the stairs, he noticed Nevia sitting at the breakfast nook on the island.

He slowed his approach to determine what she was doing before he interrupted. Her body stiffened and her head popped up. "Ethan?" she asked in a quiet voice littered with doubt.

"Yes," he said, resuming his pace to hide his surreptitious intent. "How did you guess?"

As he came around the island, he could see she had nothing in front of her. She wasn't reading, eating, or even fiddling with an inanimate object. He tilted his head, still waiting for an answer to his question.

She tapped her nose. He must not have hidden his shock, because she immediately lowered her eyes. She seemed reluctant to acknowledge her talent. "You can really tell the difference between me and someone else just by scent?" He leaned on the island.

She shrugged. "I guess."

Ethan noted the embarrassment that filled her face again. "Am I interrupting you?" He pulled himself off the counter to give her literal space to answer the question.

"No, I was just... thinking. I can't sleep in strange beds."

"Is Danato's room alright?"

"Yes, it's like a hotel. Is that the house's doing?" she asked carefully.

"No, it's always like that." Ethan actually didn't know why the country cabin décor had never overflowed into Danato's bedroom. "He just doesn't need much," he added, which was admittedly true. For all the power Danato had over budget, the only luxuries he afforded himself were liquor, coffee, and reading material.

"It's very comfortable. I'm just a little too preoccupied to sleep."

"I see that." Ethan headed over to the fridge and pulled out the milk. "Do you always sit alone, staring into nothingness when you can't sleep?" He grabbed a saucepan and poured the milk in before setting it on the burner to warm.

"I was thinking about... everything."

"Care to pick a topic?" He grabbed cinnamon and honey from the cupboard, along with two matching mugs, and set them by the stove.

Nevia took a pregnant pause before licking her lips to speak. "I was thinking what a horrible mistake this was."

Ethan pulled a wooden spoon from the drawer on the island. "Coming here, you mean?"

"No, taking this job. I'm so far out of my league."

"Superhero powers got you down?"

"Superhero?" Her eyes flashed with anger, though he got the impression it was directed at the word, not him. "I'm a drug-sniffing dog!" Even as she said it, she must have realized how loud she had spoken. She glanced behind her. "I'm sorry."

Ethan pursed his lips and shook his head as if to say, *don't worry about it.* He didn't bother explaining that the bedrooms were virtually sound proof, unless the house deemed otherwise.

"I'm not even that good," she continued. "You could probably train a dog faster than me." She ran her fingers through her hair. The short Hershey-brown tresses spiked up, giving her a little tangible attitude. "I'm so stupid."

"Easy, girl. You're gonna scare your own shadow away with that talk. What about just now? You could smell me before you could even hear me. I mean, how is that not talent?"

"Ethan." She locked her fingers in front of her on the counter, as if she were trying to keep her gestures under control. "You chased werewolves. You brought in all your bounties in record time. The only thing that slowed you down was the paperwork."

Ethan shook his head. "What do I have to do with this?"

"I'm your replacement."

He chuckled. "Yes, but that doesn't mean you have to do what I did. Find your own way to contribute."

"I was training to be in the FBI. I'm a great marksman, but I can't run more than a mile without puking. I was planning to get a desk job tracking potential terrorists. I can't compete with…" She ripped her hands from their self-imposed restraints and raised them in a wide, all-inclusive arch. "…this. I don't know where to begin to take in all this information, let alone physically confront the reality of it."

Ethan smiled, thinking back to his first tour of the prison and the laundry list of dangerous creatures. "I know that feeling, Jordan. I'm the successor to run this freak show. I've been in this world for going on three years and I still have to ask questions. You're never done learning, and when you are, you're dead."

Ethan turned down the heat on the milk and stirred in the honey and cinnamon. "Are you sure I'm the only one that is intimidating you?" She looked up at him, but looked down just as quick. He divided the milk mixture into the mugs and rinsed out the pot. "I've known Daniel for almost two years. I worked with him for six months. It's a wonder that I didn't get the opportunity to see his power until now." He brought the mugs over to the edge of the island and sat down beside her on the saddle stools. "I'm not sure I'm done recovering from that, but I have other things on my mind to distract me from the trauma of finding out my best friend is a... whatever he is."

Nevia took the cup of warm milk and sipped it. She let out a sound of appreciation and took in several more sips before releasing the cup to the counter again. "I'm not easily shocked." She looked back at Ethan, as if that point needed to be established first and foremost. "I don't scare easily. I don't cry at the drop of a hat. I don't guffaw raucously at jokes when they are funny. I don't fly off the handle when my anger peaks."

"You keep your emotions under control."

"Yes," she said, drawing the milk back up for another sip. "Most people think I'm a cold fish. Stone-faced, you know? I just don't put everything on the outside. Some people bottle their emotions. That's not me either. I can handle what I feel. I just don't display my reactions."

"I sense a 'but' coming up."

She drew herself from the counter to face him. Her knees brushed against his as she did, so he scooted back to give her room. "Daniel is..." She paused in reflection.

He took a drink of his milk, which he found too hot to sip as freely as she had hers. He sensed movement from the balcony. He looked up over the rim of his mug and saw Daniel leaning against the railing of the balcony that overlooked the main floor. Daniel raised a finger to his lips to shush him.

Ethan looked at Nevia to see if she had seen him shift in attention. She was still contemplating her response. She was holding her milk close to her mouth in anticipation of another sip. He wondered if the beverage was preventing her from smelling Daniel's presence as she had smelled him. Or perhaps her mind was just too distracted by the conversation.

"Daniel is... creepy, sadistic, lecherous?" Ethan supplied, lowering his cup to the counter to cool off.

"Amazing." She looked up at him with an almost scolding stare. "To say the least."

"You weren't freaked out by his display?"

"No. I know I should be. I should have run screaming like any reasonable person would want to, but..." Ethan glanced up at Daniel, who was intently listening to Nevia. The scowl on his face was out of place. "I'm looking forward to seeing what else he can do."

"Really?" Ethan asked.

"I know that must sound morbid as hell to you."

"If you're so fascinated by his power, why don't you want to continue being his partner?"

"I'm a born leader."

"Okay." Ethan wasn't sure where that personality trait was hiding, but he could at least humor her.

"I can't follow. I had no problem being the new kid that would eventually earn the respect of my peers, and become the person they sought out for advice until I inevitably became the frontrunner." Nevia leaned forward. "I don't think Daniel's going to let me call the shots, ever."

"Not outside of the bedroom, anyway." Ethan shook his head, dumbfounded that he would use that old joke at this moment. "I'm sorry, habit."

"No, I know what you mean. If I was the type of girl who could rule through pillow talk, I'm sure I would be upstairs instead of in this kitchen, but that will never be good enough for me. I'm worth more than that."

Ethan nodded. "I'm starting to see that." Daniel moved away from the balcony and slunk back to his room. He must have heard enough. "Why don't you explain to me what exactly you do, so I can attempt to talk you out of transferring?" She scoffed at the suggestion. "I'm serious. I'm curious anyway. Is it really just scent?"

She shook her head. "It's like wine tasting. Wine is wine, but there are subtle variations in the flavor notes. The really good wine connoisseurs can taste and smell where the grapes were grown. For me, it's like men and women are red and white wine. Instead of tasting the difference, though, I can smell it."

She scowled and shook her head. "No, it's not just that. It's like I feel the difference. It's almost tangible. My nose is the conduit to detect the differences, but it's not any different to me than... just knowing. It's almost cognitive, and for many years, I thought it was. In fact, if it weren't for those stupid lab tests, I wouldn't have known I wasn't just psychic."

"So, you've always had this ability?" he asked, sipping his milk.

"Let's just say the other kids didn't like playing hide and seek with me."

"Mmm," Ethan said into his mug as he swallowed to respond. "That's funny. So what do I smell like?"

Nevia laughed. "I knew you were going to ask me that. It's not just scents, its pheromones, and colors, and vibrations."

"Really?"

"That's the tangible part. I don't know how to explain it."

Ethan put down his mug. "Okay, do it. Smell me."

Nevia shook her head. "It's just too embarrassing. To get a good read, I need proximity." Ethan nodded. She rolled her eyes and took a deep breath before setting down her mug. She scooted to the edge of her stool and leaned into his neck to smell him.

She drew back and lifted his arms slightly. She drew her nose across his chest, inhaling slowly. She repeated it and leaned back, biting her lower lip. He arched a brow in anticipation.

"Human," she smiled. "Male. Younger than I thought. Just into your twenties. Heterosexual."

"You can tell that?"

"Of course, pheromones. I know that you find me attractive, but you aren't actively trying to attract me. Which tells me you're sexually unavailable. From that, I would deduce that you are married or in a committed relationship. You have a purple color."

"Is that my aura?"

She shrugged. "I suppose. I see purple on men often. It's synonymous with pride. Yours is deep purple. I think your image is important to you, but it's more important to you that your image be viewed well by others. Your vibrations are erratic. You're under a lot of stress."

"Not really anything that you don't already know. Anything that you couldn't know?" he challenged playfully.

"I know that Daniel was just listening to our conversation from upstairs a few minutes ago."

Ethan's mouth turned up into a smile. "You weren't exactly shy about talking in front of him."

"I don't do shy."

Ethan nodded. "You really aren't the least bit afraid of him, are you?"

"I don't do fear either, at least not when I'm armed."

Ethan laughed. "I really hope you change your mind about staying with them. I don't think you'll be playing second fiddle to anyone. From what I can see, you're just what Daniel needs."

"In the bedroom," she kidded.

Ethan chuckled and shrugged. "Who knows, maybe both?" Ethan gave her a light chuck on the shoulder before downing his warm milk. "Try to get some sleep." He slipped off the stool. "I look forward to seeing your best work tomorrow."

She nodded, catching his meaning. She squeezed his forearm, giving him a taut smile. "I will do my very best, Ethan. It doesn't take a nose to see how much you miss her."

He cleared his throat, feeling the emotions he was burying start to rise. He nodded, and she released his arm. "Good night."

He went back to his room, intending to sleep, but the grief lingering in the pit of his stomach twisted into disgust. Shame and anger marred his memories of the last few weeks. Fists alone couldn't slake his lust for revenge. That frustration led him to carry out his revenge on the apartment that represented nothing of himself, and even less of Cori.

He ripped the frail translucent dividers to shreds and threw them into the living room. He shattered the painted vases against the wall intended for a television. The matted swan drawing was no match for the porcelain shards.

The large silk pillows, a painful replacement for furniture, expelled their stuffing under the pressure of his grip. Three samurai swords that were stacked delicately on their wall display took their turn at perforating Ethan's bed—a belated response to his unintentional five-week affair.

After he destroyed everything destroyable, he sank to the floor and cried, a response he had desperately tried to avoid. He wasn't above the expression, as Nevia claimed to be, but he didn't want to let it out. He didn't want to admit to himself how close he was to losing Cori.

22

D ANIEL HEADED TO THE cafeteria as soon as he woke in the morning. He could have stayed at the house and had coffee and a jalapeno cheese omelet with the others, but he wanted to get away from Nevia. He hadn't meant to spy on her conversation with Ethan last night, but when his name came up, he couldn't help but listen in.

What he'd heard, however, perturbed him. Her fascination with his eyes already baffled him. He found her interest more unsettling than the aversion he usually received from people. Now that he knew she wasn't in the least uncomfortable with his power, he couldn't stand to be in the same room as her.

He was a freak. He knew he was a freak. He was fortunate to have a few close friends that honestly accepted that about him and moved past it. At least, he hoped Ethan could move past it. He hadn't really had a chance to have a heart to heart with him about it. Not that he would instigate one.

Nevia should have been running away screaming at the sight of him. She should have been shooting judgmental looks at him. She should have been the one running away to the cafeteria to get away from him. The fact that she wasn't made *her* the freak.

Daniel slammed a beige coffee cup under the coffee spout at the beverage center. The impact separated the handle from the cup. "Son of a bitch!" he yelled louder than necessary. "Does everything in this place have to be old as shit?" A silver-haired woman peeked out from behind the food line before dismissing him with a headshake and returning to work.

"Do you want good coffee, or good cups?"

Daniel turned and found Belus standing behind him. His short stature never matched his voice. Though he rarely raised his volume, his hoarse bass always sounded gruff.

"Coffee," Daniel answered solemnly, just short of kicking the floor with his shoe like a scolded little boy. He tucked the handle into the cup and slid it to one side. He grabbed a new cup and filled it to the brim. "You too?" He looked back at Belus, pointing at the machine.

"Yes, thank you." Daniel poured him a cup and pointed to the array of coffee polluters that lined the table. "Black is fine," Belus said, taking the cup from him.

They gravitated to a table to sit together. "What puts you in a foul mood this morning?" Belus asked, positioning his coffee on the table before climbing into a plastic chair.

"A woman," Daniel chuckled.

"How can that be? Cori's detained."

Daniel raised an eyebrow mid-way to his first drink of happy caffeination. "Was that a joke?"

Belus shrugged. "Apparently not."

Daniel smiled. "You never cease to subvert my expectations of you, Belus."

"I never will. What's the girl trouble, if not our resident pain in the ass?"

Daniel perked a brow at him. "I thought you liked Cori."

"Never said I didn't. Is this about your new partner?"

Daniel nodded. "Are you sure you really want to listen to my girl troubles?"

Belus looked at his watch. "Not if it's going to take all day."

"Okay, okay, ahh, she likes me." Daniel threw up his hands as if it was a grand revelation he had built up to.

"Yeah, so?"

"Come on, she saw me kill a transmorph. She looked into my eyes. I mean, *really* looked."

"*I've* looked into your eyes. Do we need to go to couple's therapy?" Belus asked, stone-faced.

"It's different when you're looking at me from behind bars."

"Is it? I knew what you were capable of when they brought you in. I wasn't afraid to stand before you. I wasn't cowering at the sight of those black holes you call eyes. Not everyone is afraid of you."

Daniel leaned back in his chair in frustration. Belus was right. The first time he had been in this prison was as a prisoner, not a bounty hunter. Prior to being a hunter, he had been seeking out transmorphs. He'd killed without distinguishing between good and bad. He had hurt a lot of people before he fully understood his power, and even more after he did. He had rightly deserved to be imprisoned.

Belus had argued on his behalf, when no one else would. He saw something in Daniel that no one else did, including Danato. If it weren't for Belus's interest in him, he may not have been recommended for paroled employment. He wouldn't have learned to distinguish between dangerous transmorphs and benign ones. He also wouldn't have refined his ability to release humans from enveloping transmorphs, and he would be sitting in a cell upstairs with all the other subservient, uncategorized creatures.

"What does that mean if she doesn't run screaming from me?" Daniel asked.

Belus tipped his brow. "What do you think it means?"

"That she's like my soul mate."

Belus laughed boisterously. "Should I be jealous?"

Daniel smiled despite rolling his eyes. "I'm serious. What's wrong with her?"

"Nothing," Belus drawled. "She just isn't a chicken shit. She has a rational mind, and she isn't intimidated by things that are out of the ordinary."

"She's a female-Belus," Daniel admitted. "Well, she's certainly small enough." He smirked at his joke. Belus raised a finger in silent objection to any comments about his height. "Why weren't *you* afraid of me?"

"I'm not easily shaken, you know that."

Daniel leaned over the table and lowered his voice. "I'm a murderer, Belus. I killed my father. I've killed transmorphs, good and bad. I think you and I both know my father wasn't the only human blood on my hands when I entered this prison. Why? Tell me why I was any different from your other prisoners."

Belus leaned over the table, mimicking his secret exchange. "You want me to tell you about some redeeming quality I saw that made you worth fighting for?"

"Yeah." Daniel nodded.

"I can't. You were a half-cocked asshole with anger management issues, psychological problems, and a supposed affinity for watching transmorphs implode."

"What made you save me, then?"

"The *supposed* part was what saved you. The reason you can't stand that Jordan isn't afraid of your power is because you can't stand that she isn't, and you are." Daniel leaned back, unintentionally validating the accusation.

"Listen, kid, you put your trust in a fearless little man many years ago, and he gave you your freedom and your self-respect back. I don't mean to tell you what relationship you should have with this new partner, but you should take into consideration what she can give you if you put your trust in her like you did me." Belus shrugged and took his coffee to go, leaving Daniel to contemplate what to do with a woman he couldn't stand the sight of before he'd even slept with her.

23

Daniel was the last to arrive on the transmorph level. Ethan had taken over the responsibility of chaperoning Nevia through the cells. Instead of letting her go into the cells as he had; Ethan dragged the offenders out and used his forceful grip to hold them in place while she did her assessment.

Heaton was hanging back, sipping his morning tea. He glanced at Daniel as he strolled over to him. "Where have you been?" he asked.

"Nowhere, sweetheart. Why; did you miss me?"

"Fuck you too," Heaton said casually, more than caustically.

"Cafeteria. I needed to think." Daniel huffed out a breath as he watched Nevia do her work.

"Uh-oh. What about? You slept with her, didn't you? That's why you didn't stay for heartburn city this morning?"

"No, I didn't. I'm not going to either."

Heaton turned slowly and gawked at him. "Who are you?"

"Shut up. I can work with a woman without sleeping with her."

"Um, no, you can't. Don't get me wrong, I'm not interested in being the third wheel to your awkward ex-lover partnership, but you are incapable of the level of forethought that it would take to say no to sex."

Daniel frowned at him. "Why are we friends?"

"Nobody said we were good friends, *sweetheart*," Heaton said with a wink before turning back to the entertainment.

"Why is she smelling all the transmorphs again? She already narrowed it down to two." Daniel watched Ethan move onto the next cell, which had not been in Nevia's previous list of candidates.

"She wants to be sure."

"Damnably slow process, if you ask me," Daniel said. "She would be useless in the field. I can't just go around holding down random people so she can sniff them."

"I don't know," Heaton said. "She seems to be getting better."

"Why do you say that?"

"Ethan told me she knew you were listening in on them last night." Daniel's mouth dropped. "He said you were over twenty feet away upstairs, and you never made a peep."

"Japers, I wanted to see what she was going to say about me. That means she knows I know what she said. Damn, that's not even fun. That's just honest dialogue through a third-person mediator. I might as well pass her a note to see if she likes me."

"Since when do you care if you're not going to sleep with her?" Heaton pointed out.

"Shut up," Daniel mumbled.

Down the corridor, Nevia finished reading the last transmorph and said something to Ethan. He took a step away from her and looked at the floor. She gestured emphatically as she spoke again, but that only prompted a lowered head nod from him.

"That doesn't bode well." Daniel headed over to the conversation that was draining his friend's spirits. "What's the verdict?" Ethan glanced up at him, but turned away. He stalked off, hiding whatever reaction he didn't want Daniel to see. Nevia looked at Daniel with sympathetic eyes. "What did you find?"

"It's still down to two transmorphs," she answered.

Daniel stared at her. He could feel his face translating the anger he was trying not to feel. He broke his eye contact and ushered her gently away from the cells, and out of earshot of the transmorphs. "Listen," he said, locking his hands on her arms and trying to emphasize his earnestness with a strong grip. "I know you are struggling with your proficiency, but this isn't a time to be reserved in your evaluation. If it's 60-40 we go with 60. Do you get me?"

Nevia's hands whipped up and rotated, knocking his hands loose. Her face was still sympathetic, but her voice was stern. "I am not being ambivalent. I'm being honest.

I smell Cori on both of those transmorphs equally. I can't give you an explanation for that, and I won't give you a percentage. As near as I can tell, she could be in either one of them right now."

"You must be wrong."

"Clearly, Daniel, because her body is not split in half. But at one point, very recently, she was in each of these transmorphs. I don't know, maybe they were passing her back and forth. The fake Cori could have been releasing them to exchange the body and share in the torture. I don't know. *You* tell *me* what these creatures are capable of."

Daniel looked back at the cells. They were definitely capable of that and much more. "I'm sorry," he grumbled. "I shouldn't have questioned your skill."

"Don't be. I haven't demonstrated enough competency to go unchecked. I would do the same in your shoes. The truth is, I smell Cori on all the transmorphs. I've been as judicious as I can in identifying these two for you."

Daniel nodded, admiring her resolute, all-business demeanor. "Listen, I need to go talk to Ethan. We need to figure out another way to pinpoint her. I think later, though, when we aren't trying to save our damsel in distress, we should talk."

"About what?"

"About us."

Her brow tipped, and she pulled her head back as if the topic had actually impacted her. "There's an *us*?"

"We, us." Daniel motioned back to Heaton, who was conveniently hanging back to give them room to talk. "This partnership."

"I see. You may have missed some of last night's discussion, because this…" She motioned to Heaton, him, and herself. "…isn't going to work for me."

Daniel swallowed hard, feeling the unfamiliar sting of rejection. "Well then, that's what we'll talk about." He cleared his throat and walked on, giving Heaton a wave to follow.

24

"I DISAGREE," HEATON SAID vehemently for the fourth time.

"I know you disagree," Ethan said, sitting in Belus's usual spot on the file cabinet while Heaton stood behind the office door. Belus and Daniel were, for the most part, keeping quiet. Belus had taken Danato's chair whilst Daniel and his expansive breadth consumed one of the chairs before the desk. "Why do you disagree?"

"Because you haven't witnessed the degree of control that Daniel needs to perform a human extraction. If he tries it on the wrong the transmorph, then we don't get another go at Cori for at least three weeks. Daniel, tell him."

"I could try to—" Before Daniel could finish his addendum, Heaton slapped the backside of his head. Daniel was out of his chair and facing down his friend in a heartbeat. Heaton shifted off the wall to intercept him. Ethan watched the anger build between them, but instead of coming to blows, they seemed to reach an impasse. Neither man would throw a punch, so it was just a matter of who was going to bend. "Three weeks," Daniel snarled and sat back down. "Or I risk losing my strength halfway through the procedure."

"A wounded transmorph will kill its host in order to survive the attack." Heaton shifted to lean over the desk, updating Daniel about the risks as much as Ethan. "Daniel needs to be at his strongest to make sure the only casualty is the transmorph." Heaton stared at Daniel a moment before continuing. "We both want to help, Ethan. Daniel, in his half-cocked way, is willing to put himself in the grave to release Cori. I am being loyal to both of you and Cori by informing you of Daniel's limitations."

"Heaton's right," Belus interjected. "We need to exhaust all possibilities of identifying Cori's true captor before we risk losing three more weeks. Her mind is already in danger of being entangled; we shouldn't waste our efforts because we are too impatient to wait another day or two for a better solution." Belus tapped a pencil on the desk. "Perhaps the scent will fade in a day or two."

"It doesn't sound like it has faded much from any of them," Daniel said. "I guess we're lucky to have a definitive choice of two. Should we try your brain-sucker again?"

"No!" Ethan said more sharply than he'd intended. "He couldn't distinguish between Cori and the other minds before. He doesn't seem to handle multiple minds well."

"What about a stronger reader?" Heaton interjected. "Has anyone else in the prison read Cori?"

"No." Belus shook his head.

"Actually..." Ethan corrected. Belus's eyes searched him for the answer. "Mezula has."

"What asinine fool gave Cori permission to go near her?" Belus barked. "Cleos is one thing, but that woman is a sadist."

"I sort of did a stupid thing right before she ran off with Vince."

Belus perked his brow. "And Danato let you live?"

"I think the only thing that saved me was the distraction of Cori escaping with the werewolf."

"I imagine so. Mezula might be strong enough to read through the minds," Belus informed Heaton.

"Good," Daniel said. "Let's go get her."

"I don't have to remind any of you that she's a prisoner, do I?" Belus glanced at Ethan.

"She'll be in shackles the whole time." Ethan jumped off the file cabinet and headed out the door with Heaton and Daniel.

25

"Oh, sweet mother Mary." Daniel stood before the beautiful redhead in her long, black, high-slit dress. "Where have you been all my life?"

"Right here, sweetie." Mezula extended her hand through her bars for Daniel to kiss. "Waiting for you," she drawled.

Daniel reached for her hand just as Ethan and Heaton opened their mouths to object. Daniel paid no heed to their sputters and kissed the woman's hand. Ethan threw his arms up in exasperation and turned away.

"Hello, Ethan," Mezula said. "Haven't seen you in a while."

"Hello Mezula. I've been busy."

"I heard you married your pet crush." She smiled, pulling her hand from Daniel, who was taking more than a gentleman's share of kisses. "Happily ever after, then?"

"No. Yes! But no, we... she's been taken by a transmorph."

"Oh, I'm so sorry." Even though she sounded sincere, Ethan couldn't believe she felt any concern for Cori. "What brings you by to see me?"

"Ethan here—" Daniel leaned on the bars, flashing an easy smile. "—he says you've read Cori before. Is that so?"

"Yes, but it was a long time ago."

"How long?" Heaton asked from beside him.

Mezula shifted her attention to him. "Over two years, I think."

Daniel backed away from the cage and conferred with Heaton. "Two years? Will that still work?"

"I don't know," Heaton grumbled. "A positive location?"

"If she's strong enough." Daniel veered back to Mezula's cell. "Are you strong enough?"

"Strong enough for what, dear?" She shrugged.

"We need you to find Cori," Ethan said, stepping forward.

Mezula eyed him curiously. "She's entangled. How long has she been under?"

"Five weeks," Ethan said, biting back the guilt, so it didn't come through in his voice.

"Wicked creatures, those transmorphs. You have my sympathy."

"Do we have your support?" Daniel asked.

"Ethan always has my support. I can't let that devout of a love go unquenched." Ethan waggled a pair of handcuffs in front of her. "Oh, my. Speaking of quenching." She smirked.

26

MEZULA STROLLED THROUGH THE transmorph level as if she were walking through a park on a fine summer day. Nothing about the prison ever seemed to fluster her. Ethan imagined he could scream in her face, and she would simply pull out her compact to check if his hot breath had disturbed her makeup and hair. The calmer she was, the more restless he felt.

Although he was happy to be free of using Cleos as a crutch, he wasn't any more contented with recruiting Mezula. She seemed genuine in her interest to help them, but he couldn't help but remember how brutal her readings were. Belus was right: she enjoyed the pain she inflicted on people.

She approached the cell of one of the transmorphs and Cori number one met her at the bars. "Christ, Ethan, you are getting desperate. Why don't you just admit defeat and leave us to our revenge?"

"Do you know what has happened to your sixth?" Ethan asked, staying behind Mezula. Heaton and Daniel stayed even farther back with their arms crossed in duplicate observation of the show.

"Yes." Number One looked down at her feet in solemn contemplation. "We felt her loss."

"Did you feel her pain?" Ethan asked. She looked up, holding a sneer, but didn't answer. He took it as a yes. "I will order that for each and every one of you, unless you reveal and release Cori."

Cori-1 tipped her head and smiled coyly at him. "Bring it on, bitch," she said with Cori's exact inflection.

Ethan nodded to Mezula. She reached between the bars like a predator to its prey. She latched onto Cori-1's hand. The only thing missing in her devious smile was salivating fangs. Cori-1 screamed in agony from the reading. Ethan closed his eyes and reminded himself that she was not his Cori.

After Cori-1 collapsed, Mezula stumbled away from the cells. Ethan caught her before she lost her balance completely. "Well?" he asked, letting her head lean back on his shoulder so he could see her face. "Is she there?"

"I must sleep," Mezula said with half-closed eyes.

"Bullshit!" Ethan pulled her around to face him. "We don't have time for you to sleep."

"I must," she whispered.

Ethan shook her. "Tell me!"

"Wake me in an hour," Mezula mumbled before she closed her eyes and wilted against him.

"Damn it!" Ethan lifted her unconscious body up and turned back to Heaton and Daniel. "I forgot about the sleep thing."

"Will she be doing that after every read?" Heaton asked.

"I guess so," Ethan said. "What do we do now?"

"We wait," Daniel said, uncrossing his arms. "She's still our best option. Until we know which one is the real Cori, we can't proceed."

Ethan placed Mezula on the floor, being careful to pull her high-cut skirt over her as best he could. He stepped over her and joined Heaton and Daniel. "What exactly happens when we do find her?" he whispered, so the transmorphs didn't know every detail of their plan.

Daniel nodded for them to go into the next section. Once through the airlock, they stepped into the room they had been using for interrogation. Ethan sat on the table and propped his foot on one of the plastic chairs. "I know you aren't going to do what you did to Erica."

"It's not that different," Heaton said, leaning against the doorframe.

"It's not an all-inclusive destruction like it was with Erica," Daniel said, lounging on his little yellow chair like it was a recliner. "It's more of a surgical technique, assuming I want to kill one of my patients."

"You can do it, though?" Ethan felt like he had asked this question a hundred times already, but he still wasn't confident with the answers he was getting.

"It's difficult to control. My precision is not without its errors, but yes."

"The process of removing her body is like sand-blasting the caramel off an apple," Heaton explained. "You'll definitely get the caramel off, but a lot of the peel is going to go with it."

Ethan's hopes dimmed. "What are we talking? A bad skin peel or downright filleting?"

"I can reverse most of the damage." Daniel gave Heaton a sideways glance. "I've done this numerous times without skinning anyone alive." Heaton moved over to him and pulled up his right sleeve. "Heaton, damn it!" Daniel growled.

Heaton shoved his arm out for Ethan to see. The skin looked perfectly normal until Heaton turned his wrist to reveal the soft underbelly of his forearm. The rippled scar tissue had healed as a permanent shiny mocha color.

Ethan touched the marred skin, unable to believe it was real until he did. His stomach lurched as he looked at his friend's damaged flesh—yet another secret, revealed at the worst possible time in his life. "You did this?" Ethan looked at Daniel for the answer, but his eyes glazed into a hard stare. "You just said you can reverse the damage."

"This *is* reversed," Heaton snapped. "I almost lost my arm because of this incident."

Daniel shook his head. "You're a fecking ass to show him that right now."

"He needs to know that what you do isn't *magic*," Heaton said firmly. "It's dangerous, and I'd be lying if I said it isn't scary as hell."

Daniel stood to face his friend. Heaton straightened and stepped closer to meet his challenge. "And that's how you've always felt? Or just since you stuck your hand in my way?" Despite the civility in Daniel's voice, Ethan stood in case he needed to break them up.

"Yes." Heaton didn't specify which it was. Given the extent of the scarring, any wavering opinion he might have had about Daniel's work would have been solidified after that much pain.

Daniel's jaw clenched and unclenched before he spoke. "Thanks for sharing. I'm sure Ethan appreciates you adding to his worries."

"I'm being honest." Heaton glanced back at Ethan. "He needs to know what you are."

"And what am I, Heaton? What do you see when you stare into my eyes?"

Heaton seemed taken aback by the statement. He looked at Ethan and then at the floor. He pulled down his sleeve and moved to the door, stopping only to give Daniel a stern glare before leaving the room to walk off his irritation.

Daniel rubbed his face and took in a soothing breath. "Of all the days for him to let that bitterness out." He sat back in his chair and leaned forward over his knees. After a beat he looked up at Ethan mournfully. "He got in the way. He didn't understand. He thought he was helping. I was at my full strength. I couldn't undo all the damage." Daniel's eyes were begging for understanding. "He's right though. I am extremely dangerous. What I am proposing to do may injure her, but I *can* get her out. I'm being honest as well. I wouldn't attempt this if I wasn't confident I could do it."

Ethan nodded. "I don't think Cori would begrudge you a few scars if it meant saving her life. You've always had my back before. I know you have it now."

27

"TIME TO WAKE UP, love." Daniel gave Mezula a nudge with his foot. She had slept for just over an hour.

When the prod didn't rouse her, Ethan crouched down and shook her shoulder. "Mezula!" he shouted, but she remained blissfully asleep. Ethan looked up at Daniel. "Maybe we should get some cold water."

"Nah." Daniel shook his head. "Just... you know..." He waved his hand in a slapping motion.

"What?" Ethan asked, knowing full well what he meant for him to do.

"Just a little." He made the motion again and shrugged.

"You do it." Ethan stood up. "I'm not slapping any woman that can cause that much pain just by reading your mind.

"I thought you were the brave one. Mr. Leaps Off Tall Buildings Without a Second Thought."

"Nah," Ethan mocked. "I think I'll let you take this one. Now that I know you can defend yourself."

"Sure, sure, but she knows you. She's less likely to stay angry at a friend."

"We aren't *friends*," Ethan said, rejecting the word in case it might stick.

"Oh, to hell with this." Heaton pushed them both away from Mezula. He picked her up by her shoulder and gave her an unforgivably hard slap across the cheek.

Ethan took another step back, gaping at his friend's intensity. Daniel stifled his laughter and ducked behind Ethan to shield himself from whatever violence Mezula was about to unleash. Ethan was hardly adequate coverage for his football-player frame, but he seemed more interested in hiding his face than his body. After a few muffled snorts of repressed laughter, Daniel popped his head out. "What is she doing?"

Heaton moved away, revealing Mezula's freshly awakened face. A shiver ran up Ethan's back when he saw the red mark on her cheek paired with her simper.

"Mezula, are you okay?" he asked warily.

"Of course." She stretched her arms and groaned. "Thank you for waking me." She turned her attention to Heaton. "I don't know that I got *your* name." Her tongue dragged against her front teeth as she looked him up and down. "Don't worry, sweetie." She slipped her leg free of her long dress, exposing her thigh up to her hip. "I like it rough."

Heaton blanched and backpedaled away from her. If he hadn't regretted slapping her before, he would now.

The statement should have been a turn-on for any hot-blooded man, but Ethan got the distinct feeling that when she said *rough*, she meant bruises and cracked ribs. The attraction to masochism was short-lived for most men, when it went beyond playful spanking.

"Mezula—" Ethan sputtered, a laugh he hadn't intended to let out. Daniel quickly echoed it as he leaned against him for support. After the fit passed, he cleared his throat and forced himself to get back on track. "What did you read from the first Cori?"

Her smile waned as she looked back at him. She raised her hand, requesting his help to get off the ground. His initial instinct was to back away, but he pushed through his baser fear and did his gentlemanly duty.

When they came face to face, he could see her eyes were bloodshot. The readings must have taken a toll on her body, as well as her victims. He wondered if there was any hope of her reading anyone else today.

"Their minds have melded," she stated, as if that were the only explanation Ethan would need to understand the situation. "She is among them, but equally distributed."

Daniel joined the discussion. "That's a bunch of blarney to us. You're going to have to put it a bit more simply."

Mezula gave Daniel a cold, cursory scan. Apparently, they were no longer on a hand-kissing basis. "All five of their minds are intertwined with hers. I read six minds in Cori-1, and not one of them is stronger than the others.

I have no doubt all five will be the same. They've masked her."

"Fecking transmorphs. Nevia must have been right. They were passing her around, so each of them could get a lock on her mind to impersonate her better."

"Yes, it appears that way. They've also implanted their consciousness with her," Mezula said.

"Consciousness?" Ethan asked.

Daniel put a hand over Ethan's chest as if he were blocking him from advancing on Mezula. "Can you even tell which mind is Cori's?"

Mezula shook her head. "I can't be sure. They are mimicking her in every way. I'm so sorry, Ethan." She offered her condolence with a deep brow and tilted head. Ethan might as well have been standing next to Cori's coffin.

"It's fine. We'll just find another way to identify her. Right?" He looked at Daniel for confirmation.

Daniel nodded even as he glanced at Heaton. "Right."

Ethan glanced between the two men, sifting through their perpetual subtext. "What aren't you telling me?"

"You haven't told him?" Mezula glared at Daniel.

"Told me what? What more can there be?"

"Nothing new, Ethan," Daniel assured him. "We've discussed that the longer Cori is inside of that monster, the more at risk she is."

Ethan turned to face Daniel. "I don't care how much you are trying to protect me. I don't care how much you don't want me to worry. I want to know what just changed! What did she say?" Ethan pointed accusingly at Mezula.

Daniel tried to put his hands on Ethan's shoulders. He pushed them away more forcefully than he'd intended. "Save your anger management lessons for someone who isn't trying to save his wife. Talk to me Daniel, or I swear to God I will roll you!"

"Ethan." Heaton came to stand off to the side of both of them. His diplomatic voice was now the mediator. "He won't fight you. Just stand down and we'll tell you what our concerns are."

"You said six weeks wasn't long enough to be a threat to her," Ethan said, backing away from both of them. He rested his hands in front of him and stood in his attentive, wide stance.

"It isn't," Daniel said. "Physically, she's dehydrated, malnourished, and probably exhausted from trying to fight. Atrophy of the muscles takes months. Most hosts lose their hair after the one-year mark. A slew of other health problems related to malnourishment come into play at the one-year mark."

"We aren't concerned about her physically, though, are we?" Ethan said, containing his anger at Daniel's persistence to skirt the issue.

"No." Daniel ran his fingers through his auburn mop.

"We can't remove the mental residue of the transmorphs," Heaton said, taking over the explanation.

"Once we separate her, we remove the source of the minds, but… it's like having a hypnotic suggestion left behind. Cori will be influenced by it. She'll be… different. A secondary risk to that kind of mental trauma is susceptibility to further psychic attack. Which, as you might imagine, isn't a good thing in this job."

"Why didn't you just tell me about this before?" Ethan asked.

"Six weeks is still a short time to expect any major mental compromises."

"But?" Ethan provided to move things along.

"But…" Heaton nodded. "She has five transmorphs tapping into her psyche. More minds jump up the timeline and increase the likelihood of problems." Heaton looked over at Mezula. "How entangled is she?"

She shook her head. "I don't think she will be herself for quite a while. So much of her mind has been weakened by the invasion. I would be surprised if she didn't lose her memory. With five other minds crowding her, she may fracture."

"Fracture?" Ethan asked.

Mezula bit her lip before answering. "She could create split personalities just like the five Coris you see here."

Ethan lifted his hands onto his head and leaned over, taking in a few cleansing breaths. He wanted to scream and punch the walls. Instead, he let out a loud elongated curse that made everyone in the room look at their shoes as if it was a call to prayer.

"Ethan." Daniel approached him when he was calm again.

"No, don't." He held up his hand. "I know you want to give me hope. I know you want to say something encouraging, but right now I can't hear that. I need to talk to Belus. We need to figure out which one of these bastards has her. We'll deal with... amnesia and split personalities later." He backed away from all of them. "Put her back in her cell, will you?" He left without offering an apology for anything.

28

D ANIEL HEADED BACK TO the house while Heaton took Mezula back to her cell. After the unabashed sexual innuendos she had thrown at Heaton, Daniel decided it was best to give them time alone. Heaton, of course, objected fervidly to being alone with the masochist, but Daniel had reminded him that she was still handcuffed and had no superhuman strength. The last he had seen of them; she was tugging on his earlobe with her teeth as the elevator doors closed.

When he came in, he found the house dark except for the light burning in the fireplace. Nevia was curled up under a blanket on the couch, catching up on the sleep she had missed the night before.

He loathed waking her, but he knew it might be his only chance to speak with her alone. He sat down on the coffee table before her and watched her chest rise and fall. Her mouth was slightly open. He smiled at the book that was open under her arm. She hadn't had a chance against sleep reading about the lineage of hobgoblins. Many had tried and failed to finish that particular volume.

He reached out his hand to touch her face. He pulled it back, concerned how she might react to the familiarity. If she were any other woman, he would have had the audacity to wake her with a kiss. But she wasn't any other woman; she was his partner, and he wanted to keep it that way.

"Daniel?" she said. Her body hadn't stirred at all. Only her lips were awake enough to get his name out.

"Yes," he said, disappointed that he didn't have to debate how to wake her any longer.

"Did I miss it? Did you save the day without me?"

"No, you didn't miss anything." He leaned his elbows on his knees and enfolded his hands. "We used a reader to distinguish Cori. No luck. Ethan and Belus are brainstorming to come up with another way to identify her."

"I'm sorry. Where's Heaton?"

"Hopefully getting laid."

Her eyes flapped open like rebounding shades. "How's that again?"

Daniel shook his head. "Never mind, he's busy." He stood up and moved closer to the fire. He didn't care for the intense heat, but he didn't want to be so close to her while they spoke. "I was hoping we could talk. Before things get hectic again."

"And what will we talk about that wasn't made perfectly clear last night?"

He ran his fingers through his hair to push down his unruly locks. "You know, Heaton and I have never really had a leader. When Ethan came along, we would follow him on his wild goose chases, because that's what he wanted to do. Heaton spends just as much time trying to focus my attention as I spend trying to loosen him up. The jobs get done nevertheless. No one really leads, but everyone follows."

"And you think that will be enough for me? Just sit back and be the third wheel in the boys' club. I'll be the dog to flush out the fox, you'll be the hunter, and Heaton gets to carry your extra ammo."

"I'm not the hero in this, Jordan. Heaton's put a lot of time and effort into his captures. I don't keep count. We're partners."

"It doesn't matter, Daniel. Even if I thought you could both stand being partnered with a woman, I can't be the nose you need me to be. You can report to Sophie that I failed my field test."

"You didn't."

"I couldn't pinpoint her for you. Her mind is at risk, because lab flasks and multiple choice don't emulate real life. I'm resigning—"

"Shut up." He slashed his throat to bring home the point. "Bloody hell, you're a sore loser. Listen, Cori *was* being passed between the transmorphs. Their minds are entwined in hers. That's why you couldn't tell between the two. They were the last two to have her, and one of them still has her."

Nevia sat up, pushing the blanket to one side and tossing her book on the coffee table. "That's good to know. I only wish I could distinguish between them."

"Damn it, woman, you did a good job. We would still be grasping at straws if it weren't for you. You've got a weird-ass little skill, but it is worth something. I don't say that lightly because I thought you were bullshit two days ago."

"Now, what do you think of me?"

He turned away to fiddle his fingers on the mantel. He looked back at her over his shoulder. "You want honesty?"

"If you're capable of it. You know I wouldn't spare your feelings."

He looked down at the fire before answering. "You worry me." He heard her stand up, and she came up on the other side of the fireplace to join him.

"Worried that I might get hurt?"

"No... well sure, but I worry about that for Heaton too. He's a daredevil."

"What about me worries you?"

He looked her over, trying to convey what he felt without actually having to speak it. He removed his tinted glasses and set them on the mantel. It took all of his will to force himself to look at her. He paused and waited to see if her response would change from the last time she had looked at him without his shield.

Her eyes flickered over his face, taking in all of his features. When her gaze finally settled on his, her feet gravitated forward. It was the exact opposite reaction he'd gotten from every single human being he had ever encountered, save Belus... and his mother.

He wasn't fully aware he had raised his hand to stop her until she bumped into it with her shoulder. He looked down at the delicate frame that was pushing against his hand. Instead of moving his hand, he latched onto her. He expected this would stop her advancement, but it didn't. She pushed forward until her body was mere inches from him. She stared up at him, unnerving what little bravado he had for sober proximity.

He felt his hand shaking against her shoulder, and his breathing increased to match his pounding heart. "This," he said, bringing his hand up to rest on her right shoulder. "This worries me."

"Are you afraid we won't be able to work together after?" she asked, bringing her hand up to the opening in his shirt. She rested her palm on his bare chest.

"After what?" Her hand felt cool compared to the heat of the fire.

"After we have sex."

"What? No, that's not what I mean."

"Are you sure?" Her free hand came out of nowhere and grabbed at his pants, searching for his answer directly from the head of activities.

He snatched both her hands instantly and placed them in prayer, sandwiched between his. "Oh, wow, you are a delightful surprise." He lowered his hands to her wrists and kissed the back of both her hands. "Very delightful." He cleared his throat and moved away, grabbing his glasses off the mantel as he did.

"I don't understand. You don't want me?" she asked. "I was told you would screw a nun if she bent over to pick up a penny."

"Who said that?" He turned back at the edge of the living room area. "That's horrible!"

"Clearly an exaggeration, but if you're not worried about a potentially awkward after-sex relationship, why are you acting this way?"

"Because," Daniel stepped forward again, putting on his glasses and shoving them high on his nose, "you aren't afraid of me."

"Oh, you're not one of those role players who like bashful schoolgirls and virgins, are you?"

"What? No... well sure, who doesn't? But... crap, woman, why don't you get this? I'm a freak! I have black holes for eyes, which you are compelled to come closer to while everyone else pulls away. You've seen me incinerate a transmorph, and you can't wait for a repeat performance. You should be scared of me."

Nevia took in the statement while she walked around the couch to the kitchen. "You want something to drink? I bribed a cafeteria lady to get us more beer."

Daniel watched her pull out two beers and pop the lids off against the counter. He couldn't place the emotion on her face. She looked bored. She met him between the couch and dining room table and handed him the beer. He watched her take a long swig. When her lips were free, she let out a sigh of enjoyment.

"Are you intentionally tormenting me?" Daniel asked.

"I don't really have anything to say to you, Daniel. You've just informed me that my lack of fear for you has driven *you* to be afraid of *me*. I told you before; fear doesn't look good on me. I'm not sure you're wearing yours very gracefully either, but feel it and get over it. I'm not the one with the issue here. Either you need to trust me, or you need to trust yourself. Whichever it is, this isn't going to be solved tonight. So, have a beer." She tapped the long neck of her bottle to his.

He smiled, wondering why he'd stopped her advance. He could have been down to bare skin with her. "I don't want you to transfer," he said, remembering the reason he had started this whole conversation.

"I'll think about it," she said. "Now, drink up."

"Yes, ma'am." He smirked and lifted his bottle for a drink without taking his eyes off her.

29

WHEN ETHAN GOT BACK home, the lights were off in the house. Daniel and Nevia were sitting in the living room drinking their beers by the firelight. They both looked up at him as he entered. He thought for a moment that he might have been interrupting, but his sympathy waned along with his compulsion to scold them for having open beverages in the living room.

He switched on the kitchen light and headed straight to the fridge in search of something to feed his guests. There wasn't much he could make heads or tails of. His culinary abilities dimmed with repetition. He should have just kicked everyone out to eat in the cafeteria, but the manners that Danato had instilled in him demanded otherwise; the same manners that made him cringe to see food leave the confines of the dining room table.

Ethan pushed his hands through his hair and linked them behind his head as he stared into the fridge. He wasn't looking for anything anymore, and even if he was, he wouldn't have seen it. His eyes had blurred into the relaxation of a mental stupor.

"She's not in there," Daniel said from behind him. He hadn't heard him come over, which was evidence of how unfocused he was.

He felt the sudden urge to turn around and grab Daniel's self-appointed black shirt uniform and throw him against the counter. He knew he could do it. Despite Daniel's linebacker frame, he was no match for the muscles that dragon sperm built.

If Heaton was right, Daniel wouldn't do anything to defend himself. Despite his purported anger issues, Ethan had never seen Daniel lose his temper. His voice never rose more than a few decibels before being reined back into a quiet disciplined volume. Ethan didn't have that control. His years of arguing with Danato, Belus, and Cori had left him with a healthy voice box.

At that moment, though, he didn't have any interest in *yelling* at anyone.

"Daniel," Nevia's voice cautioned from the living room. "Go check on Heaton."

"What?" Daniel asked, confused by her order. There must have been a good deal of nonverbal discussion going on behind his back, because Daniel eventually circled around the island and threw on his coat. "Back in a few," he said before slamming the door on his exit.

Ethan looked over at Nevia. She was still on the couch, watching him. "I wouldn't have done it," he said, defending the anger she no doubt smelled on him.

"Are you sure?" she asked.

"Yes." *He wasn't.*

"Then no harm either way," she said. "Do you want to talk about it?"

"No." He slammed the refrigerator door. He wanted to punch the stainless-steel appliance until it looked as bad as he felt. "I HATE THIS!" He yelled at the top of his lungs, clenching his fists until his knuckles were white and his palms threatened to bleed. Nevia stood, quietly observing the scene with far less judgment than he'd thought anyone capable.

"I need to save her! I love her too much. I can't lose her. We fought so long to get here, and we are still fighting." He braced his arms over the stove and looked at her through venomous eyes. "You shouldn't have sent Daniel away. I need someone to yell at who can handle a good ass-ripping."

"You won't break me."

He looked down at the stove. "We've looked through every scenario. We can't distinguish her. All the medical tests showed nothing."

"Then you should give up," Nevia said matter-of-factly.

His eyes shot up at her. "I will never give up!"

"You already have."

Ethan stepped around the island. "Do you really want to try reverse psychology on me right now?"

She shrugged. "You've tried sniffing her out, reading her mind. Medical identification is next to useless, apparently. You just said you've tried *everything*. You're done. Let's pack it up and throw Daniel at one of them."

"I'm trying to be patient. If we choose the wrong one, then Daniel will need weeks to recover. Her mind is already at risk."

"Mmm." She took a long swig of her beer. "So find another way to find her. Something you haven't thought of."

"Look!" His finger flew out before he was even ready to make his point. "I've spent every minute of every day for the last three days thinking of nothing but how to get her free."

"No, you haven't," she retorted, blank-faced. Ethan felt his face burn with heat. Some part of the house was about to feel his wrath. "You've spent every minute of the last three days thinking about how scared you are of losing her." Nevia stepped from behind the couch, swirling her beer. "How much you love her? How angry and guilty you are? You've been thinking about saving her, but you haven't actually been thinking about how to save her."

Ethan watched her approach. It surprised him that in the face of his anger, she was still moving toward him. She stopped in front of him, crossed her arms, and tapped her beer bottle on her elbow.

He watched the movement. When she paused, he noticed the shaking in her hand. She was coming to him against her own better judgment. Her taunts had a purpose, and she was risking a black eye to enlighten him to it. He felt the fury that was keeping every muscle in his body tense, release. He may have been mad enough to pick a fight with his best friend, but he certainly wouldn't take out his anger on Nevia.

"What are you saying I should do?" he asked.

"Start simple. Cori is a human being. Transmorphs are not. Start there. Look for answers in the obvious places first. It's usually what we overlook in panic mode that's the most useful. That's why children are so smart—they aren't educated enough to be stupid like adults."

Ethan nodded. "My brain is so fried right now, I don't know if I can."

Nevia moved forward suddenly and grabbed his arm. She did a double take on his bicep before she spoke. "Patience is still good advice." She drank down the last of her beer and let out a healthy feminist burp. "Now, you can get us a round of beers and I'll help you out with supper."

He took in a much-needed breath. "Thank you."

"Don't thank me yet. I'm not that handy in the kitchen," she said, moving around him.

"No." He placed a hand gently on her shoulder as she passed. "Thank you." She nodded and continued into the kitchen.

By the time Daniel came back with Heaton, Ethan and Nevia were two beers in—three for her—and concocting what would hopefully be a tasty Mexican-style skillet dinner. Daniel approached the island and looked over the two of them cooking together at the stove. He gave her a questioning look that might have been him asking if everything was okay, but she didn't offer an answer.

Daniel glanced at Ethan from across Nevia. "How you doing?"

"Good." Ethan nodded to Nevia. "You've got a good partner here. She's the whip cracker you needed."

Daniel locked eyes with Nevia. "Yeah, I'm trying to convince her to stay with us."

Nevia ignored him, putting her attention on the skillet. "Heaton, where have you been?" she asked Heaton before he could make it to the couch.

He glanced back at her with a concerned look on his face. "Nowhere."

"Mmm." She glanced at Daniel, cocking an eyebrow. "It doesn't smell like nowhere."

Ethan looked over at Heaton's progressively panicking face. "What?" he sidled up closer to Nevia. "What do you smell?"

"Who do I smell?" she corrected.

Ethan looked at Heaton to confirm what Nevia was implying. Heaton rolled his eyes, refusing to admit to anything.

"Where did you find him?" Ethan asked Daniel.

Daniel broke his trance on the stovetop and smiled broadly. "Gobshite was in the infirmary." He busted out laughing.

"Infirmary?" Ethan darted looks between them. "Tell me you didn't have trouble with Mezula."

"Oh, I think he had plenty of trouble with Mezula," Daniel said.

"It's not like that!" Heaton stammered, trying to regain some control over the assumptions being made.

"Pray tell, what *is* it like?" Nevia inquired with a grin.

"I..." Heaton huffed and sat down on the couch before he could make the situation worse.

"Heaton," Ethan scolded. "Did you actually... with Mezula? Do you know what would happen to you if Danato was here?" Ethan struggled to control his laughter. He knew he should be furious. A half an hour earlier and Heaton might have turned out to be the deserving target of his rage, but after the grounding of a couple of beers, he couldn't help but find amusement in the situation.

"Can't be any worse than what she did to him." Daniel snorted and broke into laughter again.

"What did she do to you?" Nevia asked the back of Heaton's head.

"She—" Daniel leaned over the counter; his voice restrained by his uncontainable laughter.

"Shut up!" Heaton yelled at Daniel. "This was your fault to begin with!"

"Crap, Heaton," Ethan said, losing some of his amusement. "Did she hurt you?"

Daniel toppled out of view to the floor behind the island. Only the hisses of his laughter revealed his location.

"He's very embarrassed," Nevia mumbled.

"You might as well tell us, Heaton," Ethan said. "You know as soon as Daniel has control of his faculties, he's going to tell us, anyway."

Heaton jumped up and came around the couch. He made a quick beeline for the fridge, not missing the opportunity to kick Daniel's body on the way by. Daniel let out a solemn grunt from below, but the assault only produced more laughter. Heaton retrieved a beer, twisted the top off, and tossed it on the counter by the sink. He took a long swallow of his liquid courage before looking either of them in the eye.

"I wasn't going to do anything, to be sure, but she's very..."

"Yeah." Ethan remembered Mezula's generous offer to help him forget Cori.

"I kept her locked up. I'm not that stupid. She liked that. She came at me, and I pinned her hands to keep her off me. She liked that too."

Ethan bit back his smile, trying not to disrupt the story with anything resembling the entertainment he was getting from it.

"She was demanding further rebukes and abuse, but..." Heaton clenched his eyes shut as if the imagery of the memory was as appalling the second time around as the first. "I... ah... couldn't provide her the abuse she wanted nor the enjoyment she wanted."

Daniel's head popped up behind the island as he climbed to his feet. A shit-eating grin plastered his face, but he'd managed to mute his body-quaking laughter. Heaton scowled at him. "She offered to help me stay... attentive to her. Offered," Heaton scoffed. "She foisted her help on me."

Ethan leaned to one side to hide his smile with Nevia's head. He wished he could see her expression. He wondered if she was able to keep a cool head even in this situation.

Heaton cleared his throat. "She..." His eyes glazed as another memory superimposed over his train of thought.

"How did you end up in the infirmary?" Nevia said in a sweet, quiet voice, saving Heaton from giving any more details about the encounter.

Heaton clenched his jaw and took another long drink of his beer. "After a while, it was clear her help wasn't going to wear off anytime soon."

Ethan sputtered out a laugh that couldn't be contained. He leaned on the counter like he was in deep contemplation, but the shaking that was inflicting his body said otherwise.

"I tried to wait it out. I tried to ice it down. I finally went to the infirmary and told them I had a bad reaction to Viagra."

Daniel joined Ethan in sputtering uncontrolled laughter. They both sank to their knees gasping for breath, while Nevia kept enough control of herself to finish cooking the meal.

"I'm so sorry, Heaton," Nevia said as she pulled the skillet off the heat. "That's an easy lesson hard learned."

Daniel guffawed and once again disappeared into rolling laughter. Ethan smacked the counter, trying desperately to breathe.

"You are all wankers!" Heaton yelled at them and returned to the living room to pout.

After a halfway decent meal, Ethan started cleaning up the dishes. Nevia joined him to help dry his washed dishes. It only took a minute of them playing out their domestic roles before Daniel wandered into the kitchen to contribute by grabbing another beer.

Ethan suspected Daniel was uncomfortable with their quick connection, so he tested the theory. He reached behind Nevia to grab a dish that she had already dried. "Excuse me, I see a spot I missed." He gave her a smile as he grazed her back to retrieve the pristine bowl.

He glanced back at Daniel. He was leaning on the counter next to the stove, fixated on where Ethan's arm was touching her back. He saw a familiar look in Daniel's eyes, the territorial instinct that every man was born with it. Since Daniel never kept his claim on any woman, he never had cause to be jealous of anyone.

As he returned the clean bowl to the soapy water, Nevia looked up at him with an unspoken question. He shrugged at her and pointed back at Daniel with his eyes. "Interesting," he said.

"Yes," she said with a slight frown. "We'll see how long that lasts." She rolled her eyes and looked back at Daniel.

"Are you going to help, or are you just going to stand there staring at Ethan's ass?"

Daniel flinched and for a second looked as if he might try to defend his sexuality, but it soon changed to a smirk. "It's such a fine arse. I think I'll just keep looking, thank you."

"Mmm." Nevia looked behind Ethan. "It sure is. Cori's a lucky girl."

Although he knew she was just trying to add to Daniel's jealousy, Ethan felt his cheeks warm with blush. He looked away to cover his smile. When he looked back, he was surprised to see Daniel walking away. He joined Heaton in the living room, and didn't look back at them once.

"See?" Nevia tipped her chin toward Daniel. "Weak heart." She looked at Ethan and tapped her chest. "There's no fight left in him. Too many women, not enough love." She tipped her brow and went back to drying. "After all, the last time he fought for a woman, his father ended up dead."

Ethan frowned and stared after his friend. He wondered if that wasn't an explanation for so much of Daniel's behavior.

Later that night, Ethan did his best to depict an ice skater for their game of charades, but it turned out to be futile since Daniel had mistaken his triple Salkow for a pirouette. The word ballerina was repeated more than once, along with *poof* and *tosser*.

"Time," Heaton shouted.

"Figure skater!" Ethan yelled in exasperation.

"Oh, please, like I would know that. The only ice I care about is covered in scotch."

"I want a new partner." Ethan collapsed onto the couch next to Heaton.

"You drew the short straw." Nevia stood to take her turn. Daniel extended the bowl of folded papers he and Ethan had written up for their team to act out.

She drew out a paper and shielded it behind her hand to read it. "I am not acting this out." She crumpled the paper and threw it at Daniel.

"What? You said we have to take what we get." Daniel opened the paper to see which one she had gotten. "Oh, damn! That was a good one."

Heaton reached over and took the scrap paper to read it. "Dude!"

Ethan leaned over to read it. The crumpled paper held the words of a specific oral fixation of Daniel's.

"I was hoping Heaton would get that one," Daniel defended. "Either way, I'm perfectly happy to watch one of you embarrass yourselves."

"Redraw." Heaton motioned to Nevia to do so.

"That's alright. I have plenty more of that variety." Daniel handed her the bowl.

She drew out another paper, which she looked at and promptly crushed. "Are you ever off?" She picked out another. Her face crumpled with confusion as she read it. "I don't even know what that is."

Daniel leaned over to see which one she'd grabbed. He smiled and winked at her. "I'd be happy to show you."

"So you claim." She gave him a scolding look before grabbing for another paper.

"I'm not flexible enough for those moves anymore, anyway," Daniel mumbled as he settled back farther into his chair.

"Okay," she said, looking over her paper. "Shit."

Daniel waved his hands insistently, wanting to see her choice. She handed it to him. He nodded. "That's one of Ethan's. Good choice. Deceptively difficult." Daniel threw him a thumbs-up.

"Ready," Ethan said, taking the timer from Heaton. "And... go."

Nevia started her performance. She brushed her hair with an imaginary hairbrush, emphasizing the length before opening an imaginary window and tossing it out. Her theatrical depiction included her heart pounding affection for her secondary character, the knight who climbed her proffered hair.

"Rapunzel!" Heaton blurted out.

"Yes!" Nevia clapped her hands together before giving him a high five.

"Damn it!" Daniel grumbled. "That was a hard one, too."

"Your turn, sourpuss," Nevia said. "Who needs another round?" she asked, brandishing her empty beer bottle at everyone.

"Me, if you want me to participate in this bullshit," Daniel answered as he stood and picked a paper from Heaton's bowl.

"I better not," Ethan said, eyeing the empty bottle sitting on his side table. He couldn't remember what number he was on.

Nevia stopped next to him. "I'm sorry. What did you say?" She held her hand to her ear. "You put your balls where?"

Ethan chuckled. "Fine, one more."

"Heaton?" Nevia hollered as she headed to the fridge.

"Beer me, babe," he called back.

"Babe?" she questioned.

Heaton grimaced. "Sorry, just trying that out."

"Did it fail?" she asked.

"Yup."

"Good."

Daniel watched her dig in the fridge as he unfolded his paper. "I misjudged her," he mumbled. Ethan wasn't sure if he meant to address Heaton or him, or both, or neither. "I thought she was shy. She's just pensive; pensive and sassy." His brow furrowed. "Is that even possible?" he asked Heaton. "Isn't that like being book-smart *and* good at sports?"

Heaton glanced back at her. "Maybe she's a *just-add-beer* sort of personality."

Daniel nodded. "Maybe. That's good though, right? For a partner, I mean. Smart and tactical on the job, fun and flirty off the job?"

"Flirty?" Heaton exchanged a sidelong glance with Ethan before answering. "Sure. Sounds just about right to me."

Ethan knew Heaton was seeing the same thing he had seen in Daniel earlier. He was developing an abnormal interest in Nevia, as unfamiliar to either of them as it was to Daniel himself.

Nevia returned to hand out the pre-opened beers like a woman familiar with waitressing. Daniel took a long swig before finally reading his selection. "Oh, bloody hell! I demand a redraw."

"On what grounds?" Nevia asked, curling up in Danato's chair.

"On the grounds that this is a shit game." Daniel gave a wave for Heaton to start the timer. He made a valiant effort to sway his hips while waving his hands on either side of his body.

"Hula dancer," Ethan guessed.

"Thank God." Daniel threw his paper on the fire and plopped into his chair. "When the dancer in our bowl comes up, I expect one of you to do it justice."

"I'm not stripping," Nevia said flatly.

"Damn it, woman! What is the benefit of having a female in the group if you aren't going to show some skin?"

"Benefit? Hell, after a month, you two won't know how to live without me."

"Hear, hear." Heaton lifted his bottle of beer. Daniel gave him a glare, but he just shrugged. "She's got a Glock, a sniper rifle, and she can hold her beer. That's three things Ethan didn't have."

"Hey!" Ethan protested, although he knew it was true.

"Sniper rifle? I didn't know about that." Daniel looked over at Nevia, perturbed by his second-hand information.

She waved her hand at the expanse between them. "See? You're already hooked."

Daniel stared at her for a moment longer than an indifferent man should have. "Who's up?" he forcefully interrupted his own contemplation.

"Me." Heaton tossed Ethan the watch before stepping up to his place. He took a paper out of the bowl. "Alright, I can do this." Heaton walked around the couch.

"Go," Ethan said, watching the clock.

Heaton walked casually toward the stairs. Just across from Nevia, he stopped and drew his imaginary gun. He threw his right leg back to lower himself, and whipped his left arm out away from him as he shot his imaginary gun.

"James Bond," Nevia guessed.

"Yes!" Heaton shouted.

"No way!" Daniel objected, throwing a handful of papers from his bowl at them. They fell ineffectually on the floor in front of his chair. "How did you get that?"

"That's the classic James Bond gun-barrel sequence," Nevia said, pointing at Heaton, who was doing a little dance to celebrate his success. "Sean Connery, to be specific."

"What?" Ethan joined the rabble-rousing. "You can't know that!" He could believe she knew James Bond movies, but he didn't understand her rationale behind the specific actor.

"Because," Nevia said patiently, "Connery was the only one to swing his left hand way out. The original Bond movies had a stuntman doing the sequence, and he had a little hop in his turn. George Lazenby went so far as to kneel on his sequence. Roger Moore braced his shooting arm with his left hand. Timothy Dalton and Pierce Brosnan may as well have been posing for an Uncle Sam 'I Want You' poster."

"What about Daniel Craig?" Ethan asked.

"They didn't do the gun barrel sequence for him."

"You guys are missing the key point here." Heaton waggled his head. "We are kicking your ass."

"That's because this is a girl's game," Daniel said. "Oh, excuse me, girls and wankers."

"Well, the girl and wanker are still kicking your ass," Nevia pointed out.

"Hey!" Heaton objected. "Let's not keep that going."

"Alright, that's enough smack talk. If this game turns into a brawl, Danato will never let me have guests over again." Ethan peeled himself off the couch. As he stood, he felt the rising number of empty beer bottles come back to haunt him. His brain felt foggy and distant. He wished he hadn't let Nevia emasculate him into having another one.

He was definitely enjoying himself, but he was beginning to think he should withdraw from the festivities and refocus on helping Cori. He already had enough guilt about not noticing she wasn't *his* Cori. He didn't need to feel guilty about having a party while she was in mortal danger.

With beer in hand, Ethan took his scrap paper choice and centered himself. He opened the paper and stared at the tiny word. *Yogi*. He had never really seen the word on paper before. He knew what it was. He even knew how he could act it out, but something was sticking to the word. It was snagging on the beer webs in his mind.

Several thoughts started to boomerang around in his mind: ballerina, sexual positions, hula dancer, Yogi.

Dancers.

Flexibility.

Ethan's beer slipped from his hand and thunked against the floor. It tipped over, hiccupping its contents all over the bear rug.

All eyes were on him. Whether it was the shock of him spilling in the sacred living room space, the expression on his face, or simply the trauma of wasted beer, they all instantly knew he wasn't playing the game.

Ethan looked between Daniel and Heaton. "I know how to find Cori."

30

E THAN DIDN'T WAIT TO hear the slew of questions that would have followed his statement. He ran out of the front door without his coat. To his surprise, there weren't any frantic calls bellowing after him as he raced up the path to the prison. He did, however, hear footsteps trying to keep up with him.

He burst through the main entrance and leaped up the stairs leading to the offices. He made it to Danato's door just as Belus was pulling it shut for the night. The dwarf looked tired and strung out. Ethan could only imagine how many hours Belus had spent researching different options to save Cori.

"Belus!" He stopped just short of bowling him over. "I know how to pick her out."

"How?" Belus narrowed his eyes and surveyed him carefully. Ethan knew he smelled like alcohol, but if the solution to Cori's predicament was found at the bottom of a bottle, it was worth the indignity.

"Music!" he said with delight.

Daniel, Heaton, and Nevia clambered up behind him, eagerly listening in on the hallway gossip.

"Music?" Belus questioned, eying his entourage with a similar disapproval.

"Humans are more flexible than transmorphs. We need to play some music that Cori can dance to. Whichever one has her will have more movement."

Belus's expression changed from censure to distress. "Assuming she is conscious in there, how do you know she will dance?"

"She has to. It's ingrained in her poor music-starved brain. She can't not dance when there is music. Hell, she dances when there's just a tune in her head."

Belus nodded. "That's an excellent plan, Ethan." He looked down at the office doorknob and tapped it with his finger. "I'm afraid I can't let you enact it, though."

Ethan felt his heart sink into his stomach. If his run hadn't sobered him, that statement did. He couldn't even formulate the words he needed to question Belus, let alone object with the ferocity that his clenched fists were demanding.

"What the hell do you mean?" Daniel pushed past the others and said what Ethan's muted voice box wouldn't. With Daniel on his left and Ethan on his right, Belus was caught between a rock and a hard place. He didn't look up at either of them. "If it's a plan that could potentially work," Daniel said, "we should at least try it."

"Ethan knows we can't have music here." Belus looked at him with a hard stare. "He also knows why we can't."

Ethan did know why. The wavelengths broadcasted by audio equipment would provide the magical entity that controlled the time bubble a path to get into human minds. It was one of the strictest rules of the prison. It was also the reason he had to suffer without cable.

Ethan slipped to his knees. Had it been Cori in his position, she would have just acted on the instinct without getting permission, but that wasn't him. He was the disciplined one. The good one. How he wished now that he wasn't. "Belus, we have to try. Just a little music. I only need a minute, two at the most."

Belus looked back at the ever-entrancing doorknob and tapped his finger on it again. "Ethan—"

"Belus," Daniel said with as much supplication in his voice as Ethan. "We have to risk it. We have to. Ethan can't lose her."

Ethan glanced at Daniel, seeing the panic in his face. Every effort he made to save Cori had so little to do with her. Daniel hardly even approved of Cori, let alone knew her well enough to fight for her. The effort he put toward saving her was for Ethan's sake. It was honorable, but in the end, it made Ethan feel like he was the only one truly on Cori's side through this whole thing.

If Danato were standing in front of him right then instead of Belus, it wouldn't have taken more than the mention of saving Cori's life to convince him that the risk was worth it. Danato wasn't there, though. It was only Belus to decide Cori's fate.

Belus and Cori had a volatile friendship. She was the mutiny to his conformity. Although she was at odds with her own character, she had been trying to play by Belus's rules to gain his respect. Ethan had always thought that under his gruff exterior and castigation, Belus loved Cori as much as he and Danato did. As he looked at the stoic man standing in the path of her rescue, he wondered if he had been wrong.

Belus glanced at Ethan before turning to face Daniel. "As the warden's second, I can't permit using any telepathic channeling devices within the confines of this prison. I won't authorize it." Ethan felt his chest tighten, and he pressed his lips together to cover the curse words he was about to let out. "If you have a problem with that—" Belus nodded to him. "—take it up with the acting warden."

Acting warden?

If Ethan had been wearing a name tag, he would have flipped it up to check the name. *He* was the acting warden. It didn't matter what Belus said. Before Danato left, he named Ethan the acting warden. By merit of a very long test and a very big dragon, he had the final say in what happened at the prison.

He hadn't taken the role very seriously and was more than happy to defer to Belus. Now, however, Belus was deferring to him. As elated as he was to have that control, he recognized the burden that had just been passed back to him. As a husband begging for the life of his wife, it was easy to ask for permission to save her. As the warden of a prison, debating between protecting Cori's mind from further entanglement or upsetting a magical deadlock that could cost lives, he had to weigh the outcome rationally. He couldn't simply pick Cori by default. Not when he was responsible for everyone.

Ethan stood up, relieving more than his knees. He rolled back his shoulders, took in a deep breath, and took his title back from Belus.

"We'll give her two minutes." Belus's shoulders sagged, but he nodded. "If she can't break through enough to give us a clue, then Daniel will break one of them tomorrow. I'll risk the additional three weeks for your recovery." He nodded to Daniel, who nodded in return. "We'll need the floor cleared of unnecessary personnel.

"You are forgetting one thing," Belus said. "Even if we could get a radio signal this deep out, we destroy every radio that comes into the prison."

"Maybe, but I'm willing to bet that not everyone follows the rules—and I know just the man to ask." Ethan passed between Heaton and Nevia and headed back down the hallway.

"I'm not going to like this, am I?" Belus called after him.

"Nope," Ethan answered.

31

"Is this what you had in mind?" Duke entered the transmorph level carrying a fifty-year-old turquoise radio.

Ethan was congregating with the others, trying to convince them to leave the area so they didn't risk their free will. He hadn't made much progress, but Heaton had at least agreed with him that Daniel shouldn't be present. Daniel, however, was insistent that he wasn't susceptible to such things.

"Duke, that's perfect. Does it still work?"

"What the hell is that?" Belus came in behind him, seeing part of the radio in Duke's arms. Duke turned to show him, and Belus's face darkened with outrage. "I didn't know that thing was still here. We can't use that."

"Two minutes, Belus," Ethan said, bracing himself in his military at-ease position. He had conceded to two minutes. He would not lose any more.

"That shouldn't even be here. It is beyond dangerous."

"He's right." Duke nodded and patted the radio. "More than one man has made the mistake of listening to the sirens on this beast and come up with a case of the nut-jobs."

Ethan smiled at Duke. The man freely acknowledged the danger of the object he held, and yet there he was, still holding it. He didn't have the enthusiasm for caution like Belus. If there was something weird and unusual in the storage room, he called the "prop room," Duke not only knew about it, but it had likely harmed him.

Belus eyed Duke. "Who else knows about this radio?"

"Upon penalty of death, Mr. Belus, I have no idea what you're talking about. I just found this radio a few minutes ago." Duke set his eyes forward and thrust his chin out, refusing to divulge any more information.

"We knew it would be dangerous," Ethan said.

"No, *a* radio is dangerous. This is *the* radio. That thing is what caused the murders in the 1960s. It already contains the entity."

Ethan knew he should take that into further consideration, but it was always going to be dangerous. Everything about the prison was dangerous, from the prisoners to the furniture. The only person in the world that made all that peril tolerable was Cori.

He didn't want her to lose her memories. They had fought too hard against themselves to be together, and he didn't want to start from scratch. He already knew what one-sided love felt like; he wasn't going back to that.

"Let's get a signal, Duke?" Ethan could tell Belus wasn't happy, but the dwarf gritted his teeth and bore the insult to his pride, just as he would if Danato had overruled his concerns.

"It's a mighty fine machine now that it's possessed. No station needed." Duke brought the tacky radio to him. "Just dial her knob a little. It will play anything you want it to. And by anything, I mean, whatever song you happen to be thinking about at the time."

"Psychic radio," Ethan scoffed. He took the radio from Duke and set it down near the transmorph cells. He looked at Belus. "I don't suppose ear plugs will make any difference?"

"Rain jacket in a flood, unfortunately," Belus answered somberly.

Ethan looked back on the growing tension in his audience. Heaton and Daniel were mirror images of loyalty. Their hard supportive stares and crossed arms told him they were not leaving his side. Nevia tucked herself behind them, playing the part of the wallflower, although she wasn't. She didn't seem as resolute in staying, but he wasn't about to insult her by asking her to leave when Heaton and Daniel were staying.

Belus and Duke hung back with opposing moods. Belus's bitterness would certainly last a while. He wasn't the type to give up a grudge, even if everything turned out for the best. Not that it bothered Ethan. He didn't need or want his approbation like Cori did.

Duke, on the other hand, was grinning. He looked thrilled to be a part of this search and rescue, despite the potential for psychic rape. Any day that didn't begin and end with roof duty or food delivery was probably a nice change of pace for him.

Ethan stood and walked the line of cells containing his duplicate wives. The guards had placed Cori-5 and Cori-1 in the closest cells, so he could watch them simultaneously. They were his target pair. One of them was housing the real Cori.

Cori-1 came to the bars as he passed and spat in his face. "She'll hate you, you know." He stopped to wipe the spit from his cheek. "You've failed her. You've cheated on her. She won't let that go."

"I know," he said.

"Then why go through all this?" Cori-5 rushed to her bars. "Just keep one of us. Or all of us," she said sweetly. Ever the manipulator.

"I'd rather have her back and hate me than trapped and loving me against her will."

"You are so pathetic," Cori-1 snarled. "She regrets marrying you, you know."

Ethan could feel his jaw set. He knew it wasn't true, but it still hurt to hear, especially coming from her lips. "No, she doesn't. She loves me."

"She's not capable of loving you." Cori-1 wrapped her fingers around the bars. Her boney knuckles looked more like claws. "Her heart died with Vince."

He stepped up to the bars. "When will you mind-suckers realize, just because you have her memories, it doesn't mean you know who she is?"

"Ethan, don't listen to her. I do love you." Cori-5 reached for him from her cell.

"I'll give you one more chance to release her voluntarily." He raised his voice so the other transmorphs could hear him. "If you don't, tomorrow morning, one of you will die."

"Back to threats, are we?" Cori-1 mocked. "I just hate it when people play up their hand when they are clearly losing."

"I'm just telling you what's going to happen, in case you want to prevent it." Ethan looked down the line of transmorphs. "That goes for all of you. Free Cori, and you will be spared. Don't, and I will make sure that I am your next target of revenge." Ethan paused, hoping that one of them might be smart enough to protect herself.

"You didn't actually think that would work, did you?" Cori-1 leaned her face against the bars and chuckled.

"No." He stepped close enough to whisper. "But I want to be able to put my ultimatum in my report. That way, the board will be more forgiving of my tactics."

"Careful, boy." Cori-1 spoke with the depth of Danato's bass. "You don't want to make enemies of a transmorph."

"Then you shouldn't have made an enemy of me." Ethan marched away before she could offer a rejoinder. He stooped down for the radio, but stopped just short of the dial. He looked back at Belus and raised two fingers. He knew Belus would keep him at his word, no matter what was happening at one minute and fifty-five seconds.

Ethan touched the dial, but he couldn't think of a song. Not a single tune came to mind. Even his childhood lullabies were too deep to conjure. He moved his body so no one could see his mouth as he whispered to the device. "I need a song for my wife. Wake her up and make her move. Make her dance."

He felt stupid speaking to the radio, but if the magical entity controlling the time bubble was sentient, there was no reason to assume it wouldn't understand him. Whether it would listen was another matter.

Without a particular song in mind, he rotated the dial, searching for the prophetic radio station. After a few slow turns, the radio crackled into a crisp, clear, fast-paced country song. He grimaced, unable to recall a single time when Cori had sung a country song. The ditty reverberated through the hall in a way that one small radio shouldn't have been able to do.

The electric guitar may as well have been in the same room with them. Ethan wouldn't have been shocked to see a man with a microphone standing right behind him. He understood now what Belus meant about bringing raincoats to a flood. Earplugs would do little to knock out the permeation of this music.

He walked along the cells and watched the Cori's glare suspiciously at him. He was surprised to see two toes tapping on the floors already. He was right. Real Cori or not, if they were in her mind, they wouldn't be able to resist dancing. And once the real Cori moved, her flexibility would surpass that of her shell, ultimately revealing her location.

He smiled and glanced back at Belus. He was already moving toward the radio. He wasn't taking any chances. Duke, meanwhile, was enjoying the song as well. His head was bobbing as he mouthed the words. Ethan could easily picture Duke at home in Texas with cowboy boots and a cowboy hat, line dancing in too-tight jeans.

He looked back and saw Cori-1 and 5 shifting their shoulders back and forth. The hip shake was overcoming any resistance. He needed more, though. They needed to do something that a transmorph was incapable of.

Cori-1 waved her arms. Ethan could sense the potential for Cori's signature belly roll, the transmorphs could never duplicate.

The radio stopped. The sound of metal meeting concrete immediately followed the instant silence.

Ethan whipped around and saw Belus smashing the radio further with malicious kicks to the speakers and dials. He obviously had no intention of ever discussing the use of this radio again.

It was what he had agreed to, but the two minutes had gone far too fast. He should have said one song. Five minutes. Anything more than two minutes. He could have popped popcorn in two minutes, but did he really expect to lure out a near-dead, mentally tangled woman from captors that had been holding her for six weeks?

Belus panted from his destructive exertion and stared back at Ethan. His usual stoic façade reflected Ethan's own despondency. He wasn't happy about adhering to the timeline either, but someone had to be the *good guy*.

Duke's voice broke the silence as he sing-talked the next lines of the song. Everyone gaped at him. He continued unfettered by his audience's stares and shimmied up to the cells.

As a man familiar with line dancing, Duke trotted left, then right in front of the cells. With a quick step turn, and a hip thrust that deserved to be applauded, he drew smiles from the Cori doppelgangers. They were eager to play along, mimicking his moves with a clap, twist, and twirl.

Nevia's melodic voice joined Duke in the chorus. She jumped into line with him and added her own hip sway and shoulder toggle to the dance. Duke grinned ear to ear, more than happy to have backup.

Ethan took a few steps back and watched both transmorphs. Cori-1 added the same hip sway and shoulder toggle as Nevia. After that, the move changed slightly. Ethan held his breath as the transmorph thrust her chest out and kicked her butt back. The body roll was too complex for the creature's overtaxed flexibility.

Will the real Cori please stand up?

Ethan smirked and looked at Belus for his consensus. He nodded, relief flooding his face as well.

Duke and Nevia finished their song and looked over at him to see if they should continue. Ethan clapped for them, as did Heaton and Daniel.

"You know what this means, Jordan?" Daniel hollered over to her. "Heaton and I are going to have to find a country bar."

She smiled and shook her head. Duke gave Nevia a pat on the shoulder for a good dance. She gave him a curt nod, shying away from his brilliant smile.

"I take it you like that song?" Ethan asked as he approached them.

"Yeah." Duke frowned at him. "Sorry about that. I must have been thinking about it when I was carrying the radio."

"It's alright, Duke." Ethan glanced over to the broken radio. "I have a feeling it knew you knew the song."

"Good thing, I guess. Mr. Belus has got a red streak for that thing." He nodded to the mess of parts on the floor.

"It was a very good thing. Thank you." Ethan shook his hand. Duke probably didn't even fully understand the importance of the music in detecting the real Cori, but it didn't make any difference. He would never refuse to help over something as trivial as lack of comprehension.

"Which one is it?" Nevia asked.

"Number one," Ethan said. Cori-1 glared through the bars at him. "Don't be mad. I warned you what would happen."

"And I warned you," Cori-1 whispered. "He'll kill her trying to get her out. I'll make sure of that."

Ethan looked back at Daniel. He and Heaton were listening intently to Belus. They broke from the inaudible conversation and stared down Cori-1 with concentration that could only be described as predacious. She shrank back and cowered in the depths of her cell. She knew her time was running out.

32

"YOU'RE NOT READY." HEATON leaned forward to glare past Ethan at Daniel. They were all loaded into the elevator, minus Belus, on their way back to the house. It had taken the lift nearly three minutes to arrive, so his former partners had plenty of time to begin bickering about the balance between heroism and stupidity. It was a laughable disagreement to Ethan, since Heaton was just as likely to let his bravado exceed his capabilities in an emergency.

"I can do it. Let's get this show on the road," Daniel griped through clenched teeth. He was determined to take on the transmorph that night instead of waiting until the morning. It was a noble idea, but Ethan didn't like the idea of Daniel fighting a transmorph when he still had beer in his system. "You're treating me like a damn child," Daniel snapped. "You know as well as anyone how capable I am."

"In the bedroom," Ethan and Heaton both chimed in. Nevia glanced back at them with an amused grin.

"Bang on, but that's not my point," Daniel complained.

"We know your point," Ethan jumped in. "We know you can do it, but Cori will be there in the morning. Her mind won't be that much worse off in eight hours than it is right now."

"I know, but..." Daniel trailed off. He could have ended that sentence any number of ways: *I just want to help. I can't stand to see you like this. I want to prove what a good friend I am.* Ethan wasn't sure what he'd had in mind when he started, but instead of finishing his thought, he slumped into the corner of the elevator and pouted.

Nevia peeked back at him. She must have had an idea of why he was so distraught, but she didn't share. Instead, her eyes settled on Ethan's. "Why are all of you still so worried about her? Aren't we going to save her, after all?"

Ethan frowned at her and looked at Heaton for the complex explanation. They had already gone over the many risks of a long-term encasement, but Nevia had missed out on the conversation about mental entanglement.

"Of course we're going to save her," Daniel defended.

"We can save her body," Heaton explained. "We are just concerned about her mental state once she is released. With five transmorphs fighting for a temporal grip on her consciousness, she's in danger of losing memories, or worse yet, she could have a mental breakdown that will cause her mind to fracture. She could develop split personalities, schizophrenia, or any number of mood disorders or manias."

Ethan grimaced at the extended description. Heaton hadn't given him the long version of possibilities, but one or two worst-case scenarios had been scary enough.

"I can remove her mind and body from the transmorphs, but I can't remove the transmorphs from her mind." Daniel's voice dripped with frustration. Ethan should have turned around and reminded him that removing the body was far more than he could have achieved without him, but that wasn't what he did.

"They stay with her, even after the physical connection is gone? They control her?" Nevia asked.

"It's not an active connection," Heaton said. "They aren't plugged into anything; they are just residual. It's like they leave a stain on her. She can't just scrub it away, though. It interferes with her cognitive abilities."

The elevator ponked. Everyone stepped out and headed to the lockers near the exit. "If she is left in there long enough," Heaton continued to explain while Nevia's face distorted with pending questions, "regardless of her physical condition, it could interfere with her motor skills. That's why some hosts have to learn to walk and talk again after the encounters. It's like getting a massive concussion. The brain is permanently damaged, unless it can find new pathways for the synapses."

"Christ, Heaton," Daniel mumbled and gestured to Ethan.

Heaton looked back at him sheepishly. "Ethan, I'm so sorry. I just get into teacher mode."

"Wait, no." Nevia stepped in front of Heaton before he could get to the exit. "In an accident, there is *physical* damage to the brain, but you aren't saying that there is physical damage."

"No, her mind is healthy, but it's overwhelmed. Two minds can't inhabit one brain, let alone six."

Nevia tipped her head. "But they aren't thinking anymore; they're inactive." Nevia glanced between all three of them for verification.

"Yes, they're inactive," Daniel moaned. "What the feck is your point? This isn't helping Ethan."

"Actually, I'd like to hear this." Ethan was starting to understand the answer she was fishing for. He was stupid not to have been asking these questions himself.

"What do you want to know?" Heaton asked.

"What's actually preventing Cori from recovering?" Nevia touched her head, frustrated by her lacking terminology. "What's left to block her... original synapses when they leave?"

Heaton's face contorted with condescension. "The memories of five other beings," he drawled sarcastically. "Her brain wasn't designed to hold that much information. Her brain will be overloaded, and the result will be either a memory dump or... that other stuff."

Ethan laughed.

His long boisterous chuckling must have made everyone question his sanity, but he couldn't help it. "Son of a bitch," he mumbled and walked back to the elevator.

He pushed the elevator retrieval button, but naturally the doors didn't pop right open.

"What is wrong with you?" Heaton asked, seeming almost annoyed.

"Memories." Ethan tossed up his hands. "Too many memories. That's what you're worried about?"

"This is serious," Heaton said sternly. "Her mind is human."

"I'm not laughing about the risk to her mind," Ethan said, feeling the levity of the situation morph into what it was concealing. "I'm laughing because I have to go ask that son of a bitch for help again."

"Who?" Daniel asked.

"Cleos." Ethan pushed the elevator button again.

"The mind-sucker you punched out?"

"Yes, but he isn't just a mind-sucker. He's a feeder." Ethan watched enlightenment flood the faces of both his friends. Nevia looked at him, still lost. "Cleos can eat memories," he explained to her. "He removes them from your mind. Once they are gone, you can never remember them. He can also replace memories, or conjure memories that you have long since forgotten."

"I see." Nevia smiled, but pulled her lips back taut when she saw he didn't share her appreciation for the serendipitous realization. "But you hate this person."

"I never thought of him one way or another, until..." Ethan didn't want to be having this conversation with anyone, especially Daniel. "Until it was clear that Cori was more interested in his guidance than mine."

There it was. The dirty little secret in his marriage.

He had been unknowingly cheating on his wife with a transmorph. His wife, up until being taken, had been having an emotional affair with Cleos. He knew it wasn't physical, but he still couldn't stand that she didn't confide in him.

In many ways, he was still dealing with the same issues he had from the very beginning. She was trying so hard to be independent and strong that she was pushing him away. He'd thought when they consummated he would be her one and only rock. When that didn't happen, he'd rationalized that marriage would bind her to him, but that clearly didn't happen—thus their current predicament.

"Can he help?" Heaton asked, stepping up to bat away the awkward silence.

"Yes. I assume, anyway."

"Will he?" Daniel asked. "Would he hurt her, just to hurt you?"

"No." Ethan hated that he didn't have to speculate about that answer.

"Can you trust him not to… take advantage?" Heaton asked, no doubt sensing where Ethan's concerns were landing.

"That's what I need to go find out. Either way, though, I don't really have a choice. He's the only person who can put her back together." The elevator doors opened, and he stepped in. "Because he knows her better than anyone," Ethan snarled and slammed his palm into the B button. The doors closed.

33

ETHAN MADE HIS WAY down to Cleos's cell. It was late enough that he expected him to be asleep, but he wasn't. He pushed the button on the intercom. Cleos was sitting on the edge of his bed like he had been waiting for him. He jumped up when he saw Ethan.

"What's happened?" he asked with worry etched in his face.

Ethan didn't answer right away. He enjoyed torturing him, but the increasing anxiety coming from Cleos irritated more than amused him. His alarm was genuine. It only reminded Ethan of the relationship he had with Cori, and how important it was to him.

"She's fine. I mean, she's still in the transmorph, but we know which one. We will get her out in the morning."

"Good." Cleos relaxed and took a step away from the glass. "I hadn't expected you to share any information with me about your progress."

Ethan stared back at him. "I'm not here to fill you in."

Cleos looked him over, a not-so-cursory examination of his body. "You seem to be back to yourself again, looking more like a soldier. Did Belus hand over the reins, or did you finally take them?" Ethan only offered more of the same silent glare. "I take it you need something from me."

"I need to know if you can remove the extraneous memories the transmorphs will leave behind in Cori's mind and replace any dumped memories."

"Transmorphs... plural?"

"They were sharing her. Five of them have tapped directly into her mind."

Cleos's eyes shimmered with what looked at Ethan like delight. "I can remove them. It may take several long sessions alone with her to do so," he said with tormenting satisfaction.

"Whatever it takes to get her back to herself again. You can do that, can't you? Get her back to herself, her real self?"

"Are you asking if I'm going to change her?" Cleos crossed his arms. "Why would I do that? The original Cori and I got along so well. Are *you* sure you want the original back?"

Ethan knew if there had been bars instead of glass, he would have reached through them to strangle the man, but then again, Cleos may not have been so bold if that was an option. "I want my wife back. Just as she was when I married her."

"Before or after you sent her running to me?" Cleos smiled, but he showed a hint of anger. Ethan knew as well as he did that the night she left hadn't been good for either of them. "She will always come back to me, you know."

"Yes, I imagine she will return to this cage from time to time. As long as she's home for dinner and beside me when I sleep, I don't think it much matters anymore to me."

Cleos's chin tipped up, and he shook his head. "Oh, I think it does, Ethan. In fact, I know it does. You know I could help you with that. Give you some pointers to get you back on track with her."

"The only thing I need from you is to clear her mind after she's out."

"You hardly need to ask," Cleos said. "I'm more than happy to help save Cori again."

"You don't want anything in return?" Ethan looked around his cell. He could easily take advantage of this opportunity to upgrade his scant furnishings.

"No," Cleos said, returning to sit on his bed. "I have everything I want from you."

34

ETHAN WAS HAPPY THAT he had left his coat at the house. The frosty air biting at his ears and fingers cooled his temper. He had spent the last few days being worried, angry, and ashamed. He wanted to feel relief. He knew Daniel would free Cori, just as he'd said. He knew Cleos would save Cori's memories. In the end, it didn't matter how it was done, as long as Cori was alive and back to normal.

He was a little disappointed when he got back to the house that no one was around to talk to, but he was glad that everyone was getting the sleep they needed to face the morning. He didn't care to put off Cori's release any longer than it took to eat breakfast and chug a cup of coffee.

He headed upstairs and opened the door to his apartment. He had forgotten about the terror he'd wreaked on it the night before until right then. The modest, perfunctory gray interior hit him like a smack in the face. His king-sized bed sat against the far wall, sandwiched by two simple wooden tables. Two identical lamps lit the room, under beige, creased lampshades. The sea of taupe that colored the walls blended with the gray in the carpet. Two wooden chests of drawers, no closets. A small door leading to what was undoubtedly the smallest bathroom he had endured in a number of years.

He leaned his head against the doorframe and rubbed the wood. He knew the house was upset. He couldn't blame her. After trashing his room the way he did, he was lucky he had a bed at all.

She had tried so hard to find a happy medium. She might have even been signaling him to the sudden change in Cori, but he was too much of an anthropoid to notice her warnings.

Looking over the staunch surroundings, it reminded him of Danato's room. This was the room Danato had endured for years. Yet the remainder of the house was in good condition: undated, attractive, bright, and warm. Ethan wondered what Danato had done to his bedroom to cause the house to seek such a long punishment on him.

ated his futile attempt at sleep

35

DANIEL TRADED HIS FUTILE attempt at sleep
for lounging on the couch and staring into
the hearth. He loved firelight. He wasn't sure it was
an unnatural affinity, or if he just liked to watch it.
Unfortunately, it was the penetrating heat he usually
shied away from. He was probably the only person that
would be happy when the next ice age arrived.

He couldn't quite shake the thought of what he
had to do tomorrow. He should have been used to the
killing by now, but he wasn't. He dreaded it every time.
He would have much rather gotten it over with tonight,
but he could hardly fight Ethan on it.

To an outsider, his power might have seemed dramatic
and even romantic, but he knew what it really was. He
ripped people apart one molecular bond at a time while
they screamed and begged for their lives, vocally and
mentally. He wasn't a psychic—far from it—but under
the guise of opening someone up from the inside out;
it included the dispersion of their thoughts. *Not* hearing
their minds would have been like trying to cut up a body

without getting blood on you. He couldn't block their thoughts even if he tried.

"Is that fear I smell?" Nevia asked behind him.

Daniel jumped at her sudden presence, but he didn't look back at her. "Just nervous," he mumbled. He was suddenly glad again that he hadn't tried to sleep with her. There would be no hiding anything from her.

"Do you want company for your insomnia?" she offered.

He wanted to say no, but he couldn't imagine that it wouldn't sound rude. "Sure."

"You can say no if you want to be alone."

He looked back at her. Her drawstring newspaper-print pajama bottoms hung low on her hips, showing off her navel ring. A loose white top slumped off her bare shoulder. There was some kind of black lace under it. Her hair was bed-head spiked, giving her the rebellious look that her button-down shirt and trousers couldn't convey. "I'm not much for conversation right now."

"Who says we have to talk?" She walked over and sat on the coffee table in front of him, leaning over her knees. Her shirt had since adjusted itself to cover whatever layer of black undergarment he had seen before. She sat for a moment quietly and then smiled at him. "Okay, that's weird. We have to talk."

"Have you decided to stay?"

"Not yet. I'm kind of hoping to see what's available for me before I commit. Heaton tells me there isn't much beyond hunting, unless I want to take over Sophie's job and climb the corporate ladder."

He shook his head. "You're so much better than that."

"That seems like high praise from a man who's been calling me a bloodhound."

"I'm an ass. You know that already."

"Why the sudden change of heart? Why do you suddenly want me to stay?"

"Is it too late to say I want to be alone?"

"Mm-hmm." She nodded.

He cleared his throat. "Belus thinks you might be good for me."

Nevia shook her head, as if her ears weren't working. "Belus? The short man everyone stops short of saluting when he enters the room?" He nodded. "How does he know anything about me?"

"He doesn't. Only what I've mentioned, but he does know me; better than I know myself, if history is any indicator." She raised her brow when he didn't immediately explain the statement. He groaned and leaned forward, cupping his hands over hers. "Can we do this some other night—preferably not the night before I perform an intricate extraction?"

She moved her right hand out of the shelter of his hands and caressed his cheek. He instinctively closed his eyes to feel her soft hand against his face. It was the strangest feeling to him, more intimate than a kiss, and yet purely platonic.

He had done the same thing to many women right before he kissed them. His signature move, in fact. But he had never felt a woman do it to him, save his mother. His eyes flapped open at the thought of that relationship.

He withdrew from the contact and relaxed back into the couch. He almost laughed. Was he really that fucked up? He rubbed his face, trying not to think about how much emotion she might detect from him.

After a moment of silence, he found his voice. "After I killed and disposed of my father's body..." He paused, trying to find some excuse not to tell her any more about his past. He had revealed all of his past to Heaton through many years of cathartic beer binges, but he had never told anyone anything sober, nor had he told anyone less than a week into their acquaintance.

He looked up at her and saw the diplomatic observation that made her seem cold. He may have shocked her with his honesty the first time he'd revealed his secrets, but he had a feeling nothing about him would ever shock her again. "I took over as the area's requisite transmorph hunter. People knew me by my father's reputation. The first jobs I was called to were sort of horrific."

He shifted, trying to get out of his own body as he spoke the words. She leaned forward and put her hands on his knees. She wasn't holding him down, but he felt the weight of her compassion like a boulder. He growled and took in some quick breaths before continuing. "Needless to say, the hosts did not survive. I didn't work for a few years. Without my father's guidance, I had no way of understanding how to control my power. So, one day, I found one. A transmorph, you know? It was purely by accident. Telltale signs in the evacuation process. I won't bore you with the details." He shifted again, not wanting to relive any of this sober. Nevia moved onto the couch, kneeling beside him. She squeezed his arm reassuringly.

"It was at a bar." He stared into the fire, finding some comfort in the whiplashing flames. "I pretended to be interested in him, an act I don't think I could have pulled off if I hadn't had such an agenda in mind." Daniel finally stood up, unable to keep his seat any longer. He could feel his eyes well with tears. He leaned on the mantel and begged the reaction away so he didn't have to expose that part of himself.

He stood there for a long moment before he finally looked back at Nevia. She was still kneeling on the couch, patiently waiting for him to collect himself. Her shirt had slipped off her right shoulder again, revealing the black lace. He could see now that it was a tattoo. Another opposition to her clean-cut FBI façade.

He found some vestigial courage and continued with his story. If she was going to stay, she should at least know what kind of monster she would be working with before she made any commitment. "I took him back to my apartment. I didn't know about straight and narrow transmorphs at the time. I just assumed they all occupied people. I was a vampire hunter, by killing photophobes. I just didn't get it.

"I tied him up, gagged him, and tortured him. I used him for months. Focusing my power on his fingers, toes, hands, and feet. Transmorphs can regenerate over time. By the time I was strong enough to use my power again, he had recovered from my last torture."

"Did you kill him?" Nevia asked while he paused in remembrance.

"He was begging for death after two months. I kept it going for eight." He smacked the mantel. "By the time the hunters came for me, my skills had improved significantly. One man tried to save the transmorph and got caught in the crossfire. I killed him instantly. Another man got away, but without his right arm. After I turned the transmorph and the hunter to ash, I decided it was time for an abrupt change of scenery. I found the hunter I'd crippled in the hallway, bleeding to death. I was going to kill him, but somehow I reversed the damage just enough to stop the bleeding. It saved his life. Certainly didn't bring his arm back, but that was, and still is, beyond my capabilities.

"My father told me once that women paid him good money to remove scars, but I'm not sure he didn't just use that as an excuse to go to strange women's houses and shag them behind my mother's back." He could hear the acrid tone in his voice, but he couldn't help it. As much as he hated being the reason for his father's death, he truly hated the bastard as well. "That was the first time I had ever tried to use the reversal skill, and truthfully, I think if it weren't for my intense guilt over killing yet another human being, I wouldn't have been able to do it."

"So, you went on the lam. How long?"

Daniel scoffed. "Once my survivor reported my abilities to the bigwigs, they sent out the collectors. They had my scent from my apartment, and I was legally detainable under the supernatural paradigm clause that the prison abided by."

"The collectors are different from hunters, I take it?"

Daniel smiled. "Yeah, bloodhounds like you, only not nearly as cute." He winked at her. "Those demon-beasts caught my scent and had me hogtied within eight hours of my so-called escape, and that was just travel time for them. I was incarcerated in this very prison less than a day after I killed that hunter."

"That's when you met Belus?" she asked, getting them back to the original topic they had started with.

"Yeah, Belus and Danato; Ethan and Cori weren't around yet. Danato was a hardcore asshole in those days. He had lost his wife not long before my arrival, so he had no sympathy for any part of my situation. Belus, for God knows what reason, did. At the time, no one knew much about... whatever I am. They were interested in my abilities as a weapon in the fight against what was becoming an unavoidable rise in parasitic transmorphs. Apparently, there were a few too many females in our gene pool and not enough experienced males.

"Belus was convinced that I was a good person. I wasn't, but for some reason, he fought tooth and nail to get me assigned as a hunter. It took him a full year to cook up a release program for me. Danato was pissed about it, but he went along with it. Mostly, I think he was just sick of Belus bitching to him about it. So I left the prison on monitored trips to hunt down known transmorphs and remove them."

"I assume you were better this time around."

"Barely. I got better, though. Eventually they pardoned me, but I was put on permanent parole. If I so much as lose a human finger on my watch, I could be thrown back into this prison."

"After this long, you should be free and clear of that threat, don't you think?"

He shook his head. "No. Heaton is essentially my parole officer. He reports back everything I do to Sophie. We're partners, as I said. He is my most trusted confidant in the world, but if I screw up, he's obligated to report me."

"Seems like an odd relationship."

Daniel shrugged. "He keeps me in line. I like it that way. I like having someone there to snap me out of my hostility when I need it. I like having to ask permission before I do something. It takes away some of the guilt. Marginally, but still."

"So, when you said that Belus thinks I would be good for you, what did he mean?"

Daniel moved back to the couch and sat down beside her. She adjusted to a sitting position, so she wasn't looming over him. He put his arms over the back of the couch. "He's the only other person who can look me in the eye like you do without pissing himself. He figured he was meant to help me and maybe you might be able to help me too."

"Help you with what?"

"I don't know. Maybe redeem me. Help me balance the population of transmorphs. Make my job not suck so much."

She smiled a taut smile. "Not suck so much?"

"It would be nice to find transmorphs before they've ruined the minds of their hosts and the lives of their families."

"I see. So, that's why you want me to stay. To save these people while they are still recognizable."

He nodded. "Is that a noble enough reason for you to stay?"

"I think so."

Daniel couldn't resist any longer. He reached over to her slouching collar and tugged it over to view the patterned black ink that covered her right shoulder. "What is that?" He tipped his head, trying to identify the shape.

She turned away and pulled the white shirt over her head to reveal her bare back. Over her shoulder, a scaly serpentine dragon crawled down her back, its head positioned just over her low back while its clawed feet walked down from her shoulder blade.

"That's beautiful," he said, instinctively reaching to touch the artwork. After touching the ink to make sure it wasn't just drawn on, he pulled away so he didn't take advantage of her exposed skin. She turned around to face him, but didn't put her shirt on to do so. The serpent's tail trailed over her shoulder and curled around her pert right breast.

He gulped, looking over her milky skin and pink nipples freely open to his gaze. He forced his gaze upward to her eyes. He shifted slightly, feeling a change in the spare room in his boxers. "Beautiful." The word caught in his throat. He kept his eyes on hers, desperately trying not to ogle her like he wanted to—like he would have any other woman, without hesitation.

She set her shirt down on the couch and crawled over him, straddling him. "Nevia," he whispered.

"Jordan," she corrected.

"God damn it," he cursed in a whisper. "I hate calling you that."

"Why?" she asked, settling her hips onto his and unbuttoning his shirt.

"Because." Despite the objection he was about to give her, he shifted himself into a better position for her to get on target. "Nevia is such a beautiful name. Jordan is so harsh. You are too beautiful not to call you Nevia."

She leaned in to whisper in his ear. "I'll make you a deal. You can call me anything you want while you're inside me." She brushed her lips across his ear as she leaned back on him again.

"Nevia," he said again, grabbing her hips to stop the motion that was driving him to rise against her. "I'm trying not to do this with you. I don't want to sully our partnership." His hands were shaking, and he was having far more trouble keeping his eyes off her breasts, which were in perfect position for him to... "Damn it, woman!" He clutched his eyes shut and gritted his teeth. "I'm trying not to be an asshole to you. Why won't you let me not take advantage of a woman for once in my life?"

"Daniel. Open your eyes." He complied. "You aren't taking advantage of me. I'm taking advantage of you. Now, I'm going to slip your pants down, and mine. I'm going to have my way with you, and you aren't going to say another word unless it's moaned in ecstasy, understood?"

He huffed out a breath of relief. "Yes, ma'am."

As she'd promised, she undid his pants and slipped out of her own. As she took him in, he reached tentatively for her chest. She pushed his hands against her and he felt his trembling reservation stop. He pulled her against him, letting his mouth clamp onto her breasts while his hands pulled on her shoulders, driving him deeper into her.

He pulled her face close for a deep kiss, but she veered off to kiss his neck instead. He suddenly realized that she was indeed using him. He felt somehow violated by that thought. He had just given her everything of himself. Every detail of his shady past was lying on the floor like her pajama bottoms, but she was still withholding part of herself. He had never felt so naked and open with a woman before, and she couldn't have been farther away to him.

He glanced over to the stairs as she voiced her pleasures. "Don't worry," she said. "I'm watching."

He took his eyes off the stairs and let her stand guard for them. He watched her have her way with him. When her hands raked his shoulders and chest, signaling her height of pleasure, he allowed his own to overtake him.

Shaking and out of breath, she slumped and immediately dismounted him. She grabbed her shirt and pants from the floor. He grabbed her wrist before she could stumble away.

He pulled her over and touched her cheek, all but demanding the kiss she'd refused him before. She leaned into him and surrendered to a sweet, albeit guarded, kiss. He tried to draw her in for more, but she pulled away and went back to Danato's room, pajamas in hand.

As Daniel pulled himself together and zipped up his pants, he noticed a smattering of blood along his bare stomach. He looked after Nevia and wondered if he could be mistaken about the reason for that blood.

He headed to Danato's door and hovered his fist over the oak wood as he debated whether to knock. He couldn't imagine for one second she had been a virgin. Not the way she had come after him. He knew she was young, but she certainly would have had a relationship or two in college.

He suddenly felt like a dirty old man. He was over a decade her senior.

He should have felt privileged to be her first, but he felt bad. Her first experience was ten minutes with a womanizing, sociopathic freak on a couch in a stranger's house. That wasn't the way anyone should lose their virginity.

He wanted to beat down the door and demand an explanation. Maybe it was like she'd said: She was using him. Maybe she just killed two birds with one stone. Get the awkward sex with your partner out of the way, so you can continue without the usual sexual tension that arises because of close proximity. Plus, she gets to cure herself of the nasty burden of virginity.

More than an explanation, he just wanted her. He wanted a redo. He wanted to take her again in a proper bed, with a proper embrace. He wanted to lie with her afterward in quiet revelry instead of slipping away into the night.

For the first time in his life, he hadn't been the one slinking off to get away from his lay.

For the first time in his life, he was disappointed he wasn't even being given the option of falling asleep at her side.

He backed away from the door, wondering a hundred more things that wouldn't get answered standing outside of her door. He forced himself to go back to his room. He was finally tired. And, for the moment, he was no longer concerned about the events of tomorrow.

36

PER BELUS'S SUGGESTION, ETHAN had Cori-1 moved into the gym, so her fellow transmorphs didn't have to watch her being disintegrated. Ethan would have been happy to have the beasts see what happened to anyone seeking vengeance on someone he loved, but Belus reminded him they didn't need any more invitations for retaliation.

"Are you really going to do this?" Cori-1 asked as he dragged her into the gym in shackles. He sat her down on a workout bench and looked over the mismatched gym equipment to see if anything would be dangerous enough to use as a weapon if she tried to escape. "Are you really going to watch me die?"

Ethan looked at her. He still had to remind himself that this Cori was only a shell. She looked more disappointed in him than scared. "Unless you give her up right now."

Cori-1 shook her head. "Not after what she did to us."

"Still mad about the acid in the face, huh?" Ethan shoved a few spare dumbbells out of the way, just in case.

"Among other things. She was always so undisciplined around us. Dancing and singing as if we were her playthings. We knew it would be her undoing in the end, so we played along."

Ethan smiled. "Funny, it was yours, too." He glanced back at the gym door before crouching down in front of her. "What did she do wrong? How did you get her?"

The transmorph's face crumpled, almost instantly tearing up. "I was so mad at you for making me read that file."

Ethan clenched his teeth. "Don't do that." He started to stand, but her hands clasped onto his face. Her skin was still too soft, but the touch, the way she held him, was the same. He probably should have seen the slight changes in her personality, but there were hardly any abnormalities in her body.

"Please, Ethan, let me explain." He pulled her hands away, but stayed next to her to hear her version of the events. "After I read the file, I went straight to Cleos."

"I know, but why?" he asked, hoping that he could get answers. "How could you stand being in his presence after what you read?"

"I don't know." She shrugged.

"Bullshit, Cori..." Ethan hung his head. He was arguing with the wrong woman. She did, however, have Cori's mind. She had the answers. "She read that report. He destroyed five women's lives—five innocent women. One day, they were healthy and happy; then they met

Cleos. It must have taken him weeks to devour their minds."

"Stop it!" Cori-1 shook her head, hiding her face in her hands.

"Why can't you hear this? He's a monster! Always was. You just didn't want to know about it. You refused to see it. You are *still* refusing to see it!" Ethan pulled her hands away from her face. This might be his only chance to say what he really wanted to. It might have been cowardly to say these things through the shield of a transmorph, but he knew he would never be able to say them to the real Cori. "He lobotomized those women, feeding on their every memory. Friends and family, gone! Childhood, gone! Personality, gone!"

"He *must* have had a reason!" Cori-1's body rocked with the same tears Cleos saw the night she confronted him. She was so determined to see beauty in the beast.

"That's what she thinks, isn't it? How is that possible? How could there ever be a good reason to strip someone of every memory they ever had?"

"I don't know, but there must be. Ethan, he is kind. I have seen it in him."

"Why? Because he helped you study?"

"He is my friend."

"He's using you!"

"I don't care!" she screamed in his face. He could feel the flare of her temper as tangibly as the heat of her breath. "He's my friend!" She pushed Ethan away. He fell back, catching himself with his hands. "I won't choose between you," she hissed.

"You won't choose between a brain-washing fiend and your husband?" He wanted so much to believe this wasn't what Cori's real thoughts were, but he knew they were. These were her uncensored and candid thoughts. "I thought I finally had you, Cori. I thought, after everything we had been through, that I could be your confidant, your hero, your..." He pushed himself back up and stood. He had more to say, far more, but this wasn't the real Cori. There was no point in discussing the future of his marriage with this imitation. "You went to Cleos. You wanted him to tell you why he did it, but he wouldn't. Then what?"

He could see the pain and sympathy in her eyes, like she knew what discussion was being sidestepped. "I..." Her voice caught. "I was angry, hurt, and betrayed by both of you. I felt alone. Danato was gone. Belus couldn't give a shit about my problems." She laughed through her tears. "I just decided to go to work. I took on some new duties, like Belus had suggested. I went up to the transmorph level, and I started logging in the prisoners."

"Then what? Did you trip? Did you get tricked?"

Cori-1's face blanked as she tried to remember. "I saw something."

"What did you see?"

"Something very wrong. Something that shouldn't be."

"What did you see?" Ethan moved back to kneel before her. "What distracted you?"

Her eyes narrowed. "I can't quite remember. All I remember was being grabbed—a strong arm, stronger than I ever thought it would be. It wrapped around my neck. It was in my mouth and nose. I couldn't breathe. I couldn't see, and then... nothing." She lowered her head and wept quietly. "I'm so sorry, Ethan. I shouldn't have left. I should have stayed with you that night." She looked up at him through red, puffy eyes. His heart ached to hold her. "I'm so stupid."

His hand reached for her cheek without thinking. "Don't say that. You know that's not true."

"I don't mean to screw everything up. I love you so much."

She leaned forward to him, and he couldn't resist kissing her lips. They were her lips. He only hoped that those were also her words. She leaned in slowly, wrapping her arms around him. He let his arms rest on her back. He wanted so much to fall into the embrace, to forget just for a moment about Cleos, the transmorphs, and the arguing, but he couldn't.

Cori-1 was not his wife. She was standing in the way of him hugging his real wife, and she was about to die for that offense. Whether or not he wanted to, he had to break up this little heart to heart and get himself back on track.

It wasn't until he reached to pull her back that he realized her hands were fully embracing him, beyond the latitude that the cuffs allowed. He shoved her away, but it was too late. Her transmorph embrace had locked onto him. She pushed him back to the ground for a truly smothering kiss.

37

D ANIEL KEPT THINGS CASUAL through breakfast, but he wasn't sure how much longer he could take being around Nevia without discussing last night. In a million years, he had never expected trying to be alone with a woman after he had slept with her. He usually ducked out as fast as he could, or just acted like a complete jackass until they left. It was harsh, but he always figured it was easier than watching them panic when the blinders of alcohol wore off to reveal their unfortunate choice of bedfellow.

Ethan had already headed over to the prison. Heaton was just finishing his tea, and would no doubt expect to be leaving with Daniel in tow. Nevia was in Danato's room, unpacking her gun. She had barely gotten permission from Ethan to bring it into the prison before he left. Daniel got the impression that her anxiety about the coming events was making her trigger finger itch. Everyone had their security blankets. Apparently, hers was a semi-automatic pistol.

Heaton rinsed out his cup and placed it in the sink. He looked back at Daniel's mug. Daniel picked up the empty cup and pretended to sip from it. "Why don't you head over and remind Ethan about getting his paws in the way? I'll wait for Miss Bond."

Heaton looked him over like he was deciphering his lie. All he had to do was determine which lie it was this time. The "*I'm not sloshed*" lie. The "*I wouldn't do that*" lie. Or maybe today it was just the same old "*I love my job*" lie.

"He's going to try to save her," Heaton said. "You know he will. It won't matter how much we explain it."

"I know. Just go show him your arm again, and remind him what a dumbass you were once."

Heaton stepped over to him, glancing back at Danato's door. "What are we going to do about her?"

"What do you mean? I thought you liked her."

Heaton shrugged. "I do, but can she do the job?"

"She can smell—"

"No, I mean the other hunts. Far be it from me to pass up the opportunity to save people from mental anguish, but let's face it, most of our work is still vampires. Do you really want to spend time saving the damsel in distress every other hunt?"

Daniel would have banged his own head into the counter if it would have knocked any sense into him. In his haste to approve of her staying with the team, he had only thought about saving his transmorph victims—and himself. He hadn't thought about the many cold nights he and Heaton had spent trudging through sewers, stalking through caves, and all-out running for their lives from the many sub-creatures in the vampiric genre.

There was something to be said for being a trained FBI agent, but she didn't have the strong athletic body it would take to fend off even the weakest vampire attack. He had encouraged her to stay without considering the risks to her.

"I guess we'll have to talk about that with her. I don't even know if she wants to stay, but you're right. If she's a liability to herself or us..." He paused, thinking how ironic it was that he wanted her as a partner and now he couldn't have her. "...we'll have to let her move on to other career choices."

"That ought to be a fun conversation with Sophie." Heaton smirked. "I'll head over and talk to Ethan."

"Thanks."

As soon as Heaton was out the door, Daniel headed to Danato's room and tapped on the door. He pushed it open slowly, not waiting for a response. He found Nevia slipping on her holster over her white button-down shirt. She nodded to him as she slammed a cartridge into her pistol and slipped it into the leather cradle under her left arm. "Are you ready?" she asked.

He wasn't sure if she meant ready to go to the prison or ready to kill a transmorph. "Yeah, but I wanted to talk to you about last night."

She tipped her head and frowned at him. "Really? You want to do that? Isn't that the kind of thing men like you avoid?"

Daniel had never denied his character to anyone, but he hated the way it sounded from her perspective. "I suppose so. Normally, but this is different."

"It's sex, Daniel. Good or bad, it's still a cock in a slot." Nevia slipped on a blue blazer that neatly covered her gun. All she needed was an ID badge to flash, and she would fit right in with the FBI, aka America's yuppie police.

"It's different if one of you is a virgin."

She slid her hand over the blazer to dust off any residual fuzz balls it may have gained from sitting in her suitcase. The pause in the movement was so slight, he wasn't entirely sure he had seen it. She shrugged her shoulders even before her eyes made a hit-and-run on his. "Not really. Have to start somewhere."

Daniel knew that wasn't true. He didn't care who, when, where, or why. Everyone's first time was *different*. Good or bad or indifferent, it was going to be forever engrained on your mind. It was the backdrop of your sexual identity. It wasn't baggage, but it was definitely the luggage cart on which all your future disappointing relationships would be stacked.

"You shouldn't have started with me, Nevia." He leaned on the doorframe.

"Jordan," she mumbled, kicking her suitcase lid shut.

"You could have found a nice guy, someone who could be *with* you, not just *in* you."

She glared back at him. "How did you even know? Was I that pathetic?"

"No!" He laughed. "You were..." He wasn't sure what adjective to put with last night's events. He wasn't sure asking for another round would project the proper compliment at this point. "Perfect. You were perfect. I only knew because you bled."

Her brow dipped in confusion. "Fine, you've deduced my secret. I'm a virgin whore. What do we need to discuss?"

Daniel wished he could smell her emotions. She was expressing hostility in spades, but he knew there was more to it than that. Last night *hadn't* been perfect. It'd lacked intimacy. She'd offered her body as a platter, or perhaps *he* was the platter. Either way, her heart hadn't been in the picture.

That shouldn't have bothered him, but it did. Maybe he really was a sociopath. Maybe he only wanted to have her heart, so he could break it. After all, how could he ruin any chance he had with her if he didn't leave her emotionally stunted?

"Is that all you wanted from me? Just to—"

"Pop the cherry," she suggested, taking a step forward. He nodded reluctantly at the vulgar phrase. "Yeah." She crossed her arms. "Should I send a thank you card?"

He knew he had done this same act with a hundred other women—well, maybe dozens—but he had never been on this side of it. He'd never realized how much it stung to have someone reject not only your future connection, but to belittle your current one.

For a split second, he thought about how angry Sophie was with him. He wondered if she had put Nevia up to this to hurt him. He couldn't put it past her, but he was certain that Nevia couldn't fake the bravery she had shown with him. He also doubted that she would sacrifice her virginity just to settle a debt of revenge.

"Do you even like me?" he asked, feeling like he needed to defend himself in some small way.

She dropped her arms, and along with it, her aggressive expression. For a moment, she was with him again, present and accountable to last night's events. "I don't know what I should say to you. I don't want to be a bitch, but if I don't, you won't let this go, and then it's going to be weird."

"You did use me. My reputation preceded me, and you knew that I would..." Daniel wondered when she had decided to sleep with him. Was it before or after she knew what he was? "You never had any intention of being with me beyond that."

"Your reputation doesn't just precede you, it emanates from you. You are a throwaway lay, and you like it that way. At least, you think you do. If you thought that this was something more, then I'm sorry, but I can hardly get wrapped up in..." She twirled her finger at him. "...this emotional mess. Don't get me wrong, I empathize with your past, and I am in awe of your power, but that's all." She took a step toward him. "Daniel, you are an amazing man and someday maybe you will be a good man, but until those two things come together, we are just partners. Thank you for last night, though. I can't wait to do it again, with a *nice* guy."

Daniel stared at her. It was all he could do not to plead his case and deny her accusations. She was right, of course. "I deserve this," he stammered, finally finding words. "This and so much more, I know. I just... I thought, since you weren't afraid of me... I wasn't going to sleep with you. For once in my life, I wasn't going to."

"Daniel." She stepped forward and put her hand on his arm. "I don't have to sleep with you to help you. You know that, right?" When he said nothing, she pulled her head back and narrowed her eyes at him. "Unless you left out something about how you and Belus met."

He smiled. "Oh, did I leave that part out?"

She chuckled, giving him a rare, full smile, but it faded away quickly. She squeezed his arm. "Look, I spent a lot of time being the good girl in high school, and I spent my college days working my ass off to build a career. I just didn't get the chance to strike that off my to-do list. I know it's a shit way of going about it, but hitting twenty-four as a virgin was starting to sound like crazy cat lady territory."

He pulled her hand from his arm and kissed her palm. "I hope you don't regret it." He held onto her hand.

"Not yet." She smiled warmly even as she pulled her hand away. "Come on, you've got to see a transmorph about a girl." She slipped by him and headed to the front door to put on her coat.

He didn't want that to be the end of it. It demeaned him to chase after a woman like a love-struck teenager, but he didn't know what else to do. He wanted more. Not just another night. He wanted her, and he had no idea how to get her.

38

B Y THE TIME THEY made it to the prison, Daniel had forcefully focused himself on the task at hand. He didn't have time to worry about his feelings for Nevia and her lack of feelings for him. For the time being, Cori was the only woman he was concerned with.

He pushed Nevia's fluffy white coat into the locker and looked back at her. "Where did you get this puffy piece of shit, anyway?"

"Blue-light special," she quipped.

He arched an eyebrow, not understanding the reference. "I'm buying you a real coat when we get out of here," he grumbled, slamming the door.

"You don't have to do that," she said, moving into the main foyer ahead of him.

"I will after I ceremoniously burn yours." He followed her through the foyer. "Besides, you'll need something warm. This frigid pit stop comes with the job."

Heaton came down the hall from the gym. "Have you seen Ethan?" he asked, throwing his hands up.

"No, he said to meet in the gym," Daniel said. "Maybe he had trouble with Number One."

"Wait here, I'll go to check the transmorph level," Heaton grumbled as he moved past them.

"Alright," Daniel said and headed on to the gym.

Nevia slowed to a stop beside him. Her head whipped, and she gawked at him, wide-eyed. Before he could begin to ask what was wrong with her, she ripped her Glock from its holster and spun around, pointing her gun at his best friend.

Had he not been a hunter for the last four years, he might have had a slower reaction—which, in this case, would have been preferable. Even as Nevia yelled for Heaton to stop, Daniel had a hold on her wrists, forcing the gun into the air, where it couldn't hurt anyone.

She twisted out of his grip just as fast and gave him an expert kick to his solar plexus. An additional chop to his throat sent him back to the wall. While he tried to find his breath, she ran after Heaton, who had bolted down the corridor at her first movement.

Daniel growled and forced himself to move after them. He had no idea what was going on, but he was going to make damn sure he was a part of it.

The chase continued into the stairwell. He followed the sound of trampling feet on metal stairs. He peeked up here and there to make sure he was gaining on them. Unfortunately, he was trailing.

He jumped steps, trying to get ahead, but the banging footsteps stopped above him. They were on the fourth floor—the transmorph level. "Feck!"

He sprinted up the steps with even more motivation. He was just starting to piece together the last two minutes. Heaton must have been the transmorph. It must have escaped. Nevia smelled him. She was trying to stop him, and Daniel had gotten in her way.

With that in mind, he could only be impressed that she was willing to hurt him rather than take the time to explain her actions. Or maybe he was just impressed that she had the foresight not to kick him in the mebbs. She wasn't likely to get a lot of backup if she had.

He pushed through the door to the transmorph level and ran section to section until he came upon the party—and a party it was.

All the transmorph cages were empty. Heaton was holding his hands up high, begging for Nevia to put down her gun. She had her Glock trained on him, following him as he backpedaled.

Belus and Ethan were glancing between the two of them, trying to figure out what was going on.

A nameless guard was spinning his wheels, trying to get a grip on the situation as he kneeled down next to the *second* Nevia. She was lying on the floor, barely conscious. Daniel could already see the red mark on the side of her cheek where someone had hit her.

"Put the gun away, Jordan," Heaton pleaded, but he still kept authority in his voice.

"What the hell is going on here?" Belus asked. "Who said she could bring a gun in here?"

"I did." Ethan shook his head. "I didn't know she planned to use it on her own partner."

Daniel looked at the second Nevia. She was looking at him and pointing to the first Nevia—the one with the gun. "Nevia?" he asked, volleying his gaze between them.

"I'm here, Daniel!" the supine Nevia hollered at him.

"That's not me, Daniel," the gun-toting Nevia said.

"Well, shit." Daniel stepped a little closer.

"Stay right where you are." The Nevia with the gun poked a finger at him without taking her eyes off Heaton.

"Why?" he asked as he circled around to see her face better.

"Because I don't trust you right now."

"Don't trust me?" he scoffed. "You're the one with the fecking gun."

"Daniel," Heaton barked. "Get her under control right now."

"What the hell happened?" Daniel asked.

"She chased me up here and let all the transmorphs out," Heaton said.

"Daniel listen!" the sitting Nevia yelled from her position on the floor. "Heaton is the transmorph. He still has Cori. You have to keep him here."

"That's true," the armed Nevia agreed. "And I'm Jordan. The real Jordan."

"No, Daniel, I am!" The downed Nevia struggled to rise.

"Why should I believe you?" Daniel asked the Nevia, who was still keeping a firm eye on Heaton.

"Because I'm the one with the gun," she informed him.

"She got the drop on me," the other Nevia said. "She's tricking you. Think about it."

"When I showed up," the guard interjected, "they were rolling around on the floor. It could be either one of them."

Daniel looked between the two of them and stepped forward. "No!" Nevia-with-a-gun pointed her finger back at him. "Not until you figure out who's who."

"I'm trying to."

"Daniel." Heaton looked at him sternly. "She has Cori." He nodded at the Jordan pointing the Glock at him. "She got your girl's gun and transformed."

Daniel shook his head. "No, Cori's taller than Nevia. She's in one of you four."

Ethan stepped forward. "This is out of control. We need to figure this out."

The standing Nevia shifted her gun to Ethan as a warning before moving it back to Heaton. "You don't move either!" Ethan put his hands up in surrender.

"Okay, time to clear the playing field," Daniel said. "Ethan, Belus, and soldier boy, you go back to your cages."

"Daniel!" Belus and Ethan objected simultaneously.

"Or I will cremate you," he whispered as he gave them a look that dared them to challenge him. "I know you have shit for survival instincts, but trust me, I can make the pain last."

The three seemed resigned to their fates and sauntered back to their cells. They even voluntarily shut the doors. With three left, Daniel turned his attention to the still-kneeling Nevia. As he approached her, the other Nevia repositioned to keep him in her line of sight.

He stopped next to the unarmed Nevia and provided her with a hand up. "Two Nevias." Daniel clucked as he lifted her to her feet. "Oh, the fun that would be."

The risen woman ignored his comment and stared down her mirror image. The other Nevia glanced at him. "You've got about thirty seconds to figure this out before I start shooting."

"Hmm." Daniel nodded. "Lift your shirt."

Her brow furrowed, but she didn't take her eyes—nor her gun—from Heaton. "Excuse me?"

"Lift your shirt, now, or we'll see who the faster draw is."

She untucked her shirt and pulled it up to reveal the small silver hoop in her belly button. The Nevia next to Daniel ran, but he grabbed her collar and yanked her back. He peeked under the fabric, but there was no tattoo. "Can't mimic what you can't see."

Daniel threw the Nevia-shaped transmorph into an open cage and stalked over to Heaton. "You sure about this one?" He grabbed Heaton's arm.

"Yes," was all Nevia said to back up her accusation. He looked her over, hoping she had more evidence. She narrowed her eyes. "I'm sure."

"You can put the gun down now," he said. "The only person you're threatening right now is Cori." She flinched with the realization and lowered her gun. Daniel yanked on Heaton's arm and dragged him along. "Besides, bullets don't kill transmorphs."

Nevia holstered her gun and trailed behind him. "What about you? Any immunity to bullets?"

"Only if I know they're coming, but it's a bit like trying to catch an arrow. Sure, it's possible, but do you really want to practice?" He heard her chuckle behind him. "Good job on the catch, though. You may have just saved us from another episode of "Where's Wally.""

"Nice thinking on identifying me."

"I have a good memory for details." He wanted to make a comment about that being what made him such a good lover, but he resisted. That conversation was already over.

39

B Y THE TIME THEY made it back to the gym, the transmorph had returned to Cori's shape. Daniel knew it would be difficult for it to maintain a shape that didn't outline the person it was holding. Transmorphs rarely changed shape once they had imbibed their host.

Heaton met them at the door, rubbing his head. He bypassed Daniel and grabbed Cori-1 by the neck. "If Cori wasn't inside you somewhere, I would—"

"Your fists are a waste of time!" Cori-1 spat back at him.

"What happened to you?" Nevia interrupted the banter.

"She knocked me out with a dumbbell. Ethan was unconscious when I came in. She practically suffocated him." Heaton gestured to Ethan, who was recovering on the workout bench. He looked utterly dejected.

"Give us a minute." Daniel shoved Cori-1 at Heaton and he eagerly took over as her escort. Daniel moved to Ethan and sat down next to him. "What happened?" He already knew the answer, but it didn't mean he didn't have to ask the question.

"I got sloppy." Ethan rubbed his face, as if the mortification would simply rub off with a good scrub. "I got caught up in an argument. A fight I should have been having with Cori. A fight I may still have to have with her." Ethan's eyes watered, but he took a breath and blinked it away before it could claim the name of tears.

"Is this about that mind-sucker?"

"Cleos, yes."

"Is she..." Daniel didn't want to say the word. "Cheating?"

"No. No," Ethan repeated to assure him. He hit his fist into his leg. "It's not even that simple. I suppose it's an emotional affair, if there is such a thing. I don't even know if I have the right to be this angry. She hasn't done anything wrong, and yet I feel so betrayed... abandoned. I know why I feel like this. I get it. I've had enough fucking shrinks in my head to know that I have abandonment issues, but I do need to feel close to her, and I don't." Ethan chuckled and looked at him. "You must be resisting the urge to say 'I told you so.'"

Daniel thought about that. He had never been fond of Cori. She was cute and hot, but she seemed complicated. His brief meeting with her in the infirmary had told him two things: that she had a lot of love for Ethan, and that she was scared of it. Daniel had hoped for Ethan's sake that she would get over that fear and give herself over to her love wholeheartedly, but with so much loss in her past, it was probably difficult for her to love blindly.

"From what you've told me, Cori's got her own issues with abandonment," Daniel stated carefully. "Maybe she just wasn't ready for marriage."

"I thought it would be better." Ethan looked over at Cori-1. "I thought it was me and her forever. I wasn't planning on a threesome."

"Well, not with another man, anyway." Daniel smiled, but realized too late that Ethan wasn't ready for that kind of levity. "Cori loves you. I knew she loved you when I met her. She was willing to tackle a dragon and lose for you. She would fight to the death for you."

"But?" Ethan asked.

"But if she can't make you happy..." Daniel paused, uncertain of how influential his advice could be in this area. He glanced at Nevia. As if sensing him, she looked over. He could see her trying to determine what the conversation was about. She must have gleaned the gist of it, because she gave him a sympathetic smile that may as well have been a frown. "I don't know shit about love, Ethan. All I know is that for all the love you claim to have for Cori, all I ever see is your misery with it."

"I should have never made her read that file."

"Yeah, that was what went wrong," Daniel mumbled sarcastically. "Look, Cori just needs..." He trailed off as Belus entered the gym with two guards and Cleos in tow. Ethan followed his gaze. Daniel could see the two men evaluating each other across the room. The hatred between them was palpable.

Belus looked over the room, stopping his attention on Daniel. He gave him a stern look and an ever-so-slight nod before meeting with Heaton.

"Cori just needs to get out of that fecking transmorph, so you two can figure this shit out." He gripped Ethan's shoulder before leaving him behind on the bench.

He joined Heaton and Belus in the middle of their quietly heated debate. "He won't leave her side, I guarantee it," Belus insisted.

"We have to convince him." Heaton glanced back at Ethan. "He can't be here for this. It will be too painful for him to watch."

Daniel glanced back as well. It was probably a mistake to do so, since Ethan was already giving them a cold, steely glare. It was apparently obvious they were discussing him. "I'm not sure I can ask him to leave," he said.

"You would rather he watch you rip his wife to shreds while she screams and writhes in pain?" Heaton suggested snidely.

Daniel clenched his fists, reminding himself to keep his voice low. "I know what my job is. You don't need to remind me in Technicolor details."

"He's going to jump in the middle of it. You know he will. He doesn't understand any more than I did." Heaton rubbed at his forearm.

"Don't you flash that fecking arm at me again!" Daniel seethed quietly.

"Easy, boys. This isn't something we can just make Ethan do," Belus mediated. "We can either convince him it's what's best, or we can't."

"Convince me of what?" Ethan asked.

Daniel swung around and found Ethan right behind him. As usual, there had been no sound to his approach. "Christ, you dodgy git! How the feck do you do that?"

"What's going on? Why the secret meeting? Please tell me there isn't another detail you haven't told me." Daniel exchanged a glance with Heaton. "Stop doing that!" Ethan yelled. "What is it?"

"Okay, okay." Daniel held up his hands in surrender. "We were debating whether or not you should be here for this." Ethan's eyes widened. "Actually, that part wasn't the debate. The debate was whether or not we could convince you to leave voluntarily."

"As opposed to removing me involuntarily?" Ethan cocked his head to one side.

Daniel chuckled. "Look man, this is still just a conversation."

"This isn't a pleasant procedure to observe," Belus interjected. "Especially when the victim looks like a loved one. We are concerned you'll try to help Cori, which will hurt you, and most likely kill her in the process."

Before Ethan could voice any questions, Heaton spoke up. "Once Daniel starts the eradication, he can't stop."

"Why would I interfere? I want to free Cori."

Daniel put a hand on Ethan's shoulder. "Because you're the hero, and in a few minutes, I'm going to become the villain."

"Ethan," Heaton rallied back to the explanation. "The transmorph will maintain her form throughout the process. Can you really just stand on the sidelines and watch your wife die?"

Ethan turned his attention to Belus. He was observing Ethan, patiently waiting for the decision to be made so they could move on. Daniel glanced between the two men. He knew he was missing something, but he didn't want to trespass to ask what it was.

"Daniel." Ethan's eyes snapped in his direction. "I want my wife back. For the last and final time, can you do that?"

"Yes." He nodded.

"Let's get to it, then."

"Ethan, you don't understand," Heaton argued further. "She'll trick you, and lie to you, and..."

"I understand that this is my prison, my wife, and my choice."

Heaton glanced at Belus, looking for a more authoritative objection. Daniel could almost sense a slight proud smile hiding in Belus's beard, but since it was such a rarity, he couldn't be sure. "You heard the man, boys. Get to work." He slapped Heaton on the back before heading to the outskirts of the gym.

Ethan moved away to get Cori-1 into position. Heaton glared after him, shaking his head. "He has no idea what he's about to witness." Daniel nodded and looked back at Nevia, who was watching their conversation. She pulled herself away from the wall and made her way over. He appreciated her respect for their boundaries. She knew when to hang back, and when to join in. "You know how much he loves her," Heaton persisted. "He won't be able to stay out of your way."

"Maybe, but if he can't handle this, then he doesn't deserve to be warden, does he?"

"Fine print of the application." Heaton pushed past him just as Nevia reached them.

"Everything okay?" she asked, watching Heaton leave.

"Yes, Ethan is staying to watch despite our advice to leave."

Nevia nodded. "And Heaton's angry over that decision?"

"He's just watching out for Ethan... and me. He likes to be the mother hen, but it's hard with such stubborn chicks. He doesn't think Ethan can handle watching this." She nodded again. "What about you?"

"What about me?"

"This isn't exactly going to be pretty."

"Are you worried that I might be upset by your display of violence?"

"No, but in the span of a week, I've told you every detail of my sordid past, revealed my power, and given you my body. Don't you want to save anything for next week?"

She smiled a full smile rather than her taut, controlled one. He saw a glimpse of her tiny white teeth before she forcibly pinched her lips closed. "I already have plans for next week."

"Ouch." He touched his chest. "Dumped after only a week." He laughed to keep the comment light.

"Don't worry, my plans involve you."

"Don't tease... Okay, tease. I'll take what I can get." He lost his smile. "Seriously, though... I got enough women in my life looking at me like I'm the antichrist. I really don't want you to be one of them."

"I won't."

He stepped forward half a step and cleared his throat. "If I asked you to leave, would you go?" He hoped that sounded like an earnest entreaty for his privacy.

She took in a deep breath and let it out slowly as she looked around the room. He could tell the question annoyed her, but she was considering it. "How important is it that I don't see this?"

"No, that's not what I'm asking." Daniel stepped a little closer still. "I'm not asking you to leave. I'm asking you if you would leave *if* I asked you."

She looked up at him, flickering her eyes between his. She showed no objection to his proximity. Her lips parted and paused as if the words weren't quite as thought-out as she assumed they were. He wanted so badly to descend on those lips with his own, to mingle his tongue with hers. He hadn't realized how much he wanted that until right then.

"Yes," she said. He hadn't expected that to be her answer. At best, he'd expected a condition to that yes. "Is that what you want me to do?"

"No." He backed away from her and slipped off his glasses. "I want you to see this."

She gave him an askance look before she withdrew to observe the carnage from her wall.

40

Daniel approached Cori-1 with the critical eye of an art dealer. He knew that Cori—the real Cori—was inside somewhere, and he only had to chisel her out. He hated the term *exorcism*, but that was precisely what he had to do. A slow and exhaustive removal of an entity that did not want to leave the body it inhabited.

He didn't object that strongly to Ethan witnessing the procedure, but he agreed with Heaton. He was not prepared for the trickery that this monster had in store for them. It was only through trial and error that he had come to understand the ruses such creatures implemented. He wasn't as easily coerced as he once was.

Daniel circled behind Cori-1 and leaned into her ear. "One last chance," he said.

"Do you know what my kind calls your kind?" she asked with a slight smirk. "*Doth seola*," she whispered the secret to him. "Do you know what that means?"

"Yes." Daniel frowned. "It means you should have let her go."

"I tell you what. I'll meet you in hell." She winked at him.

He walked away and took his place to face off with her. He checked his audience placement. Heaton gave him a nod, and he turned his attention to Cori-1.

His heart slowed to a rhythmic thrum as he concentrated his energies away from his body's needs and into his ability.

Cori-1 stiffened as the initial shockwave hit her. Daniel understood from his depraved torture sessions with his captive transmorph that the first contact was an intense vibration that ignited heat in every cell of the body. It was the first and only warning shot. After he began, stopping was not an option. Stopping too soon would result in the death of the host. The transmorph, in a half-wounded state, would drain every last nutrient from the host to try to save itself. Once he started, he had to finish it or risk losing Cori.

Daniel let his body relax into the process. Cori-1 started to cry and beg for Ethan to save her. Daniel had expected as much. As long as Heaton did his job, this wouldn't be a problem either.

She started to pant and sweat as if he were focusing a magnifying glass on an ant. He, conversely, felt a shivering cold wrap around his body. His heart would eventually slow to near death. Without medical attention after the event, he risked coma and death. That was one detail he hadn't mentioned to Ethan.

A wave of desert heat distorted Daniel's view. Cori-1 screamed as a layer of her epidermis disintegrated, leaving fresh, pink, bald tissue. Transmorphs didn't technically have skin like humans, so the attack was the equivalent of cutting off her finger.

The transmorph recovered from the pain and cursed at him in a language only familiar to those who have dared violate them in this way. She ran at him, a last-ditch attempt to save herself. Flakes of her remaining tissue fell away from her and instantly turned to ash at her feet. She pushed against an imperceptible force, all the while bleeding from the new and multiplying gouges in her body.

His power had no sound, so the deafening screams of his victims were crisp and irreverent to his ears. As much as he hated hearing it, it was all part of the process.

A chunk of her face ripped away just as she reached him. "I will kill her!" her cheekless mouth yelled in his face. "Let me go, or she's dead! I'll suffocate her!" When she didn't get the appropriate response from him, she looked behind him to the audience. He didn't need to look behind him to know who she was trying to negotiate with.

41

ETHAN WATCHED IN HORROR on the sidelines as Cori-1's skin ripped from her body. He tightened his grip on his crossed arms. Belus stood at his side in the same position, with the same stern face he always wore. There were two guards at his back that Ethan knew were in position to tackle him if he tried to interfere with Daniel.

He was almost regretting his decision to stay, but he didn't have a choice. Heaton wanted to prevent disruption. Daniel wanted to shield him. Belus, however, was all but double-dog daring him to stay.

In some ways, Belus was a heartless bastard. Ethan had managed to avoid the brunt of his personality while he was in training to become warden, but now that he had achieved the goal, Belus offered no sympathy for the trials he encountered. He had finally released the reins of the warden to him, and all the burdens that came with it. The job title didn't necessarily exclude watching your best friend rip your wife apart with the power of his eyes.

Ethan knew that by leaving, he would be telling Belus that he still couldn't handle this job. He wasn't about to lose ground on his authority right after it had been handed to him. Although Belus's methodology was pitiless, Ethan could tell he wanted him to succeed. More importantly, he wanted Ethan to earn his respect.

That was probably the only thought that kept him from panicking when Cori-1's ruined face looked directly at him over Daniel's shoulder.

"Stop this or I will kill her! She will die screaming like me!" The voice was no longer Cori's. Even if it was intended to be, the gaping hole in the creature's throat wasn't permitting functional vocal cords. He looked down to the floor beneath her, where blood should have been pooling, but the dripping blood absorbed back into the body, before it fell away.

The blood and gore were all for show. This creature *was* mortally wounded, but it didn't bleed like a human. Their homogenized tissue was immune to most of the afflictions that human tissue was so sensitive to. Even heat and acid only temporarily broke down the creature's tissue.

Ethan sensed Heaton shift out of the corner of his eye. He was obviously concerned that Ethan would bolt to rescue her. He didn't bother to reassure him. He just kept his eyes fixed on Daniel's work.

42

The transmorph gripped onto Daniel's arm just as another layer of tissue unfurled from her body like a snake shedding its skin. A new, fresh Cori was revealed. The transmorph shell slipped to the floor in a clump around her legs. She gasped and coughed under the pressure of his sandblasting power. Her hair was slick with sweat, her face a gaunt reflection of starvation and dehydration. She fell to her knees, grasping at his pant legs.

"Daniel," her voice cracked. "Stop. It's me." She looked behind him again. "Ethan?"

Ethan watched Cori being uncovered. He exhaled and smiled as he saw her blossom out of the clutches of the transmorph. Her legs still seemed to be bound by the creature. Daniel stepped away from her pawing hands and refocused his attack. She groaned and tried to shield her face from his bombarding power.

Cori looked at him. "Ethan, what's going on?" She reached one hand out to him. "Help me." He crossed his arms tighter, resisting the urge to move forward. "He's hurting me!" she cried, pulling herself back, trying to avoid the impact of Daniel's destruction.

She coughed up blood. It splattered on the transmorph flesh still containing her. "Why are you doing this, Daniel?" she pleaded with him. Her body convulsed, and she screamed. Flesh ripped away from her face and arms. "Ethan!"

Ethan bit his cheek and held steady as he watched muscle tissue being exposed. Heaton shifted next to him again, tensing his muscles, prepared to bulldoze any attempt he made to stop this.

Ethan's eyes watered as Cori called his name again. It was intolerable.

Cori screamed as her muscle tissue vaporized, revealing creamy bone. Her face, a shredded mess, was birthing the faint outline of her skull. Her teeth were fully visible without her lips. Her curdling scream was more than any man should have been able to take, but Daniel was not any man.

He was a monster.

He was a *doth seola*.

He was a dead soul.

Cori's abdomen started to bloat and bleed from small tears. The lower body remained the same pile of rumpled tissue. Her hands ripped at her own flesh in a horrifically gruesome display until only her skull remained.

As the stomach bulged, he refocused his energy, tightening it on the flesh there so he could appease the anguish Ethan must have been feeling. The skin finally ripped open. Emerging from the gap was a new face.

Cori.

The *real* Cori.

She was slumped on the floor below the ghastly upper body that displayed such a devastating interpretation. Her slick head flopped down to the concrete, unsupported by her partially atrophied neck. Her eyes were closed, but he could see her back rise with a breath—an unassisted breath, not unlike a baby's first breath after the womb.

The remainder of the transmorph easily dispersed, and Daniel finally withdrew his attack. He coughed, feeling the humid air he inhaled into his cold lungs instantly frost over. He stumbled forward, trying to reach Cori to check her.

Most of her clothes were gone, destroyed by the last moments of sandblasting. He could see some skin damage, but nothing he would need to repair.

He dropped to the floor beside her. His narrowed eyes gazed across to her peeking eyes. They caught a glimpse of each other just before Heaton rolled him over. He pulled a long needle from behind his back and straddled Daniel. He wished he had the energy to scream, but he didn't.

Without an ounce of concern for the bruising it would cause, Heaton slammed the needle through his rib cage and injected the adrenaline necessary to keep his heart going. Daniel felt the pain, and the spike of muscle spasms that left him nearly seizing on the floor.

When it was all said and done, he looked back to where Cori had been, but she was gone. Only Heaton was left. His expression begged for some sign that he was okay. "Get off me, you poof. This isn't a date."

Heaton's expression immediately changed to relief, and he rolled off Daniel, laughing.

43

ETHAN WASN'T SURE WHO moved first, Heaton or Belus, but he shot out after them to reach Cori. He slid to his knees before her and lifted her limp body. Her head flopped back against his arm as he lifted her. She was sopping wet with sweat and her clothes were half disintegrated. He pulled her in close to shield her partial nudity.

He got the sense that Daniel was in danger, but he left Heaton to help him. He carried Cori out of the gym and up a flight of stairs to the infirmary. He could feel her bones pressing into his arms as he carried her. Six weeks without proper nutrition had left her skeletal and pale.

Her eyes were open, but she wasn't necessarily looking at him. "I've got you now. You're safe," he choked. She *was* safe. At last, she was back in his arms. For the time being, his anger was gone. Nothing else mattered.

"Ethan?" Her lips were as white as her skin. When they parted to speak, he could see the pale pink in her mouth that should have matched her lips.

"Yes, Cori. It's me."

"Wait," she groaned.

"What?" He slowed to a stop. "What is it?"

She turned her head slightly and expelled a grayish vomit. He crouched down and tipped her so she could release the rest of the grayish paste. He could only assume it was more remnants of the creature. An internal part, not so easily sloughed.

She turned back and looked at him, really looked at him. Her protuberant cheekbones and hollowed cheeks made her look like a Halloween witch. She didn't say anything, but he knew she must have a hundred questions.

"Cori..." His throat clutched again, and he couldn't keep his emotions back. "I'm so sorry." He gripped her as tightly as he dared and rocked her. "I'm so sorry." His tears spilled over onto her face.

"Ethan," she whispered again. He pulled back to look at her. Her eyes flickered over him as if she didn't quite recognize him with his growing five o'clock shadow. "What's going on? Where's Vince? Why am I back here?" Ethan heard footsteps behind him. Belus arrived with the guards, who were escorting Cleos. He barely had time to react before they arrived. As it was, all he could do was stare with his mouth agape. "Where's Vince?" she repeated. "What have you done with him?"

Before he knew what he was doing, he set Cori down on the floor and backed away. Belus put a hand on his shoulder, but Ethan slunk away from him as well. He hit the wall of the hallway and stopped, crouching as far away from Cori as he could get.

Cleos moved forward to her emaciated form. "Corinthia." With what little strength she had, she vaulted away from him.

"Don't touch me!"

Ethan couldn't help but be pleased by that. At least Cleos was no more a friend to her than Ethan was her husband.

"Cori." Belus approached. "We're going to help you. Ethan—"

"Where's Vince?" she growled.

Belus sighed and shook his head. "Vince is fine. *You* are not. Ethan is going to take you to the infirmary." Cori looked at him with the same confusion as she had before. She didn't recognize him, several years older, and by all rights a different man. "Do you understand?"

"Am I in trouble? Where's Danato? Is he mad?"

"Don't worry about that now. You're safe. We will take care of you." Belus glanced back at Ethan and gave him a nod. It was just a nod, but it had its own underlying meaning. Mainly, *pull yourself together and carry her to the infirmary.*

Ethan moved back to her. He wasn't that pulled together, but hearts were designed to break repeatedly, so he went back in for more of the same. He wrapped his arm under her again and she latched onto his neck. As he lifted her, she watched him. She was waking up from her brief time with Vince to find herself back at the prison in the arms of a man who she had last remembered being a boy.

As painful as it was for him, he found room to sympathize with her surreal situation.

44

44

O NCE IN THE INFIRMARY, the nurses directed Ethan to a bed. He laid Cori down on the over starched sheets while the nurses pushed in to take her vitals. One of the nurses started to remove her clothes. Cori suddenly became aware of the gaping holes already present in her clothing, and she crossed her arms to shield the peep show. She looked over at him.

He averted his eyes and turned his back to give her privacy. He tried to find some amusement in the situation. She was prudishly covering a body that he had repeatedly seen, caressed, licked, and bitten from top to bottom. He was as familiar with her body as she was his.

Still, he understood where her mind was. He only hoped that Cleos could bring her back to where she was. He didn't mind a little memory loss, especially if it erased the horrible memories of the last six weeks, but he didn't want her to relive the pain of Vince's death, nor did he want to wait through another mourning period to be with her again.

He waited patiently as the nurses debated back and forth about putting in two IVs or one. They settled on two and hooked up two bags of fluid. One was clear, and one yellow. He assumed one was for hydration, while the other provided additional nutrients the saline didn't.

By the time he was given the go ahead to return to her side, she was dressed in a blue gown, bandaged on both arms, and covered in all manner of sensors. The machines next to her beeped with the beat of her heart. A paper ticket produced from the machine marked each beat. She looked over at the contraptions as if they were offensive to her.

"What happened? Why am I here? Why do I feel like shit?" she asked.

Ethan smiled at her and took a seat beside her on the bed. She shifted a bit to give him room. "I could explain, but you wouldn't believe me. And if you did believe me, you would probably be scared, angry, and hurt."

"So, what, I just lie here in confusion?"

Ethan tried to suppress his smile. He was so happy to hear her sassy attitude he could barely keep his hands off her. As it was, he sneaked his fingers into hers. She glanced down at the intimacy. She didn't pull away, nor did she contribute to the grip. "You have memory loss. You're missing quite a bit, actually."

Cori wrinkled her brow. "How much?"

"That answer might be a little frightening. Rest assured, Cleos is going to give you back your memories." Her eyes moved to the observation window. Ethan looked over and saw Cleos standing outside with the guards. He could see the top of Belus's head in the mix. "It may take a while, but he will put everything right."

"No." Cori gripped his hand and pulled it across to enclose it with her other hand. "Don't let him near me. He's a vampire."

Ethan wondered how long it had taken for Cori to trust Cleos. He wondered at what point her need for consolation had overridden her fear. "He's a photophobe, but he doesn't drink blood. He won't hurt you. Trust me."

Cori scoffed. "Yeah, like I haven't heard that before."

Ethan frowned, thinking about the Mezula incident, which was not as far back in her memories as it was his. He scooted closer to her on the bed. She released his hand and shifted herself to sit up a little. "Cori, many things have changed since what you remember. Cleos is the only one who can clear and restore your mind. You have to let him work with you." Ethan couldn't believe he was begging Cori to let Cleos interact with her.

Her eyes flickered over his, trailing down his body. A body that, in her mind, was unfamiliar. "You look so different."

"Yes, I am different, much different from you remember. I'm Danato's successor. I'm the acting warden here."

Cori smiled. "Already? Good for you."

He smiled. "Thank you. I had some pretty tough competition to get the job." She tipped an eyebrow, looking for the meaning behind that, but all he could do was lean in and brush the back of his fingers along her cheek. Her smile faded, but her eyes stayed locked on his. He could hear the heart rate monitor pick up a few beats as he inched closer to her for a kiss.

Her lips parted, but at the last second, she drew her face away. "I... can't. I'm sorry, Ethan. I'm with Vince now."

As disappointed as he was to miss out on those sweet lips, he was glad she pulled away. If she was loyal to Vince, then she would be loyal to him. He backed away, letting the crook of his smile play through on his lips. "Of course, my apologies." He gripped her left hand. "I would never try to take advantage of a married woman." He kissed her hand.

As he drew back, he could see her staring at the gold rings lining her hands. Her eyes settled on the ring finger where a single diamond was embedded in the gold. He could see her mind trying to formulate a question.

"Cori," he said as he rubbed his thumb along the soft skin of her hand. "I need you to do something for me, sweetness." She looked up, still baffled, but ready to focus on his words. "I need you to let Cleos help you."

"But he—"

"No, Cori." He shook his head and gave her a sympathetic but stern look. "I'm acting on behalf of Danato. Consider my words as important as his. I know you don't trust me right now. I know I've disappointed you in the past, and in your coming future, but I love you and I won't let anything happen to you."

There was no more room to fit stupefied on her face, but her gaping mouth told him she was surprised to hear such a forthcoming expression of sentiment from him. He waved to Cleos while she was still in awe.

He entered the room and brought a chair over to her bedside. She shifted her gaze to him, clamping onto Ethan's hand harder and harder by the second. Cleos reached for her free hand, but she ripped it away, tucking her fingers into a balled fist against her chest.

Cleos looked at him. "I bet you're loving this," he mumbled.

"A good deal, in fact." He smiled broadly at Cleos.

"No matter." Cleos touched her forehead with a swift, gentle tap. "This will be easier if she is unconscious."

"Unconscious!" Cori yelped even as she was overcome by a yawn. "Ethan, what...?" She laid her head back and fell asleep before Ethan could offer her any reassurances.

"Was that necessary?" Ethan asked.

"Necessary, no. Preferable to you getting off on her fear of me, yes."

"Oh, please, like I wasn't owed that payback."

Cleos took Cori's hand. "This may take some time. I would prefer to concentrate alone." When he didn't move, Cleos rolled his eyes. "I can only do better with focus."

"What are you going to put back first?"

"I'm going to remove first, but don't worry, I have to replace her memories chronologically, so she'll get to fall in love with us in the same order as she did before. Within the next few days, her memories will be back in place."

"*Her* memories? Without influence from you?" Ethan stood up, feeling the need to put distance between their bodies.

"I can't influence her like that. All her memories are still in there. I just have to make room for them. There may be a few gaps that I can fill in with what I know of her, but almost everything will be original. I can't influence her emotions regarding those memories. So, if she comes out swinging at you, it wasn't something I did. She has her own mind, her own opinions, and she makes her own decisions. As I am constantly reminded."

Ethan didn't want to leave, but he could hardly argue with Cleos. If he was going to do this, he might as well have the space to do a good job. At any rate, Ethan needed to check on Daniel.

45

"Feck, feck, feck, feck," Daniel continued his monosyllabic rant even as Ethan entered the living room of the house. He was sitting on the couch, holding his chest while Heaton monitored him. Nevia was digging in the icebox.

"Dude!" Heaton jumped over Daniel's outstretched legs and met him at the door. "How is she?"

"Umm." Ethan wasn't sure how to answer, since she had basically lost two years of their life together. "She's well. Tired, confused, with some memory loss, but Cleos is working on that."

Heaton furrowed his brow. "Wait, she's awake?"

"What the feck?" Daniel paused in his rant to fit the sentence in. He twisted like a fish on land to look at Ethan. "Awake and talking? Christ, you got a hard nut of a wife."

"I take it that's rare?" Ethan asked.

"Well..." Heaton glanced back at Daniel. "There's usually residual..." Heaton waved his hand over his chest. "...stuff that interferes with the vocal cords. The transmorphs—"

"She's puked all that up." Ethan walked to the kitchen before Heaton could explain more. "What about you, Daniel?"

"Oh, right," Daniel said, remembering where he left off. "Feck, feck, feck, feck…"

Ethan laughed and helped Nevia get her ice pack put together. "I assume that's a good sign."

"It means the adrenaline shot hasn't worn off yet," Heaton said. "He'll be wired for another half hour tops, and then…" Heaton gave him the thumbs down.

"What's the ice for?" Ethan asked as Nevia took the pack over to Daniel.

"The adrenaline shot goes through the rib cage. It isn't pleasant to begin with, but the aftermath is like being punched in the chest with an iron rod."

"Oh, no more cold," Daniel whined as Nevia placed the ice pack on his chest. He hissed in pain. Ethan wasn't sure if it was the ice that was so soothing or the fact that a female body was in close proximity, but he stopped cussing and relaxed back on the couch.

"We should probably get him upstairs," Heaton said. "He's a bitch to carry when he's unconscious."

"I heard that, you skinny-ass poof," Daniel growled.

"I intended for you to, you crazy-ass dick," Heaton retorted as he headed over to the couch.

Ethan smirked at his former pseudo-married-couple partners and followed Heaton to the living room. They pulled Daniel off the couch and onto his feet.

Ethan considered carrying him by himself, but the image of delivering his male friend to his bedroom honeymoon-style put a damper on his muscular theatrics. Aside from that, there was also the issue of Daniel's malfunctioning motor skills. His arms and legs could still move, but not necessarily in the order or direction he intended.

"Sorry," Daniel apologized when his flailing hand smacked Heaton in the face.

They took a step forward and Daniel's foot kicked Heaton's shin.

"Dude, seriously, don't help!"

"I'm trying to—"

"Yeah, I know. Stop trying. Just go limp. We'll move you." Heaton scolded him.

Ethan snickered at Daniel's pouty face.

"What are you laughing at?" Daniel griped as they manually walked him to the stairs.

"I'm just going to miss you guys. I don't want to have to put Cori in danger just to have you guys back here."

"Aww." Daniel patted his shoulder—or rather, attempted to pat his shoulder; he more or less just hit him in the neck with the back of his hand. "We love you too."

"I'm sure we can find an excuse to stay longer after our drop-offs," Heaton said. "After all, we have a bloodhound in training. We may need her to start practicing on non-transmorphs."

"Damn it, I knew that name was going to stick," Nevia grumbled behind them.

"It just means you're officially part of the group," Ethan placated her.

"Hey, if you want to take on "poof" and "tosser" for a while, I will gladly be the bloodhound," Heaton suggested.

Ethan and Heaton walked, dragged, and carried Daniel up to his room. They placed him on the bed and left Nevia to situate his pillows and apply the ice pack. Ethan closed the door behind them just in case there was a need for privacy.

46

DANIEL'S BELATED "THANK YOU" fell on the closed door to his room. He did his best to lean forward as Nevia fluffed his pillows. The neckline of her white shirt provided a view of her flesh-colored bra as she leaned in to boost his neck. He knew it was a conniving move, considering she was only trying to care for him, but he strained his neck and wrapped his mouth around the mound of breast that was only inches from him.

She wrenched away from him with a gasp. The shocked look on her face made him smile mischievously. "Sorry, I couldn't resist."

"Try." She looked annoyed and unsettled. She searched around for the ice pack.

"Bedside table," Daniel instructed.

She grabbed the pack and scooted next to him. She placed the ice on his chest where a bruise had already started to form. He kept his eyes on her, but she wouldn't look at him. Not for the reasons most women didn't want to look at him, though. Despite the carnage she had just witnessed, she didn't seem to have any qualms about being near him.

"Nevia."

"Jordan," she corrected.

Daniel glanced at the closed door. "Nevia," he drawled with a stern voice. She looked at him. He smiled at her. "You can have another go, if you want."

"What?"

"Me, I'm practically a paraplegic, and will be for a while. Why don't you have another go at me? Take the edge off that desire."

"What desire?"

"You said you couldn't wait to do it again." He winked at her.

"Yeah, with a nice guy."

"Oh, bullshit." He rolled his eyes. "You didn't want a nice guy the first time around, cause you knew exactly what you'd get. A nice proper shag with carbon-copy kisses and barely a chance to get your goal before the clumsy wanker loses his jip. You wanted me because you knew I'd had enough experience to know what the feck I'm doing."

She drew back the ice pack, breaking their physical contact. She looked him over. "You can barely move. How are you going to...?" She paused, trying to find the right words.

"Already ready, love." He smiled, nodding downward.

She glanced down and shied away from the view. She seemed more a virgin now than she had ever before. He wondered how much false bravado she had put into her act the first time.

"I told you I'm not interested in anything more."

"Then this is right up your alley. Come on, Nevia. In a day or two when I'm feeling better, or Heaton's feeling bored, we'll be back in London on a job. Would you rather gamble your time on a good lay at the pubs or have your seconds right now?" Her eyes fluttered between him and the door. "The second time is always better."

She backed away from him, breaking eye contact. She dropped the ice pack on the floor and headed to the door. He wanted to object, but he didn't want to sound like he was begging for her. In reality, that was exactly what he was doing. He couldn't stop thinking about her and her body. He needed another lay to get her out of his system once and for all. Then they could work together without the burden of sexual tension.

When she reached the door, she turned the lock on the handle. He grinned widely as she turned around and started removing her clothes. The annoyed grimace on her face told him she was letting her hormones win out over her logic, and she wasn't happy about it. "This is the last time," she warned sternly.

His smile only widened. "Yes, ma'am. Wait." He lost his smile instantly, and he returned the same steely gaze she was giving him. She paused, holding her bra at a tenuous point between a lingerie commercial and porn. "I want all of you this time." He tried to point her up and down, but the sporadic movement just looked accusatory. "Lips included. No withholding kisses." She narrowed her eyes, trying to overturn his stipulation by withholding her forward movement. "I'm serious, Nevia," he said as firmly as he could without ruining the mood. "Every inch of you is mine this time, or you can just leave."

Her annoyance faded, and he saw the reluctance in her eyes once again. Her hormones were in control, but her mind was still arguing with her. He wondered if she was as concerned about their work relationship as he was. Maybe the intimacy of kissing was too much for her to simply walk away from like she did the last time.

Eventually, her bra fell away, and she removed his pants and underwear. She climbed onto him like he had just beaten her into submission. "Nevia," he whispered before she could proceed with the act in zombification. "Kiss me." She leaned down and touched her lips to his in a small, chaste kiss. "How many boys have you kissed?" She glared at him, more hurt than mad. "You really were a goodie-goodie growing up, weren't you?"

He brought his hand up the best he could to pull her head to him again. He forcefully parted her lips with his tongue. She whined and tried to recoil from the invasive kiss, but he used what strength he had left in his arm to hold her. He withdrew his tongue and smothered her parted lips with a kiss that made her whimper again. He released his arm and slowed his kiss, tickling her lips with his tongue.

He separated from her and let her wet her lips with her own saliva and catch her breath. He looked over her face.

She was still figuring out how she felt about all that. "It's all yours, if you still want it." He nodded downward.

She hesitated for a moment before repositioning to take him in. He let her get into a rhythm before demanding her presence back to his lips. This time she parted her lips readily, allowing her own tongue to leave the confines of her mouth. He sucked on her tongue, admiring how fast she was learning.

His hands were virtually useless for aim, but she helped him position them on her breasts. All he could contribute was a squeeze and a pinch, but she seemed to enjoy it. He drew her back for another kiss, which turned out to be the muffle of her ascent. He joined her at the top before she collapsed against his chest, shaking and panting.

She rolled off to his side, fitting perfectly in the crook of his arm, with her head on his chest. He kissed her again. A soft, tender kiss that was barely a punctuation for an act that had already ended in exclamation points.

After her breathing slowed, he sensed the tension in her muscles. She was ready to leave him. "Stay," he whispered just as her arm pushed her up. She stopped and looked at him. It was the same reluctance he had seen before the event. As unenthusiastic as she'd been then, she'd still conceded to his wishes. He didn't doubt this would be the same. He was only asking for what she already wanted, but wouldn't allow herself. "Just until I pass out, please."

She swallowed hard, searching the room for the objection she wanted to give. "Don't you think Heaton will suspect something is up if I stay?"

"I don't care what he thinks. I like the way you feel against me. I want to hold you as long as I can." He was using the soft, flirtatious voice that he usually used to get women into bed with him. He had never once used it to *keep* a woman in his bed. He was usually the one counting the seconds until he bolted.

"Daniel, I don't want things to get confusing."

"A few more minutes in my arms isn't going to muddy things any more than we already have." He leaned in and kissed her again. "You do what you think is best. I don't have the strength left to fight you on it, but I want you to stay with me until I pass out, which won't be long now."

He wasn't sure why he was fighting so hard to keep her by his side. He did like the feel of her next to him. That wasn't a lie, but what difference did it make? He had maybe five minutes of consciousness left.

She surrendered back to his chest, as he'd suspected she would if he asked nicely enough. He was happy with the victory, but once again, he wondered why. Was he really trying to bait her into liking him just so he could push her away? He hoped he wasn't that much of an asshole.

47

CORI SAT UP IN her bed, watching her saline drip. She was a little nauseated, and a lot confused. She could tell by the way everyone looked that some time had passed since she had left the prison with Vince. Since Cleos had left, she was remembering chunks about her life that she had forgotten.

She knew Vince was gone, and she remembered mourning him, but the details of his death were still fuzzy. She knew Ethan had mentioned her being married, but she didn't know to whom. Her logical assumption was that she was married to him, but she didn't remember falling in love with him, much less committing to him.

For the time being, everyone was being vague about everything. Even Belus wouldn't give her a straight answer. She wasn't sure how long it would take to get her memory back, but she knew it was going to be too long. She was already sick of being cramped up in the narrow hospital bed.

A commotion in the next room got her attention. Through the observation windows, she could see Ethan and a black man with spunky short dreadlocks carrying a third man into the adjacent room. A petite brunette followed behind them.

They had a brief discussion before Ethan shook hands with and hugged the black man. The woman offered her hand as well, but Ethan pushed it aside and picked her up in an all-consuming hug. He set her down and drew her back by her shoulders, smiling warmly at her. *Thank you,* Cori read from his lips. The woman smiled back shyly and nodded.

They said goodbye again, and the two strangers left the room. As they passed by the hall observation windows, Cori glanced over at them. They both did the same, giving her warm smiles and nods, but neither seemed to be exceptionally interested in her. At least she knew who she didn't know.

When she looked back at the adjacent room, she saw Ethan smiling at her. He slipped through the same hallway as the others and entered her room. "Good morning, sweetness." He came over and sat down beside her without any trepidation. He was definitely different from the Ethan she had left behind.

"Hi." She smiled, infected by his broad smirk.

"How goes the blank slate?" He gently tapped her forehead. "What are we up to?"

"Why don't you fill me in on the highlights and I'll tell you if I'm there?"

He clicked his tongue and shook his head. "Nope, Cleos said it's best to let your brain come to terms with things in the proper order. Too many details out of order and you might get your own timeline crossed."

"We certainly wouldn't want that," she admitted.

"Besides," he leaned forward and took her hand, "I'm kind of having fun with this." She drew her hand away from him slowly. She didn't want to appear rude. "Sorry, I forgot about Vince."

"I know Vince is dead."

His smile faded instantly. "Oh Cori, I'm so sorry. I didn't know you had gotten back those memories."

"I know he's been dead for a while now. I feel that time has passed since then, but I just don't have anything to fill in the blanks."

He repositioned himself nearer to her. She could sense his comfort at being close to her. She only wished she felt the same. "You will," he said.

She shook her head, forgetting what he was answering. "What?"

"You will be able to fill in those blanks. We're only days away. Believe me..." He cupped her shoulder, letting his thumb trace her collarbone. "...I want you to remember as much as you do."

His smile faded, and he looked at her with an open desire she was unfamiliar with from him. She could tell he wanted to kiss her, but she had never kissed him before. She didn't know what it meant to him, so she didn't want to pull away and hurt his feelings. She looked down at her hands abruptly, ending the gaze.

"I understand," she said. "I'll just let things happen naturally." She looked back up at him. "In their own time," she added.

His smile returned. "No problem, I've gotten used to waiting for you." She thought he was taking a shot at her. He leaned over and kissed her forehead. He moved his face beside hers, just barely brushing his cheek against hers. He spoke in a low voice close enough to her ear to feel his breath. "I'm a *very* patient man."

She was thankful the nurses had shut off her heart rate monitor, because she could feel it pounding in her ears. She knew he was toying with her. Clearly they were something to each other, and he was simply getting a kick out of making her squirm with his advances.

He pulled back and looked her over with more knowledge of her than she had of him. She felt her head shake, although no question had been asked to require it. "Who's your guest in the bed next door?"

He looked back as if he couldn't remember who it was himself. "Just a friend. I don't think you will remember him. I worked with him for a short time. He's the one who saved you. Well, it was a team effort, of course, but he actually extracted you from the transmorph."

Cori had gotten the rough version of her predicament from Belus, but she didn't know that someone specific had saved her. "What's wrong with him?"

"Nothing really. His partners got a call for a job. They are going to leave him here for a few days while they tend to it. He's been out since yesterday, so we decided to move him here so the nurses can watch him and I can get back to work. I expect he'll wake up in the next few hours."

"That's good," she said.

"Do you want me to come by later, after Cleos is done?" He was asking, but she was certain that he would, either way.

"Yeah, sure."

He paused again, looking her over. This time, however, his hunger was gone. He looked sad. "I wish you knew how happy I am to have you back. Even with all your memories back, I don't think you could begin to fathom how important you are to me. Maybe that's why..." He stopped mid-sentence and shook his head. He huffed an exhale. "Anyway, time for all that later. I'll see you tonight. I love you." He paused a half beat, as if he expected her to say it back. She could tell it was part of his standard goodbye. Had he even thought about it, he may not have said it.

"Thank you for your patience," she said, hoping that was enough sentiment for him to leave with. He nodded and left the room. He watched her through the window as he went on his way down the hall. Cori looked back at the adjacent room. She couldn't see his friend from her bed, but she imagined no one would mind if she took a closer look.

48

Daniel woke in the infirmary. He could smell the repugnant smell of sterility even before he fully comprehended where he was. He opened his eyes to the white sheets of an institution far too generous with bleach. He groaned, wishing that headaches were not an inevitable side effect of a job well done. "Feck you, brain."

He rolled over. His body didn't particularly hurt, nor was it stiff, but for some reason, after the excessive use of his power, it felt numb, like he had fried all his nerve endings. Moving wasn't difficult, but moving in the direction he intended was. He had learned from past experiences, not to keep anything breakable near him during his recovery.

He rolled himself over and looked at his surroundings. He was in the infirmary and to his surprise, Cori was sitting on a chair with her legs tucked against her chest, watching him. Her face still looked in dire need of a good meal, but her tissue looked healthy. Her blue patient gown and the IV hubs in her forearms told him she hadn't been released yet.

"Cori?" he said, trying to sit up, but he couldn't quite find purchase for his hands. "What are you doing here? You need rest."

Cori moved from her perch and came to his aid. Her bare feet slapped against the clean, glossy white floor as she did. She reached behind him and bolstered his pillows so he could sit upright. He scooted back on the pile. He panted from the tiny movement.

He leaned his head back on the pile and took in a few breaths. He felt Cori's weight sit down next to him. He raised his head and looked her over. "You're moving pretty good for being in a transmorph for six weeks."

"So I'm told," she said, looking him over. Her eyes settled on his, but quickly withdrew.

"Oh." He searched his face. "My glasses, are they nearby?"

She reached over to the side table and retrieved his glasses. He put them on and shoved them high on his nose. "How much do you remember?" he asked, seeing the lost look in her eyes.

"I'm missing the majority of the last two years, give or take."

"Damn. Is Cleos making any progress?"

"I think so." She shrugged. "I at least feel like me. Just me without a freaking clue of what's going on."

"Well, you're very fortunate to be friends with that mind-sucker. If it weren't for him, you might have had to consult your other selves before you wiped your arse."

He could tell from the look on her face that she didn't fully understand that statement, but she didn't ask any questions.

"Ethan says I owe you my life."

"No." He shook his head. "You don't owe me anything."

"You saved me, didn't you?"

"Well, yeah, but that's just what I do." She cocked a brow, seemingly trying to decide how she should respond to his forceful humility. "Giving you back to Ethan was reward enough." He laughed, finding amusement in the turn of tables: him in the bed, this time trying to give her back to Ethan, instead of keeping him from her.

"What?"

"You really have no idea who I am, do you?"

"Should I? Were we friends?"

He laughed again. "No, actually you hate me." He couldn't give up his smile, even though her expression changed to suspicious analysis. She examined his face carefully, as if the details there would explain his claim. He laughed again. "I'm sorry, if you knew our history, you... you wouldn't be here." He continued to chuckle, even though she wasn't joining in his amusement.

"Why do I hate you? What did you do?"

He calmed himself again. He remembered the conversation he'd had with Ethan right before he released Cori. He remembered how much pain his friend was in, trying to keep his marriage vows a priority when his wife was not doing the same. He lost his urge to laugh, along with his smile.

"A while back, you and Ethan were estranged. He was mad for you, but you had just lost someone." He paused to see if any of this rang a bell. She nodded, giving him permission to continue. "You were causing him a lot of pain with your dithering. I thought you were a bad choice for him. I talked him out of seeing you at a very crucial time. You were especially displeased to see me instead of him."

"And I *hate* you for that?"

"Well." He smiled. "I'm a hard man to like on first impression. Maybe I'll do better this time around."

She nodded. "If we hate each other and you don't want me with Ethan, why did you save me?"

"Whoa, whoa. First off, I don't hate you. You hate me on principle of association. Second, I don't let people die just because I disagree with their choice of lover."

Cori looked down at her hand, spinning the diamond ring that adorned her ring finger. She looked up suddenly. "What's your name?"

"Daniel McGrath, bounty hunter by trade, lover by hobby, and asshole by nature."

To his surprise, she grinned at him. "You want to make a better first impression? How about you answer a few more questions about my current history?"

He grimaced, wondering if he had made a grave mistake by talking so frankly with her. "Oh, feck, they've been keeping this all from you, haven't they?"

Cori moved up to a better vantage point. He pushed his glasses up again. "Don't you want to get on my good side?" She smiled coyly; a smile he was sure she wouldn't be using if she had even half her memories back.

"Not really. Ethan will kick my ass from here to Nova Scotia if he finds out I'm talking to you at all."

She looked him over. "Really? You're like twice his size."

Daniel laughed heartily. "I'm starting to like this version of you, but yes, Ethan can kick my ass, and my cock is big enough to not mind saying so."

Cori rolled her eyes. "I just need a few details, mainly why I am still here."

"You're lucky to be walking and talking, let alone—"

"No, why am I still in this prison? I was gone. Why did I come back?"

Daniel opened his mouth, hoping to find the answer somewhere in his memory of conversations with Ethan. "I don't really know that. I do know that you were competing with Ethan for warden."

"What?" Her face wrinkled in disgust. "Why in flippin' hell would I do that?"

Daniel shrugged. "I suppose you had your reasons at the time. From what I understand, you almost got the job.

Ethan is the successor to Danato, and you are his second, Belus's successor."

"No shit?" Cori seemed to envision that idea. He could tell it was a boost to her pride. "Well, wonders never cease. Pleased to meet *me*."

"Hey, you mind answering a question for me, if you know?"

"Sure."

"Why am *I* here?" he said, motioning to the room, which was the extent of his arm movements, as far as specification went.

"Oh," she said. "They brought you in this morning. Your partners left."

"What?" he squawked.

"They got a job or something. They'll be back in a few days to get you."

"Oh, right. One long nap, and I get dumped off at the sitters."

"You've been out for 24 hours."

"Fine, one partial coma, whatever." He pouted.

"Why did you need to sleep so long, anyway? What did you do to get me out?"

"I thought you wanted a good first impression of me." She leaned back away from him. "I'll let Ethan translate that one for you."

She nodded, looking back at the ring on her hand. "Daniel, are Ethan and I married?"

"Oh, feck girl, you really don't remember anything about you two, do you?"

"No."

"Well, let me settle this brain drain for you right now. You are head to toe in love with each other." Her eyes widened in disbelief. "Trust me. I was at the wedding two months ago."

"We've only been married two months?"

"Give or take."

"I've been in a transmorph for six weeks?"

"Yup, it was a nice wedding, but the honeymoon kind of sucked."

49

ETHAN ARRIVED AT THE infirmary a little earlier than he'd planned. He looked through the observation window and saw Cleos still inside with Cori. He was done with his work as near as Ethan could tell. He was sitting with her, talking. She had a small smile on her face that grew as he spoke.

He still didn't understand it. He didn't understand why she'd fought so hard to remain a part of Cleos's life even after she had read his file. She seemed almost desperate to find the good in him. Maybe he had misinterpreted their relationship the whole time. Maybe it wasn't as complex as Cleos made it out to be.

Cleos glanced up and saw him through the window. He took Cori's hand and kissed the back of it before standing up. She settled back into her pillows and closed her eyes. The photophobe waited for her to settle before leaving the room.

Ethan turned to him as he came out. He tried to glare at him, but he knew he wasn't quite managing it. He was hurting too much. "How is she?"

"She's regaining her memories exponentially," Cleos said, cupping his hands in front of him. Belus had given Cleos the freedom to see Cori without handcuffs. Ethan had agreed, but only because he didn't want to remind Cori that Cleos was a criminal every time he saw her. "I expect with or without my help, she will start to piece together her own memories."

"She doesn't need to see you again?"

Cleos shrugged. "Maybe once more, but of course that depends on her, doesn't it? Always has." Cleos brushed past him through the narrow hallway.

"Are you in love with her?" Ethan asked, looking in on his wife.

Cleos halted and turned back. "Cori and I are much more than lovers could ever be. I know her better than anyone."

"That doesn't answer my question," Ethan said, still not looking at him.

"Are you asking if I want to fuck her?" Ethan felt his eye twitch at the thought of it. Cleos paused a long moment before answering. "No."

Ethan looked at him then, surprised that he'd said as much.

"I care a good deal for Cori." Cleos approached him and looked through the window at her. "But no, I never have, nor will I ever pursue her physically. I really have nothing to offer her, do I? Prison puts a damper on love, especially when one is guilty of what he is imprisoned for."

Ethan caught Cleos's eye before he walked away again. The usual spiteful sneer was no longer on his face. "Is she in love with you?"

He stopped again. "Are you sure you don't mean the latter question as well?"

"Is she in love with you?" Ethan asked again, refusing to phrase it any other way.

Cleos thought for a moment. "I am a stray dog to Cori. Yes, she loves me. Yes, she will feed and care for me, but part of her knows that I am a wild animal, and that I am dangerous. She pretends not to notice my big bad wolf side, but she knows it's there. That is why I will always be a stray to her. She'll never take me in completely." Cleos leaned against the wall. "So, to answer your question, no, she doesn't desire me in any other way than friendship. She clings to me for many reasons. Reasons that you certainly should have investigated before you tried to separate her from me."

"What do you mean?" Ethan asked grudgingly.

"You know how attached Cori was to that damn tin ring Danato crushed. It was a Cracker Jack prize. She turned to me, a flesh-and-blood being, for advice, friendship, and support when you weren't around. Imagine how important that attachment was to her."

Ethan closed his eyes and mouthed a curse. He knew Cleos was right. Cori had so many crutches in her life. He'd assumed that when they got married, she would simply be able to rely on him, but she couldn't, not when she was still leaning on Cleos.

"The strange thing is," Cleos continued, "if she had discovered my past on her own, she actually may have recoiled from me. You forcing her to read it put her in a defensive state. That's why she wanted to know why I did it. She needed so desperately to redeem me in her eyes so she didn't lose both ends of her stability in this place."

"Why didn't you tell her? She begged you."

Cleos's eyes flared with a mixture of shock and hatred. "My sins, my sentence."

"You could have lied to her; told her it was an accident."

"It wasn't," Cleos stated without remorse.

Ethan let the subject drop. He had no intention of inciting Cleos's anger the way Cori had with her own objections to his silence. "You know, you always say you know her better than anyone."

"That's true."

"She's never told you one thing about herself, though."

"She doesn't have to."

"She doesn't get to." Ethan stared him down. "I may not know as much about her as you, but what I do know, she has graced me with on her own terms." Ethan looked back at Cori. "She also knows me. She didn't have to read about me in a manila folder. I told her my story of my own free will."

"Your point?" Cleos asked with measurable disdain.

"My point is I love her. I don't want her running to you every time she has a problem. I want her to come to me, her husband."

"Are you asking me to push her away?"

"The last time I tried to keep her away from you, I ended up pushing her right to you. I won't make that mistake again."

Cleos nodded. "I've seen how much you love her. I baited you with it to torment you with guilt. I can't promise that I can give up Cori. I am a gentleman, and I do respect your vows, but prison is a lonely place. I will, however, promise to advise her to seek you out when she is in need of solace or resolution."

Ethan nodded. "I'll inform Danato of your discovery of and assistance with this ordeal. I can't guarantee that he will approve of you walking freely in the halls, but he may not revoke Cori's access to you."

Cleos nodded. "We seem to have discovered a middle ground."

"Stranger things have happened." Ethan shrugged.

"You'll forgive me if I pass on the solidifying handshake."

"I'd prefer it, actually."

50

CORI COULD ALMOST FEEL the connections being made in her brain. She still didn't remember marrying Ethan, or the events that led to her becoming the warden's second, but she did remember the confusing emotions she'd felt for Ethan upon returning to the prison. She remembered the attraction she'd felt guilty about, and the sorrow demon that pressed her to avoid it.

She also remembered Cleos. She remembered asking him for help to study. She wasn't sure what had prompted her to trust him, but who better to ask about the prison than a mind-reader? The relationship didn't quite warrant the title of friend, but she assumed she might still be missing a few more pieces.

She heard the door open, and she opened her eyes. Ethan strolled in and stopped at the foot of her cot. She looked over the taut muscles that furnished his figure. He was tall and lean, with bulging biceps and a wide torso, but she still found it hard to believe that he contained the strength that Daniel had implied. Nevertheless, he was just as appealing as her memories were telling her. She had thought it impossible to be married to him before, but she was quickly seeing how her attraction might have turned to love.

She and Ethan had been through so much. Their friendship was important to her. She hated the way she had left things with him when she ran off with Vince. Apparently, she'd had a chance to make up for it.

"You want to get out of here?" Ethan asked, leaning his hands on the railing at the foot of her bed.

"God yes. Where?"

"Home."

Ethan rustled up a pair of jeans and a t-shirt that she could wear back to the house. Her coat was still in the locker where she had left it at some point prior. By the time she had a chance to wonder why she stayed at a prison at the edge of the arctic, she was pushing through the door to Danato's home.

It was surreal to see it again. She knew it had been only weeks since her body had left the place, but it still felt like months. Still further stretching her reality was that she had been in this home for a year longer than she could remember.

The fireplace was ablaze, as it often was when the house was pleased. In addition to the firelight from the hearth, was the light from the candlelight dinner on the dining room table. Ethan slipped her coat off her shoulders and hung it for her.

She looked over the table that was set for two. Danato was usually the third at the head of the table, but he was gone. Ethan hadn't really specified where, and she presumed he didn't know. He pulled out a chair for her. She smiled and took her place at the table.

He rushed off to the kitchen and fetched a bottle of wine. Once he had poured for both of them, he went back to the kitchen for the food. It was only spaghetti, but she knew it was probably one of his more reliable meals. He scooped the premixed sauce and noodles onto her plate and moved to his.

"Ethan," she said, biting her lower lip. "I haven't eaten a decent amount of food in six weeks, aside from the grilled cheese and oatmeal at the infirmary."

He smiled and returned with two more scoops of spaghetti for her. When he finally sat down, he raised a toast to her return to civilization. She wasn't sure a prison in the Kola Peninsula counted as civilization, but she clinked his glass anyway.

After she'd dug into her spaghetti like a war refugee, she realized he had hardly eaten anything. He was sitting back watching her, sipping his wine with a strange smile on his face. At that moment, she realized how vacant their conversation had been.

She wiped the sauce from her chin. "I'm sorry, I'm just so hungry."

"Please don't stop," he said, swirling his wine. "I'm enjoying the view."

"You mean you enjoy watching me slobber tomato sauce all over my chin?"

"I enjoy watching you enjoy."

She couldn't quite place his expression. It was as much carnivorous as it was peaceful. "I better stop there." She pushed her plate away and took a sip of her wine. "I don't want to go to bed on a full stomach."

A hint of a smile crossed his lips before he got up to clear the table. "Give me a moment, and I'll show you to your room."

She waited patiently, sipping her wine. She wasn't sure he meant *her* room, since they were married and likely shared a room, but she tried not to think about it. She tried not to think at all. There were far too many questions running through her mind. None of which deserved to be answered after such an effort of seduction was put in place for her benefit.

"Ready?" Ethan presented his hand to her. She attempted to drink down the last of her wine, which was unusually sweet and very palatable. "You can take that with you. The house won't mind. Just try not to spill." He winked at her as she placed her hand in his.

He led her upstairs, letting their hands sway between them as they ascended. He ushered her into their room. As she entered, he flipped the light switch on. It looked like a penthouse hotel. The pillows on the couch in the center of the room were plush and colorful. The wall hangings were the proper balance of modern and attractive.

A few wooden end tables and a large buffet-style piece lining the wall where they entered gave the room a homey warmth. Off to the right was a set of parlor doors. Sheer curtains hung behind them, allowing an opaque view into the bedroom. She turned back to Ethan. "This is my room?"

He nodded. "This is our apartment. The house is still deciding on a motif, but this is the best I've seen so far."

She strolled over to the parlor doors and looked in on the king-sized bed with plush white pillows. She could feel Ethan behind her. He reached around her and pushed open the doors. She took a step forward, trying not to get too close to the bed. The side table lamps provided tall golden columns of light. Once again, the warm wood of the furniture offset the sterile cold of the white pillows and metallic wall hangings.

She turned around abruptly. Ethan was right behind her. He looked down at her, trying to discern her sudden change of direction. "This is our bedroom?" she asked, keeping her eyes downcast.

"Yes." He tipped her chin up to look at him. "This is where I make love to you."

Her eyes widened, and she took a step away from him. She was still holding her wineglass. She stared at it as if it might somehow make everything make sense. She downed the contents.

Maybe it would.

"Ethan." Her voice caught in her throat. He took the wineglass from her and placed it on a dresser off to one side. She suddenly felt naked without anything to hold him back. She was attracted to him, but without the memories leading to this life, she had no idea how to proceed. "I don't know if I can do this."

His hand caressed her cheek before pushing back into her hair. She took in a deep breath as he leaned down to her. She waited for his lips, but they didn't come. "I'm very patient with you, Cori," he whispered in her ear. "I've always allowed you the time you need to come to me. In life and in this room, I've never pushed you to do more than you want to." He pulled her face to look at him again. "I know every inch of your body. I know your desires and your fears." He let his hands fall from her face and slide down to her waist. "Wouldn't you like a man that knows you so well, to make love to you for the first time?"

She could feel the heat from him, begging for her. She knew if she said no, he would back away and release her from any obligation to him. He would probably even sleep in another room, so she didn't have to be uncomfortable.

"Yes," she said even before she was sure.

He smiled and wrapped his arms around her waist. Without a hint of strain, he lifted her up above him and brought her down to kiss him. He slid her down through the kiss and held her tight while he got his fill of her lips.

He backed her to the bed and scooped her up to lie on it. He crawled on with her and lay down over her. She could feel his urgency to be inside her, but he was as patient as he claimed. He undressed her slowly, caressing her shoulders, suckling her breasts, and nibbling his way down her body until her yearnings were alleviated.

She gripped at the bedsheets, in awe of his ability to induce such powerful pleasure in her body. She had no memory of him as a lover, but every nuance of his lovemaking suggested that he had many memories of being her lover.

When he was at last satisfied that her longings were mollified, he crawled onto her and looked into her eyes as he found his own pleasure within her. His own ascent was matched with yet another of hers, and when he was spent, he laid his forehead against her chest. She felt his breath hot on her breast as he panted. He whispered, "I love you," so softly that she wasn't sure he intended her to hear it.

"I love you too," she responded. She wasn't sure that was how she felt, but she could hardly leave him in ecstasy's embrace without the sentiment. Even if she didn't love him at that exact moment, she knew it was only a matter of time before she did mean it.

51

THERE WAS PROBABLY SOME moral rule that dictated you shouldn't sleep with your wife when she is recovering from amnesia. Ethan wasn't sure it would apply in this case, but he was sure that it was probably wrong to take advantage of her ignorance.

It was only a matter of time before she remembered everything that had happened. The arguing would start again. She would refuse to give up Cleos and carry on her pseudo-emotional affair with him.

He could tolerate arguing. He could endure her inability to voice even the simplest of emotions. But Ethan couldn't abide her, seeking Cleos out for help over him.

It was too painful to be the third wheel in his own marriage. He had to stop pretending that it was working. He had to let her go.

Ethan looked across the bed at Cori. She was sound asleep beside him. A blissful smile was still peeking through her lips. His eyes watered, feeling the burden of the impending battle.

God damn it if he didn't love her, though. Why did it always have to be so fucking hard? Why couldn't she just trust him? Why couldn't he be the only man she needed?

He rolled over so he couldn't see her. He didn't want to look at her anymore.

52

"ARE YOU SURE YOU can travel alone?" Ethan asked as he walked Daniel to the docks.

"Yes." Daniel's foot flopped under him as he walked. He made a concerted effort to plant his foot and continue walking. "Why do you ask?"

"I'm sure Heaton will be back in another day or two," Ethan said, resisting the urge to help Daniel walk.

"I can heal just as well at home. Besides, you know how I hate missing the action."

"Are you sure you aren't just in a hurry to see Jordan again?" Ethan asked, hoping to rile his friend.

Daniel scoffed. "She's a mite more pleasing to look at than you, so yes." Daniel leaned on the door to the docks. "You don't have to wait with me. I know you're anxious to get back to her. How's the memory coming?"

"She's nearly back. She at least remembers everything up to the wedding. It's only a matter of time before she remembers everything else."

"All the more reason for me to get out of here. You don't need me underfoot for that. Have you made any decisions?" Ethan took in a deep breath and let it out slowly. Daniel chucked him on the shoulder. "Maybe she'll surprise you."

Ethan said his goodbyes and left Daniel to wait for his pick-up. He *was* eager to get back to the house, as Daniel had surmised. He hadn't had much of a honeymoon with Cori, but the last two days had been rich with doting and intimacy. He was going to enjoy every last bit of it while he still could.

When he got back to the house, he found Cori sitting on the couch. The fire had deadened to embers and he could smell meat burning in the skillet on the stove. "Cori, supper." He moved into the kitchen and pushed the skillet off the heat, and shut it off. They might have been good hamburgers when they started, but now they were charcoal briquettes. "What, did you fall asleep?"

Cori came over to the island slowly. In her hand was a manila folder. *The* manila folder. He could see the anger and hurt in her eyes. She remembered. She remembered all of it.

For a moment, he just looked at her, begging his mouth to say something that would make it all go away. Something to make her understand how much he didn't want to have this argument again.

She slammed the folder down on the island. He shifted back to lean against the sink and crossed his arms. He could see the rage fighting through the pain on her face. Eventually, the anger would win.

Just as he was about to formulate a response, she backed away and went to the coat rack. He uncrossed his arms and went after her. "Where are you going?"

"Where do you think?" She grabbed her coat, but he ripped it away from her.

"Don't do this!" He clenched his teeth. "Don't go to him!"

"I have to. I have to get an explanation."

"He won't give it to you. He's already refused you once." She yanked her coat back from him and she slipped it on. She opened the door, and he pushed it closed again. She glared at him. "Please, Cori! Please don't walk out on me! I can't take it again!"

"You should have thought about that before you forced me to read that file the first time." She ripped the door open and pushed past him, leaving him once again with a question in his mind and an answer that was becoming progressively more obvious.

$$53$$

B Y THE TIME CORI made it to Cleos's cell, she remembered his refusal to answer her questions. It only fueled her rage. She slid to a stop in front of his plexi-glass home, and slammed her palms into the wall before pushing the button on his intercom.

Cleos peeked over the book that he was reading on his bed. As he lowered it, she could see his annoyance. He calmly put the book down and came to the glass. "You remember?"

"Everything!"

"Then you know I won't tell you."

She smacked her hands on the plexi-glass again. When that didn't give her the release she wanted, she kicked and smacked it a few more times before leaning over and screaming at her knees. She stayed bent over and cried. She found some release in that.

When she came back up, she leaned her hands on the window and rested her forehead between them. "I need to know."

"You need to let it go." Cleos leaned on the glass, lowering his face to look into her eyes. "Does Ethan know you remember?"

"Yes, we fought. Again."

Cleos stood straight again. "Go home, Cori. It's important."

Cori stood up as well. "I need to settle this with you."

"No," Cleos scolded. "You need to settle things with your husband."

Cori narrowed her eyes. "This has nothing to do with him." She gestured between them.

"This," he gestured emphatically between them as well, "has everything to do with him! Do you really think I can tell you something to make you feel better about what I am? I've been feeding off you every time you've seen me, without exception. Yet, even now, knowing that truth, you are here. Why? Why are you here?"

"You're my friend."

"I'm a prisoner, Cori! The only thing between us is this glass." He slammed his palms against the glass.

Cori stepped away. "You know that's not true. Why are you saying this? Has Ethan threatened you to stop seeing me?"

Cleos shook his head. His lips pursed in disgust. "No. He said he won't interfere with you seeing me again, because he knows you'll just do what you want, anyway."

"Good, at least he's figured that out."

"That's *not* good!" Cleos circled, attempting to walk away, but he whipped back to the glass again. "I know you."

"Blah, blah, blah, would you get a new freaking line?"

"I know you love Ethan. I know *how much* you love Ethan. So much that it scares you."

"I married him, didn't I? It doesn't take a psychic to figure that out."

"Yes, but you still keep coming back to me. Even after fatherly Danato expressed his sincere concerns, you came back to me. Even after your husband asked you to read my file, you refused. After you read it, you are here begging me for a reason not to hate me."

"I know all that. I was there the first time around. What is your point?"

"You're scared of losing me, because you're scared of losing him."

Cori shook her head, trying to figure out his rationale. "I don't follow you."

"Cori, I'm always going to be here. I'm always going to be in this cell. I could beg you not to see me, but in the end, I am just an elevator away from you every minute of every day." He pushed his hand through the pass-way. She wavered a moment before she placed her hand in his. "Your dad left. Your mom and aunt died. Vince died. All you have is Ethan, but he has left you before. He could do it again, and that scares the crap out of you. You keep trying to hang onto me, so if things go south with Ethan, you can still have me to pick up the pieces."

Cori shook her head, but she realized what he was saying was probably true. "Why are you saying this?"

Cleos squeezed her hand. "I care for you." She met his eyes. "If you can accept my past, I will let you be my friend, but you can't keep coming to me to fix your problems. You've hurt him too much. What you're doing right now... is making your greatest fear come to fruition."

"What do you mean?" She frowned.

Cleos rubbed his thumb along her hand. "He begged you not to leave."

"Ethan's mad. How mad?"

"No Cori, Ethan is not mad. He is very, *very* sad. He was already contemplating what to do if you wouldn't give me up and you just walked out on him for the second time in your short marriage, prioritizing your relationship with me over him."

She shook her head vigorously. "That's not what I'm doing. You're my friend..."

"And he is your husband. As much as I want to keep your company, I want you to be happy more."

"What is he going to do?"

"Cori." He squeezed her hand so tightly it hurt, but she didn't pull away. "You need to go home to your husband. You need to make him understand how much you love him before he leaves you."

Cori couldn't believe what she was hearing. She thought Ethan was angry about her leaving, but he wasn't. He was hurt. He had been begging her to stay, so he didn't have to make the decision of leaving her to protect himself.

Her hand slipped from Cleos's as she backed away. She looked back at him, but he nodded for her to go. She bolted to the elevator.

She ran from the prison, not bothering to zip up her coat. By the time she flung open the house door, she was panting. She had managed to keep her tears in check thus far, but when she saw Ethan leaning against the island with a cup of coffee, she nearly lost control. She opened her mouth to begin her unabashed groveling.

"Cori!" Danato exclaimed.

She looked to her left and saw Danato leaning on the back of the couch with his own coffee. "Danato." She laughed, losing a few tears as she did. "You're back... early."

"Yes, I missed my girl too much." He smiled warmly and extended his arm to solicit a hug.

"I'm so glad you're back." She was glad to see him, but she wished he'd come an hour or two later. She rushed over to him and buried herself in his embrace. Even with one arm devoted to his coffee, he lifted her up off the floor for an encompassing bear hug that bordered on painful. She loved it, though. "I missed you so much," she mumbled into his chest.

He set her down and pulled her back to look over her face. She could never hide her tears from him. His sympathetic gaze coaxed several more drops to slide down her cheeks. "Why so sad, sweetheart?"

"I've just been through so much the past weeks. I just want it to be over."

"Belus and Ethan gave me the rough draft. I'm so sorry I couldn't be here to help you, but it looks like Ethan has done his job well."

Cori looked back at Ethan. His eyes stayed on Danato as he spoke. "It was really Daniel who did the hard part. You never mentioned his power."

Danato shrugged. "Why do you think you ended up on his team?" Ethan cocked an eyebrow. "You don't think I was going to let Sophie sign you up with a bunch of amateurs who couldn't protect you?"

Ethan's mouth crooked into a smile as he took another sip of coffee. "You never cease to surprise me, Danato."

"I don't plan to stop." Danato turned his attention back to Cori. "How are you feeling?" He pushed back her hair. She lost a few more tears, which he dried with his forefinger. He glanced back at Ethan as if he was detecting the tension in the room. "Is everything okay here?"

Cori nodded, but she couldn't keep her tears in check any longer.

"Danato," Ethan said before Cori could give an explanation for her emotional display. "I think you should know Cleos was the one who brought Cori's abduction to our attention." Ethan's voice was diplomatic, as if he was dictating to his army sergeant. "Neither Belus nor myself observed the subtle changes in her behavior. If it weren't for him, she wouldn't be here. Also, he was able to remove the memories of the other transmorphs so her mind didn't fracture."

"And you're telling me this because...?" Danato asked with a measured tone.

"Cori is aware of Cleos's crimes, and she is not opposed to being around him. Given his contributions to her safety, and the friendship I know they share—" Cori looked back at Ethan, but he didn't acknowledge that she was in the room, "—I don't see any reason to prevent them from seeing each other as you had previously requested." He sipped his coffee as if he was discussing business at the water cooler and not deciding the fate of their relationship.

"You know what my concerns are?" Danato asked. At first, she thought he was saying it to Ethan, but when Ethan finally looked at her, he nodded toward Danato. She looked up at his disciplining face. "You understand why I asked Ethan to keep you away from him?" Cori backed away, so she wasn't straining her neck to look up at him. She wanted to say something, but it wasn't meant for Danato. She was shaking her head. "Cleos is a self-admitted addict..."

"No." She started to cry again. She couldn't stop shaking her head.

"You have to understand, sweetheart." Danato stood to move to her.

She waved her hands. "I know. I know. I can't lose him."

Danato huffed. "Well, apparently Ethan is advising otherwise. You may not lose Cleos after all."

"No!" Cori looked back at Ethan. "You!" He looked at her, but didn't show her any sympathy. She moved over to him and stood next to him with her head as low as she could hang it. When he still didn't make any move to hold her, or even contradict her concerns, she linked her fingers in his. He didn't reject the clasp, but he didn't grip her hand back.

He looked her over with the observation of someone guarding their heart. He turned his attention back to Danato and nodded at whatever silent question he had asked. She heard Danato set his coffee cup on an end table. He moved to the door and slipped on his coat. The door opened and shut gently, as if he was trying not to disrupt the paused moment she had forced into the room.

Ethan set down his own coffee cup and turned to her. He placed his hand on her arm. For a moment, she thought he was going to console her, but he only used the leverage to drag his hand away from hers. She let out a whimper as he walked away from her. She heard him inhale and exhale before speaking. "We need to talk."

She bent over, feeling her stomach clench with disgust at those words. She couldn't turn around. She prayed he wouldn't say what she thought he was going to.

"I've packed a bag. I'm going to spend a few nights with the guards until a more permanent residence can be arranged."

She turned around to face him. He wasn't crying or stumbling over his words like she was. How could he not be? "No, Ethan. No, please!" She rushed to him, putting her hands on his face. "I won't see him anymore. I promise."

He pulled her hands away and took a step away. "I'm not asking for that. I never was. Danato wanted that. I understand the importance of your relationship with him now. I can respect that. I'm doing this for other reasons."

"Why?"

"Cori." A smidgen of pain entered his face, and she was glad to see it. At least he was not completely without empathy. "I thought we were everything to each other."

"We are!"

"No, Cori." He pointed to the prison. "If I was as much to you as you are to me, you wouldn't need to seek him out. I love you so much."

"I love you!" She tried to reach for him, but he stepped back again. Damn the house for being an open-floor plan.

"I..." He placed his hands in prayer before him. She could see the tremble there that he was withholding from his voice. "I can't be second. I can't have you in my bed, and in my heart, and not have you. All of you." She took another step forward, as if all she had to do was touch him and it would all go away. "Please, don't make this harder than it already is. I just need a little time and a little space. I just need you to figure out what you really want."

"I want *you*!" She was yelling, but her throat only allowed a fraction of her volume.

"I know, but you want him too. I know I'm being selfish, but I can't share you." His lower lip quivered. "I'm sorry." He walked right past her toward the door. As promised, he pulled a duffel bag from beneath the coat rack and slipped on his coat.

Cori could feel her grasp on the moment slipping away. She couldn't believe this was happening. She couldn't believe that she had screwed up her marriage after only a week of memorable time. She wished she had never met Cleos.

She remembered what little advice he had given her.

Ethan reached for the door, and she found enough voice to scream after him. "I never loved him like I love you!"

He paused, released the doorknob, and looked back at her. She moved a little closer, not so much to threaten his personal space, but enough so she could see his face better. "I know you were never unfaithful to me, Cori. Cleos explained—"

"Vince!" She breathed hard. She was only beginning to understand the fear that Cleos spoke of. Ethan's face froze in bafflement. She took another tiny step towards him. "I loved Vince. For six months, he revived my trust in men. He made me understand that I could still love, and he proved that I could be loved."

Ethan shifted to lower his bag and crossed his arms. It wasn't the most open body language for her admission, but as long as he didn't have that bag in his hand, she had a few more seconds of his attention.

"When he died, I was crushed and alone, and all sorts of confused." Ethan's face remained blank, but she knew he remembered how much pain she had gone through. "I loved him so much that his death almost destroyed me, but I love you more than that."

Ethan loosened his grip on his arms and shifted them to his hips.

"I kept myself at a distance even after we were married, because I was afraid of losing you. I knew losing you would be the end of me. I couldn't recover from that. I thought I was protecting myself from this, but I was creating it.

"Ethan, the day I found out my lover was dying was the most painful day of my life." Her face crumpled and another round of tears filled her cheeks. "Until today."

Finally, Ethan shifted with the discomfort of his emotions. She took a step forward. "I know I've hurt you. More than I realized I could, but please don't go." She took another step forward. "Cleos or not, I don't care. I want you. I need *you*." She took another step. She was close enough to touch him, but she didn't. "Two days ago, you made love to me for the first time and the hundredth time. You were just as gentle and generous as you were the real first time. I know that will never change. I know you will always give me time and space to figure out what I really want, but I don't need it, Ethan." She took his hand, placed it on her chest over her heart. "It's yours. All of it."

She could feel the shakiness in his hand. He looked everywhere but at her. He had been so resolute in his choice. His determination to follow through was keeping him in stilled objection. She leaned forward and picked up his duffel bag. She took his hand in hers again and walked toward the stairs. At the end of his reach, she felt a hint of resistance, but his feet followed.

Without a word, she led them to their apartment, tossed the bag on the couch, and brought him to their bed. She sat him on the bed while she undressed for him. His eyes took on an all too familiar hunger as she did so.

She sat down on his leg and kissed him as slowly and gently as he would her. She removed his clothes and offered him all the same attentions he had her on their first and hundredth night together. Her closing act was a little less gentle, however.

In the aftermath of their lovemaking, they lay together silently; her rubbing his chest, and him twirling his finger in her hair. To break the silence, she leaned into his ear and whispered, "I'm so sorry I hurt you."

He rolled her over and towered over her face, stroking her hair behind her ears. "I don't want to control you, Cori. I want you as wild as the day you came to this place. I want you to fight me tooth and nail when you think I'm wrong. I want you just as you are." His face changed to something resembling anger, but he kept his voice quiet. "But I need all of you, or it's no go. Do you understand what I'm saying? You come to me for advice." She felt a teardrop on her face, that wasn't her own. "You come to me for help. I want to be your everything, physically and emotionally."

"Done." She leaned up to kiss him. At first, he was reluctant to comply, but when he finally did, it was more than a kiss that he sealed the deal with.

54

CORI WAS HAPPY TO relive the first few nights of her honeymoon again, but missing supper was putting a damper on her sexual energy. She managed to convince Ethan that sustenance was required to continue their evening. He reluctantly disentangled himself from her and let her make a food run.

She slipped on her robe. "If you're not back in five minutes, I will come down and have my way with you in front of all the small appliances."

She smiled and laughed. "I'll have to decide on the way down if that's actually a threat or not." She slipped out the door and tiptoed down the stairs. She expected to find Danato asleep on the couch since his bedroom was open and vacant, but he wasn't. Their ordeal must have scared him off to busy himself with paperwork.

She decided on a PB&J for her semi-snack meal. After pasting together four sandwiches, she searched for her hidden chips, only to find them stolen. She cursed and settled on crackers for the crunch to contrast with her soft sandwiches. She grabbed the bottle of milk from the fridge and poured one big glass to take upstairs.

With the glass in hand, she headed over to retrieve her plate of sandwiches. The last of her memories from her abduction night came back in a flash.

The glass dropped from her hand, shattering on the floor. She stood in the kitchen frozen, mouth agape, and terrified.

She had gotten too close to the cells that night. It was a rookie mistake. One she would never have made if it weren't for the complete and utter shock of what she had seen. Someone had distracted her.

Ethan came bounding down the stairs. She wasn't sure if he had heard the glass shatter, or if he was simply prepared to make good on his *threat*. He took one look at her face and rushed over to her. Ignoring the glass, he took her hands in his. "What's wrong?"

"I remember what happened. I know why I got distracted that night," she told him in a daze.

"What happened?" He squeezed her hands.

"He was out of his cell. He was just strolling around the level."

"One of the prisoners? Who?"

She looked up at him, her brow dipped in disbelief at her own memories. "Efrat."

FELICIA JEDLICKA
BAD BLOOD
Book 4
THE WARDEN

BAD BLOOD

Sneak Peek

CORI GASPED, FALLING BACK on her butt. She crab walked away from Belus's unconscious form. Blood seeped onto the floor from his back. She could see a small hole dotted with red in his side.

A trail of bloody hand tracks followed her away from the body. She looked at her palms and saw the blood staining the creases in her hands and coagulating under her fingernails. One of her fingers looked disjointed, but she couldn't feel any pain from it. Her head hurt, and she was trembling, but it wasn't from being cold.

The walls of the infirmary hall were gone. She couldn't immediately place what part of the prison she was in, but the large and small empty cells suggested she was on the part-time level. A row of armed guards was pointing pistols and elemental weapons at her. They looked baffled, as if the orders they had been given weren't making any sense to them.

Movement on her left caught her eye. Efrat rose from his sprawled position on the floor and approached Belus's body with a slight limp. He paid her no heed as he passed her by. Awaking her muddled mind; she reached for her gun, but the holster was empty. She back peddled further along the ground, hoping to escape his attack.

"Don't move!" Danato said on her right.

She whipped around and saw him pointing a gun...at *her*. Another row of guards lined up behind her, waiting for an order, any order. "Danato!" She gasped, relieved. "What's going on? What's happened to Belus?"

Danato's eyes were hard with anger, but she saw him cringe, as if he might cry. "Do it," he ground out the words, looking at Efrat, but keeping the gun securely trained on her.

Cori looked back to Efrat, who was kneeling beside Belus with his hands at the ready over him. "No! Danato, what are you doing? Shoot the bastard!" She screamed, but Danato didn't move his gun from her.

Cori gave up reasoning with Danato. He was obviously as stunned by the event as she was, and couldn't think straight. She pushed herself back to her feet and ran at Efrat to tackle him.

Her attack was not throttled by bolts, but when she was close enough to push him away; he flipped her to her back using her own momentum. He pushed her to the floor and gripped her wrists firmly and painfully over her chest. He pressed all his weight onto her hands, pushing them into her breasts. She struggled to bring her legs up so she could kick him, but he kept his body at her side, out of range.

"Corinthia!" He yelled at her.

She had been prepared for slurs and banter, but she had not expected to hear her birth name from his lips. As it usually did, the name froze her, because she expected her mother to jump out and tell her to clean her room.

She met his eyes. A sea of beautiful blue—that had no business being on the face of a criminal—was conveying urgency and concern. "Let me save him!" He spoke the punctuating words like she was deaf or dumb. It was probably the best thing, since at that moment she understood nothing.

Cori searched his face for the meaning of this statement. His eyes flickered over hers, searching for the permission to release his grip. His face pleaded the request that she didn't want to believe from his voice. "I need to defibrillate him, or his heart will stop completely and he will die," he explained further, when she didn't visibly concede. "I can save him."

She knew she was lost down the rabbit hole, but why did the white rabbit look like the big bad wolf? She had so many questions: *How did she get here? Why was everyone here? How did Belus get shot?*

None of them mattered, though. Belus was over the threshold of death and the man that had put her into a flatline nearly a year ago was offering to save him. "Why?" She voiced the only question that refused to be put off.

He released her wrists and backed away slowly, like she might be a risk to him. He distanced himself from her body before he answered. "Because you asked me to." Efrat turned and repositioned his hands over Belus. He pressed them to his chest like paddles, and Belus's body arched from the electricity.

"Cori?" Danato called her name.

When she looked up toward Danato's voice, his eyes were filled with concern and his hands were free of the gun that had recently been pointed at her. The cages of the part-time level were gone.

Thank you so much for reading. I hope you
enjoyed the ride and if you aren't getting
off here, I encourage you to sign up for my
newsletter so I can return your generosity
with new release updates and special offers.

Sign-Up

You can also find me on Facebook or visit my
website. Keep reading!

Website

Facebook

AUTHOR

As a Nebraska native, and a small-town girl at that, I have very little to occupy my time beyond imagining a world outside of my own reality. By the grace of God and the seat of my pants, I have kept my waning attention span on the task of becoming an author.

So here I am, an indie author, peddling my words in cyberspace and enduring my comeuppances with an unwavering determination. I may not be a professional, and I certainly am not perfect, but if you've made it this far, you have to admit, this smartass yokel does spin quite a yarn.

From the self-inflicted sweatshop conditions of my unairconditioned childhood home, to the arthritis reaping positions of a sedentary lifestyle, I bring to you: my sarcasm, my oddity, and my heart. Take it with a grain of salt or a teaspoon of sugar, but take it for what it is: a story born of the mind, translated to paper, and gifted to you.

I thank you for your readership and even more for your support. Please recommend this book to your friends and family via any social media that you use. Word of mouth is still the best advertising and is greatly appreciated.

Most importantly, keep reading. I'll keep writing.